MY GRAPE CRUSH

The Trenton Troublemakers Book One

ROWAN ROSSLER

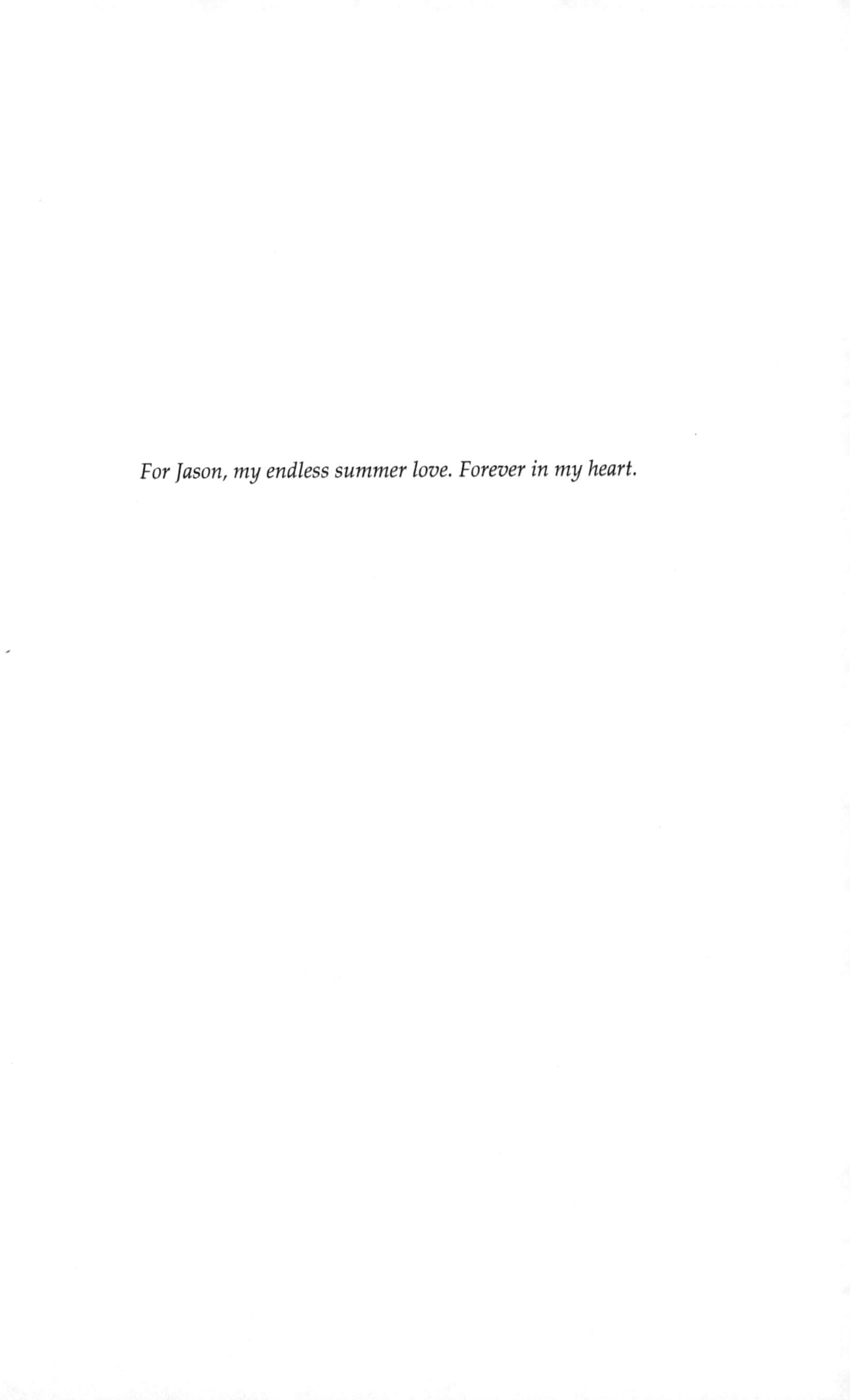

For Jason, my endless summer love. Forever in my heart.

In vino veritas
In wine, there is truth

Chapter One

DANI

I, Dani Rose Rialto, thirty-one and of relatively sane mind, blame the internet. And if you say passing the buck is an annoying millennial trend you could live without, that's fair. Own your shit, snowflake, right? The point is, no one asked me if an invention connecting humanity for better or for worse was a good idea.

I had zero say or control.

And now I'm a veritable case study on the dangers of doom-scrolling videos posted by beautiful and unattainable men.

Genuine social media addiction fueled by the World Wide Web *is* responsible for this tragedy. How else did I develop my all-consuming crush on influencer Rhys Trenton? The golden boy of Instagram lives halfway around the world on the Greek island of Corfu. He spends his mornings strolling the grounds of his cliffside palazzo flush with million-dollar brand deals and sipping craft espresso.

I drink drip coffee from 7-11. The only million I've seen is the price tag for a fixer-upper in the 'burbs that could double as a meth lab. Up until two months ago, my digs were a cramped East Vancouver apartment with the down payment funded by the Bank of Mom and Dad.

In no legitimate universe should the paths of Rhys and I ever cross.

And yet, here we are, summer thick in the air, fated together as boss and star spokesman in the sleepy summer wine town of Osoyoos, BC.

I squint into the early evening sun. Under the brilliant expanse of sky, the limo ferrying Rhys comes into focus. It snakes back and forth, switchbacking as it rises up the hill striped green with rows of neatly ordered grape vines. Welcome to Nero Vino—the Okanagan Valley's most decorated winery and my current employer, who, in all honesty, hired me as the head of marketing *because* of the internet.

Maybe I'll hold off on the blame game.

Right now, I have other priorities—like trying not to melt.

It's forty degrees in the shade and there is none in the winery parking lot where the August heat radiates around me like a sauna. My current mood is mildly irritated courtesy of Rhys being seven hours late. And he can't hold the airlines accountable because his business class flights from Athens to London to Vancouver landed on time. Plus, he had two hours to make his connection at the Vancouver airport.

Who falls asleep in the Air Canada lounge?

By missing his final flight into Kelowna, I lost an hour of my life scrambling to find a car service willing to travel four hundred kilometers on a long weekend.

One-way.

Three grand and half a day later, the angelic face hired to promote our rosé rolls up in a glossy black stretch limo. Familiar disco beats thump from the open sunroof, syncing with my thudding heart.

He's here. Like, six feet away from me.

I tell myself to play it cool, but my Ted Baker suit feels shrink-wrapped to my skin, and I'm chaos on the inside, chest pinched and pulse cranking higher.

And what is the name of that song? I know it. Before it comes to me, the limo door swings open, and a tanned foot in a white flip-flop lands on the sun-baked gravel, kicking up a puff of dust.

I feel a sudden, dizzying wave of swoon factor.

Feet factor heavily in my world, thanks to Gordon Rialto, my recently retired podiatrist father. Sadly, his Friendly Giant gene pool saddled me with flat, size-ten flippers that every dainty sandal runs screaming away from.

Rhys has flawless feet, of course. Arched and smooth with straight toes and trimmed nails. Why go to the trouble of creating the world's most arresting human without head-to-toe quality control? His feet are the only body parts I haven't memorized because he never films them.

But the rest of him? I can recite every detail with painful accuracy.

Or I could if he didn't step out of the limo and steal my breath away.

Dear god.

I blink and smile, literally digging my heels into the hot rocks to resist the force of his magnetism. Never before have I felt the desire to throw myself at someone so completely.

"Hey there," he says. "Are you Dani?" His voice sounds quizzical but also rich and decadent—the vocal equivalent of whipped cream.

"That's me. Dani Rialto, head of marketing. Glad you finally made it." I thrust my hand out, and a small beat passes before his bronzed, elegant fingers twine with mine. Was he expecting a fist bump?

"Yeah, sorry about missing the flight." He flashes a smile full of perfect white teeth. "It's not the first time I've crashed in an airport lounge."

"Happens to everyone, right?" I say, when in fact, I know a total of zero people who drop off the radar in an international airport while their agent unleashes fire and brimstone on me. Said agent—human Rottweiler Bettina Weber—grudgingly cut me some slack after I reminded her that she insisted on being the point person while Rhys traveled.

But whatever.

The warmth of his touch melts away the frantic afternoon. I'm dimly aware of pumping his hand beyond normal time limitations, buying time to trawl over his features that previously only graced my screen. The papercut jawline. Skin sun-darkened and glowing. Flaxen hair styled in the iconic feathered shag that spawned a worldwide craze—the male version of "The Rachel."

Jesus, he's breathtaking,

"I hope you didn't wear the suit and heels for me," he says, his faint European accent making him even sexier. "Aren't you burning up? It's a furnace out here."

I lick my lips, dry as the desert I'm living in. "You must be used to the heat living in Greece."

He disconnects his fingers from mine, and my brain silently screams—*No! Come back.* Then he slides his hot-pink Ray-Bans down the straight slope of his nose and studies me as if a woman rocking leopard-print eyewear is an unknown species.

"This heat feels different," he says, eyes fixated on mine. "More intense."

I feel my lungs squeeze under my ribcage.

How many nights have I spent captivated by those cinnamon-tinted irises? The in-person effect is embarrassingly the same: weak knees and a staggering surge of desire.

There is hot, and then there is Rhys.

He's taller than I imagined and adorably rumpled in a purple tee stamped with BLUE MARLIN, loose-fitting, like his board shorts. As the hypnotic music swirls around us, the song's name finally hits me. I bite back a laugh, thinking this is certifiably ridiculous. My internet crush stands before me with Donna Summer crooning "I Feel Love"?

Come on.

Like he's just tuned into the sensual, driving beats, Rhys shouts into the open door of the limo, "Hey, Colin! Can you kill the tunes?"

Donna abruptly snuffs out, and the silence somehow sounds louder. The driver's side window lowers to reveal a round-faced boomer with mutton chops and big ole affable Canadian energy.

"Hello!" He gallantly tips the brim of his ten-gallon hat. "Where should I drop the bags?"

For the benefit of both men, I point at a standalone bungalow commanding the sloped hill to our left. "That's your villa. Fully stocked and ready to go."

"10-4," Colin says. "Meet you up there, sir."

He eases the limo around us, the tires kicking up tendrils of powdery dirt. Rhys hooks his sunglasses into the V of his t-shirt, scanning his new surroundings while I steal another glance at him. Rhys and I are the same age, born and raised in Vancouver, but the similarities end there. He shines differently. I can't explain it. Is it his fame? His brand of oh-so-relatable charm? Or maybe the dust particles swirling around him like atomic streamers create the illusion.

"Do you need me for anything?" Rhys nudges me out of my private thoughts. "Or is it cool if I cut out? I need a shower big-time."

"Nothing's on the agenda tonight, but Evelyn hopes you can join her and Nicole for brunch tomorrow. Nicole's our winemaker," I explain, in case the Nero Vino information packet I FedExed to Greece two weeks ago ended up in his recycle bin unread.

His brow furrows. "But I'm not on the clock until Monday, right?"

I open my mouth and then quickly shut it. Bettina tortured me for days, grinding out the details of Rhys's contract. Drilled into me are the terms: we have him ten to five, Monday to Friday. Weekends down. Five weeks of videos, photo shoots, vlogs, and posts in exchange for a million dollars.

Could he squeeze in one extra Sunday meal on the house?

"I'm joking." Rhys knocks his elbow against mine with a grin, clearly seeing through my attempt to hide the *"Are you kidding me?"* expression. "Tell me where to be and when. I'm psyched to meet Evelyn. She sounds like a trip."

That's one way of describing Evelyn Maclaren, the madcap heiress and owner of Nero Vino. An opinionated and charismatic force of nature, she continues to milk every drop out of life at the tender age of sixty-nine.

"She's a huge fan of yours," I say, not that one more admirer moves the needle in his world. "Anyone who likes history is in her good books."

I should mention that Rhys isn't your run-of-the-mill influencer. A history buff with a reported 139 IQ, he left Canada at the age of fifteen to explore the mysteries of ancient Europe and never came home. In his videos, he rambles about the Greeks and Romans while hawking everything from beachwear to shampoo to his thirty million followers.

And he's a thinking man. Stamped on a medallion that hangs from the gold chain around his neck is a profile of Seneca, his favorite philosopher. He never wears any other jewelry.

"And you'll be at brunch?" Rhys adds, sounding hopeful, if I'm not mistaken.

"I'll be everywhere for the next five weeks. You're my responsibility. I live in that villa over there." I point west at a more modest building buried behind prickly pear cactuses and tangled clumps of sagebrush. "And Bettina said she sent you my cell number. We can communicate directly now that you're here. Text me if you need anything."

After a beat, he tilts his head. "Is that a twenty-four-seven guarantee?"

I feel my cheeks pink—something in his voice and how he gazes down at me, sweetly amused.

Holy shit. Is he flirting with me?

I dismiss it as sucking up. He knows what side his bread is buttered on. You don't piss off your boss. But laying down ground rules never hurt.

"If you run out of jellybeans at midnight," I say, "you're on your own."

He laughs, idly stroking his hair. "So, Bettina schooled you on my infamous rider. You probably think I'm some kind of high-maintenance idiot, huh?"

"Who am I to judge if you need a mattress imported from Sweden to sleep at night?" I ask with an innocent but slightly judgmental shrug.

He smiles through another laugh. "I'll sleep on rocks as long as I have my coffee and jellybeans."

Forgetting that maybe I shouldn't slag his manifesto of demands, I roll on. "At a hundred dollars a bag, that Blue Mountain coffee better taste damn good."

His eyes light on me. I like that he's loose and not getting offended. But then again, Rhys embodies carefree boho. And there is that million-dollar fee.

"Come over one morning for a cup," he says. "Happy to host."

In his voice, along with playfulness, there is kindness. But I don't want to overestimate the importance of his offer. He is Canadian, after all—being nice comes with the territory, and I've lived through the wreckage of punching above my weight. Gorgeous celebrities like Rhys have sleek Monaco supermodels on speed dial. A tall and curvy punk-rock-loving wine marketer from East Van perspiring in a suit capturing his attention?

I'm not that delusional.

But is there something else behind the twinkle in his eyes?

"Speaking of beverages," I continue, "enjoy the complimentary bottles of Pink Pearl in your fridge. You should become intimate with the rosé you're here to promote."

"Awww," Rhys says, adding "precious" to the adjectives my sister Amelia and I use whenever we fervently and frequently discuss him. "You didn't have to do that. Appreciate it, Dani." In the pause that follows, he looks at me with a focused kind of warmth. "Is that short for Danielle?"

"No," I say. "Just Dani."

He regards me a second too long for normal, eyes traveling down to my legs and back up again. It's a boldly intimate gaze.

"Just Dani," he repeats. "Got it."

He cracks a big yawn, arms stretching overhead, his shirt hem riding up to show off his lightly muscled abs. All that smooth skin stretches down to the barest fuzzy trail disappearing into his shorts. I work not to break eye contact and continue to breathe deeply through my wildly raging and improper thoughts.

Can he tell I'm ten percent in love with him?

"Well," he says, "as good as you look in that suit, I'm sure you'd rather clock out and change into something more comfortable." And just as I think I'm not imagining there's some heft to our flirty exchange, he flashes me his signature goodbye, index and middle finger shaped into a V. "Peace out, and thanks for the hustle getting me here. I owe you one."

He jogs up the slope to his villa, graceful as an antelope, and, okay, the extra three grand it cost to deliver his rather fine and firm ass at my feet? Officially forgotten. But I can still feel the spotlight of his smile like a hot lance on my skin.

That's going to haunt me all night.

Chapter Two

RHYS

I'm not the details guy. Never have been, never will. Bettina takes her cut from my earnings for the hassle of sifting through the minutiae I can live without. She feeds me the critical stuff, but the ball got dropped somewhere along the line. How did I miss that Dani was a woman? And not just your standard female, like every other blonde out there.

Serious babe-town alert.

A suit, so technically not my type, but those surreal and mystical gray eyes behind hot-librarian glasses? Sign me the hell up.

Colin rolls my two suitcases inside and pauses, admiring the villa. It's polished and sleek, with an open floor plan and furniture that's all clean lines and rectangles. Lots of greige. The kind of space Marie Kondo would take one look at and say, "My work here is done."

"You'll do just fine here, Rhys," he concludes. "Especially with a boss as pretty as yours."

His eyes are bright and playful as he shoots me a buddy wink. My own laugh catches me by surprise. Pretty? Try jettisoned onto Earth from some alternate dimension where Glamazons run free. Have I ever seen a mouth that tempting? Cherry-red blasphemy on a flawless, pale face worthy of a shrine. The immaculate luster of her hair, black as sin and hanging halfway down her back, gave rise to treacherous thoughts that continue to swirl in my brain.

Is it wrong to visualize mounting someone you just met?

"Thanks, man," I say. "And I appreciate you lending an ear."

I fish a crumpled hundred Euro note from my pocket and hand it over. Colin tucks it into his slacks, examining me with a thoughtful expression.

"I hope you find the strength to sort things out," he says. "We only have so much time on this earth."

He steps in to hug me, and why the hell not? During the five-hour drive, I'd spilled my life story. That's how it goes, right? It's far easier to vent your demons to a stranger. Well, slight correction. "Demons" make me sound rage-filled or unhinged. The trending PC word is "issues," and I have plenty of them.

One of the reasons I agreed to this gig is its proximity to the issues that need sorting.

Man-hug in the can, Colin leaves me to scope out my temporary home. Bettina assured me the accommodations were five-star—paramount for a guy who spends most of his spare time in a hammock. I wander into the bedroom for a closer look at the damn bed she insisted on. All my counterparts were supposedly padding out their riders with outrageous asks, and since arguing with Bettina is like showing up at the Battle of Normandy with a butter knife, I sucked it up.

Now I wish I'd pushed back.

Under the vaulted ceiling and extravagant tiered chandelier, the "it" mattress, filled with horsehair and guaranteed to make me sleep like an immortal vampire, looks like any other bed.

Forty grand of stupidity for a five-week stint?

What a waste of money.

I'll ask Evelyn if we can donate it to Dani later. Anyone who survives seven hours of micromanaging me through Bettina deserves a reward. Plus, Dani surprised me—beyond just being a woman. Instead of acting all gaga, like an overpaid influencer is effecting real change in the world, she had no problem taking the piss out of me and my vast credentials. And some tall women are self-conscious about their height, but she held my gaze.

All five foot ten of her, give or take.

I wash my hands in the master bathroom, deliberating long and hard on her teasing. Friendly or flirty? I can never tell the difference. Maybe a distraction is what I need. Five weeks with a bunch of strangers worried me at first, but the nerves have dwindled. Dani seems normal. And with women and me, normal is a rarity.

I seem to attract all the unstable ones.

On cue, my phone buzzes deep in my pocket. I slide it out, skim the message, and white noise roars in my ears. How did Myla Borak wrangle my number?

MB: Hiii! Miss me yet? xoxo

I wouldn't describe our time together as emotionally potent, and is it even possible to miss a first-class nut job? I shut my eyes and sink against the tiled counter edge, my mind tumbling backward into last week.

My buddy Dmitri tagged us all for a rager on his yacht, and it felt like a good idea at the time. A new house DJ would spin under the stars. Legendary refreshments. Plus, I needed a night out.

An hour into the party, I was buzzing from wicked tunes and smooth Stoli on ice when a blonde—more trashy-glam than pretty— plopped into the hot tub beside me and started talking my ear off.

Myla and Dmitri were supposedly an *item*, a term harder to pin down in the hedonistic trust-funder social groups I move in. (*"She's not your girl; it's just your turn,"* is how they explain it.) Five minutes into our mindless conversation, I surmised Myla was one of those women in the Mediterranean famous for doing nothing but hopping from bed to bed. I also have a sixth sense for when people are a little off, and the arrow tilted into the danger zone with her.

Sure enough, when two in the morning rolled around, guess who staggered into the taxi with me for the ride home?

Sleeping with her was a giant mistake.

The next morning, I peeled out of bed at noon and found her

watering my potted herbs in the kitchen. I did the polite thing and made us coffee. Then I dropped several hints about my busy day. But it went in one ear and out the other because she asked me if I wanted pasta or salad for lunch. Yup. An unmistakable Crazy. I forcibly had to eject her, and we most definitely did not exchange numbers.

My eyes pop open, and I stare at the wall, unblinking.

This all points to Dmitri.

He sailed off the next morning without Myla and sent me a thumbs-up emoji.

What a dick.

Deleting Myla's text, I try to forget how ill I felt, succumbing to a one-night stand. But sometimes the dark, empty nights are too much. Life as a famous influencer has made relationships borderline impossible, and my daily DM bombardment is a banquet of questionable opportunities from the Crazies. Marriage proposals. Dick and pussy pics. The sheer volume of batshit weirdos is undeniably frightening.

To maintain my sanity, I refuse to look anymore.

Because there's always another stan like Myla, who, after I gave her the boot, liked every single one of my posts, and that shit goes back sixteen years.

It takes a certain kind of woman to make me feel comfortable, and I've almost given up hope of finding her. But there was something about Dani that put me at ease. I felt a tenderness underneath the sharp suit. The odds of her being single feel slim, and even if she was, what buttoned-up career girl views a beach bum as a dream date?

And it's not as if I captured her heart.

She has to be nice to me.

I sigh with my entire body, exhaustion creeping in. A good night's sleep will help me reset, but adjusting to the new time zone will take even longer if I crash now.

Time to break in my shiny new espresso maker.

I hit the kitchen and pull a shot in no time. As I search the fridge for cream, my phone buzzes—a call, not a text. I have a feeling I know who it is. Sure enough, Trenton Talent Management flashes on the screen.

I'd rather not talk to my eldest brother, Sawyer, but it's better to face the music now and get it over with. I pop in my earbuds and answer with my most uninspired voice, "Hey."

A perky female voice replies, "Hi, Rhys. It's Janelle, Sawyer's secretary. I'll connect you."

Oh yeah, silly me. Agents are too important to call you directly. And now that Sawyer has had the reins of our family business handed to him by our ailing father, he's even more insufferable—if that's humanly possible.

Ten seconds later, the sunshine of my life cuts through the lame hold muzak. "What the hell happened at the airport?" Sawyer barks.

"Hi. How's it going?"

"Don't deflect," he says in that big brother tone meant to put me in my place. Practical and perfectly over-achieving, Sawyer often comes across as blunt and sanctimonious.

Because, well, he is.

"One thing led to another. No big deal. I'm here."

"Yes, it is a big deal," he corrects. "It's the optics. Act like you give a shit. They're paying you a million dollars."

I slam the fridge shut. No cream. Great. Black coffee sucks.

"Let me guess, you've never missed a flight." Sawyer's love affair with punctuality hasn't hit OCD levels yet, but any day now.

"That's not the point, Rhys. As surprising as it may seem, there's more going on with this deal than just you." His voice is very level, but there's a sound in it like a warning.

"Meaning?"

"Nero Vino hosts a summer concert series. Their outdoor amphitheater is a perfect venue to showcase some of our up-and-coming bands."

On one of our rambling FaceTimes two months ago, my middle brother, JC, a seriously talented musician also repped by the family biz, said the music division had taken a hit. Sawyer was on the prowl to sign the next big thing and leverage up the smaller players.

"So you're trying to piggyback on me." I pose it as a statement, not a question.

After a terse pause, he says, "Yes, of course. It's all about you, baby brother."

I irritate the hell out of Sawyer, mostly because I make twice the cash he does with eighty percent less effort. And because I abandoned Canada and left him to carry the burden of running the family business, he gets the joy of having to live up to the legacy of our father.

But Sawyer could have said no.

That's the thing about my older brother—for all his whey powder and workouts, he's a weakling. The world kicks out at him, and he kicks back, but not fucking hard enough.

"I've got to jump on another call," he says. "But I'm coming up on Tuesday afternoon to tour the property with Dani."

Tuesday. Damn. There goes my plan for avoiding him.

"And I was hoping you could do me a favor," Sawyer adds.

He's trying for casual, but within his usual flat and domineering delivery, I hear a sliver of uncertainty.

I slurp down some coffee. "I'm listening."

"You met with Dani today, right?"

I try to deaden my curiosity. The truth is, I'm still feeling the echo of interest in my shorts. "Yeah. Why?"

"We've exchanged a few emails since Evelyn officially booked you. She seems on it. Professional. Her LinkedIn photo is cute." He clears his throat. "Can you do some recon?"

Juggling the coffee in one hand, I use the other to slide open the patio door. "As in, suss out if she's single?"

"Don't tell her I asked," he immediately says.

I step outside and, despite talking with Sawyer, my mouth twitches into a smile. Strung between two posts and overlooking the still turquoise water of my plunge pool is the one thing in my rider I care about. Bless Dani. She picked the perfect hammock.

I ease into it, legs dangling off one side. "Does this mean you're officially out of your divorce mourning period?"

"After a year, it's about time," Sawyer admits, which, for him, is a floodgate of emotions opening up. "And, speaking of time, are you planning to visit Dad while you're here?"

I finish my coffee, which now leaves a bitter taste on my tongue. "How's he doing?"

"As good as someone forced to leave behind the only thing that matters to him can be."

Dad had a stroke eight months ago. Sawyer took the CEO reins, and from what JC has told me, he's doing a decent job of running the joint.

"I have to see what the schedule's like." I'm noncommittal as ever with the topic of my father.

"He asks about you all the time," Sawyer says quietly.

My heart does this funny up-and-down thing. The great Peter Trenton. Self-made millionaire. Universally adored. Always the brightest smile and the coldest eyes.

"Really? Does he have dementia now, too?"

Sawyer sighs dramatically. I can see him pinching the bridge of his nose, strangled by his tie and relentless commitments, sitting in his cave of an office and wondering what happened to the best years of his life.

"Why do you have to be such a dickwad?" he asks. "Ditching the family not enough for you?"

"You know damn well why I left."

"Despite what you think, Dad never hated you."

The knot in my stomach tightens. Any psychologist armed with the basics of my life could lay down a surefire assessment of why my life unfolded the way it did—why I live alone on an island and make a fortune connecting with strangers. They say success is the best revenge, but when you wake up feeling hollow inside, how is that a win?

"Yeah, whatever," I say. "Take your other call."

"Don't forget about Dani, okay?"

I hang up, the memories crowding in—blurry, yet sharp enough never to forget. I can still hear Dad's voice drifting out of his study, laying out his genius plan to straighten out his youngest son. And Sawyer, he had the chance to back me up but didn't. So, at fifteen, I bought a one-way ticket to London and left home with my heart falling apart.

And now he wants my help?

What I didn't tell him is that I clocked the no ring on Dani's finger

—a long-standing and necessary habit. The married Crazies are the worst.

I swing back and forth in the hammock, mulling it all over, the heady scent of ripening grapes dancing on the hot breeze. On paper, without any other context, I admit Sawyer is a better fit for her. But if I can rely on anything, it's the old competition between us.

The sun is starting to slip in the sky.

My second wind kicks in with the coffee.

I could text Dani about the missing cream, but it's not too late to wander over and ask to borrow some of hers.

She did make a point of telling me where to find her.

Chapter Three

DANI

There has to be a hack to survive this: endorphins pumping so hard my ribcage aches, my supposedly rational and objective view of things washed away in a chaotic rush of pheromones. Twenty minutes after *the encounter*, I'm in my office chair, eyes shut, the air conditioner wheezing on overdrive. My body temperature has recalibrated, but how long will it take for my brain to chill with Rhys and his naked finery showering a mere thirty meters due east?

Irresponsible infatuation was safer with him on Corfu. Face-to-face feels like a losing battle. A massive distraction with high cheekbones and a playful smile that inspires all manner of inconceivable things? Rhys is the last thing I need.

Crush season starts next week. Divine Debauchery, the celebrity-studded Labour Day gala Evelyn lives for, is approaching fast. Add in the Pink Pearl new brand unveiling happening at the September Wine Festival, and, hello, packed schedule.

Evelyn expects me to deliver—not because this dream job saved my shattered confidence, but because, after the heartbreak of what happened two months ago, it's my time to shine. But as I wrench off my patent leather stilettos to rub life back into ten squished toes, the sublime thrill rushes through me again.

Hotter than blood.

Rhys didn't look at me with hearts in his eyes, but he did *look* at me.

"Hello?" The distinctive warble of Evelyn Maclaren carries from down the hall. "Is my secret weapon still here?"

"In the office," I call back.

I tidy my desk and brace for the equivalent of a Bell 212 helicopter about to land. Imagine Dorothy and Blanche from *The Golden Girls*. Dump both into a blender with a scoop of glitter, add a liter of moxie, hit FRAPPE, and, voilà, you have Evelyn.

She swoops in like the gale-force wind she is, tall for her age, hellishly fit, and regal-assed in a pastel vintage Pucci sheath. Elegance personified.

"Sorry to keep you, dear," she purrs, designer kitten heels click-clacking on the tiled floor. "The traffic was horrendous. I forgot about the long weekend."

"How was lunch?" I ask.

Evelyn sinks into the antique Bergère chair on the other side of my desk, and my nose wrinkles. As usual, there isn't enough space in the room for both of us and her cloud of *Opium* perfume.

"Oh, we gabbed about the weather and wine," she says breezily. "That our husbands are either dead or deadbeats."

Evelyn spent the afternoon in Kelowna, lunching with her partner in crime, Yvette Van Ness. Both discarded multiple husbands over the years, racking up insane wealth and copious amounts of land after each divorce. Known as the Diva Dowagers, they are the most powerful duo in the Okanagan wine industry.

Is it any surprise that two clever, crafty, and successful female multi-millionaires have collected a few enemies along the way?

"Is Yvette thrilled to have Garth back?" I ask.

"Poor thing," Evelyn tuts. "Just when she was getting used to the taste of freedom. He's a bit clingy after his stint in that executive jail. You'd think they had him in solitary on Alcatraz!"

There's a saying in wine country—if you want to make a small fortune, start with a large fortune. Yvette's husband opted to give away none of his fortune, which is why he's fresh out of prison for tax evasion.

"Is she still cool for the Friday photo shoot?" I ask.

To kickstart the Pink Pearl media campaign, we hired Luca da Silva, a high-fashion and high-maintenance photographer from Barcelona. He talk-shouted through a tedious Zoom call last month with flinging arm gestures about how he would convert Yvette's sprawling lakeside manor into a Romanesque tableau.

We needed skimpy togas! Gold cuffs! Gladiator sandals and sex appeal for days!

I'm a teensy bit jealous of the willowy blonde model we hired to play Rhys's foil. Not only is she pretty, but they'll both be half-naked and getting cozy right in front of me.

"The show must go on," Evelyn states, touching up a snowy puff of hair styled into the beehive that's as famous as her wines. "And speaking of that, how is our studly promoter? Aside from late."

I slide my gaze off hers. Evelyn knows nothing about my crush. And I plan to keep it that way.

"He seems nice," I say. "And he apologized for the runaround."

"Typical Sagittarius," she muses. "Head in the sky and a pain in the bloody ass. Assumes the world revolves around them. Frank's a Sagittarius, so I should know," she adds, continuing the disturbing trend of referring to her fourth husband as if he's still alive, instead of cryogenically frozen somewhere in the California foothills.

"I mentioned brunch tomorrow, and he's fine."

Her clear aquamarine eyes taper onto mine with a scrutinizing look. "Tomorrow is Sunday; loosen it up a bit. I mean, nice suit but so serious. The black and the glasses—it's all a little Cruella de Vil, don't you think?"

"Maybe I borrow one of your caftans?" I tease.

She sniggers quietly. Despite her closet full of swirling rainbow-hued dresses, we both know the *Joseph and the Amazing Technicolor*

Dreamcoat look would drape on me like a potato sack. "You are a riot, dear. Somewhere in your closet lives a flirty sundress. Spaghetti straps, your cleavage tucked into a cute little ruched bodice—it says *I still own your ass no matter what I wear.*"

I bite back a smile. "Okay, then. Skimpy cotton flying in."

She presses a hand onto my desk, the ropey blue veins on the back the only evidence of her age. Evelyn plays doubles tennis four times a week and can polish off a twelve-ounce ribeye. Her next adventure is a springtime trek in the Himalayas.

Fierce is only the beginning.

"Thank goodness for you, my dear, dear savior," she says. "I will milk you for what I can while you bide your time with me."

"I like working here," I say, defensiveness creeping into my voice.

"I know you do. But one day you'll move on. All the good ones do."

And all the bad ones, like my predecessor, Al Porter, get run out of town for good.

"My new life's mission is to put Pink Pearl on the map. You're stuck with me until that happens," I half-joke.

"Dani," she says, waving off my sad warning. "The heavy lifting is done. The labels you created are incredible. And that sunscreen brand Rhys promoted a few weeks ago? Sold out worldwide. His reach is incredible. I'm in good hands." She eases out of the chair with a small grunt. "On that note, I better press the flesh and say hello. And it's quitting time, dear. Time to shut it down."

"I might hang in here for another hour," I say. "The air conditioner conked out in my villa last night. It's a bloody inferno."

She gives me a long stare. "Did you call Zachary?"

Our winery handyman is known for pulling miracles out of his ass, but good luck trying to find a replacement part on a long weekend with potboiler temperatures expected.

"He's on it," I assure her. "But with the holiday, he said Tuesday is the earliest he can track down parts."

"Be on him," she says, pressing hard on the words. "Remember, make your voice and needs heard. You matter."

I feel a lump spreading in my throat. Evelyn is the closest thing to a fairy godmother, and she arrived when I needed one the most. Not only has she forked out a hundred and fifty grand a year for my services—my highest salary ever—but after my former boss and lover did a number on me, she bolstered my bruised ego.

A note to career girls: please avoid the minefield of sleeping with your boss. Especially when he promises you the world and then proceeds to strip you of your dignity. Oh, and then gleefully enforces a draconian non-compete clause that makes it impossible to land another advertising job in Canada for two years. Through sheer audacity, luck, and a well-timed bottle of wine, I salvaged my career.

Point is, one workplace romance blew up my heart *and* life, leaving me an island of a woman with a mind filled with doubts. Why create fresh havoc? Forget the butterflies that exploded in my stomach when Rhys and I shook hands.

He is a serious no-fly zone.

And only a fool makes the same mistake twice.

Y

My villa, and I use that term loosely, is an old tractor shed Zachary converted into overflow housing for seasonal workers, a quaint and cramped five hundred square feet decorated with the best of IKEA. No one famous will ever set foot here. And the current indoor temperature feels like a tropical heat wave.

Jesus.

The still, heavy air smacks me in the face like a frying pan. I'd crank open every window for airflow, except there is none. While Evelyn schmoozes with Rhys, the profusely sweating part of me regrets declining her last-minute invite to bunk at her place for the night. But the other, determined part of me applauds the move.

After hiring me, Evelyn insisted I live rent-free for the summer to *test out* winery life before sourcing a permanent place. Every perk and advantage she's offered without hesitation.

But too much reliance on generosity can become a crutch.

I came here to stand tall in a new life.

That means accepting the good, the bad, and the ugly.

And the occasional night of brutal hell.

In my tiny bedroom, I peel off every article of clothing that clings to me like a lost child. Unclasp the Tiffany watch Mom and Dad surprised me with before they left town on their South American adventure. This week, they're deep in the Colombian jungle on a trek to Cuidad Perdida. Out of the cell zone for two weeks. We're a chatty family, so the radio silence has been unusual.

But my younger sister, Amelia, more than makes up for the silence. And she's calling me right on time. Eight p.m. is our magic hour, when my godsons, Alex and Elliot, are passed out full of breast milk, and her husband, Dean, is at the gym, sweating out the stress of stockbroker life.

I've barely said hello when she blurts out: "Give it to me straight. How hot is Rhys in person?"

"On the perfection scale of one to ten?" I ask. "Two million."

"Every detail please," she moans. "I am an endless vessel of gossip need. Feed me."

The thread of desperation in her voice is real. Before her pregnancy, Amelia flirted with low-level stardom as a celebrity gossip podcast host. For an ADD chatterbox fixated on dishing dirt and rumors, *Easy A Gets the Scoop* was a near-perfect vocation. And, continuing the annoying trend of being the first at everything—periods, boyfriends, kids—Amelia discovered Rhys long before he infiltrated my world.

"He seems pretty down to earth," I say. *A little flirty,* I don't say.

"Did you two vibe?"

Amelia white-washed over her jealousy when she found out I would trump her in the meeting-Rhys department, but I hear the slight edge that has crept into her voice.

"I'm his boss," I say. "Will we become besties? I highly doubt it. After his five-week tour of duty, he'll be on the first plane out of here. Paycheck cashed." I stare down at the swollen slabs of flesh supporting me. "Woman with two pieces of plywood for feet long forgotten."

Amelia makes a frustrated sound. "First of all, get over your feet. Secondly, I will trade you six ways to Sunday for my giant ass."

"Men crave a big booty," I counter, although I'm secretly glad she has some flaw. "No guy ever said square and arch-less size-ten pontoons gave them all the feels."

"Speaking of crave." Her voice drops to a conspiratorial whisper. "Any idea if the rumors are true?"

Men make up fifty percent of Rhys's fan base, and they shamelessly post cringe-inducing comments on his feed. My gaydar is far from bulletproof, but he did not give off those vibes in the slightest. Not when the fire of his obvious head-to-toe reduced me to ashes.

"Uhm, sorry, sis. You and *Just Jared* are barking up the wrong tree."

"We have no idea what happens off camera," she flips back. "Sixteen years of posting and not a single pic or video with a girlfriend? Doubtful that a hottie influencer in his sexual prime chooses celibacy."

The sun has started to set, casting a golden hue outside the "clothing optional" Dani Rialto Resort. My skin feels clammy from sweat leaking out of every pore. I pace around the couch, afraid to sit and getting stuck to the pleather.

"Is it a big deal either way?" I ask. "And why do you care so much?"

I know the answer she will inevitably skirt around. Rhys represents a lifestyle Amelia aspired to as a teen—luxury, the high life. She started her podcast to be one step closer to that fantasy world. Permanent hiatus be damned, the burning need to spread hearsay like butter rages endlessly within her. I've often wondered how she sustains her marriage to Dean, her nerdy high school sweetheart and the quintessential guy next door, who considers *Family Guy* reruns and changing diapers the height of a Friday night.

"I don't really care," she says, backpedaling like I knew she would. "But we have discussed this, and you have on-the-ground intel."

Her bruised tone lands heavily like the ferocious heat my one struggling fan in the bedroom can't keep up with. I need airflow, or Dani will melt into a puddle. Me and my nakedness beeline for the barn-style door that acts as the east-facing wall. It swings out instead of in, and because of its age and lack of use, the wood has tightened against the frame. It takes serious beef to wedge it loose.

Another thing Zachary said he would fix and hasn't.

"I will suss things out," I say, appeasing her. "And I promise to report back." Pressing the phone between my shoulder and ear, I turn slightly and prepare for contact with ancient wood. "But the odds of Rhys and me hooking up are tinier than an atom," I add. "And remember what happened with—"

"Do not utter the name that shall not be repeated in our lifetime," Amelia interrupts. "And on that slimy note, I have a great story to share."

Before another batch of gossip rolls off her tongue, I bang my raw, athletic ability against the door. But instead of the defiant squeak of resistant lumber, the door flings open.

It all happens so fast after that.

I hear a dull *thud*, followed by a cry of surprise, and then, "Ow! Shit."

The phone slips out of my outstretched hands, disappearing into the abyss of the wide-open space I fall into. My stumbling ass lurches into a shell-shocked Rhys as he staggers on the frazzled grass with a crimson stream gushing from his nose.

Then we're both falling, the ground rushing to meet us.

Chapter Four

RHYS

Shock washes over me—from the fall and a bucketload of bombarding sensations. A rush of warm blood spills out of my nose onto my lips, the stickiness saturated with a metallic tang. The swell of Dani's bare breasts crushes against my chest, pinning both lungs. I feel the hammer blows of my pulse and fight to take a deep breath. Then another.

The move here is to ask if she is all right, but *you* try to talk with a divine entity sprawled on top of you in the buff.

The idea of asking for cream now?

File that under wildly inappropriate.

Dani slowly lifts her head off my chest. Everything has gone very quiet. I feel dazed like I've been touched by black magic, but she looks like a stunned deer chased out of the woods by a hunter. I wait for the awareness to hit her—that the flimsy barrier of my clothes might erupt into flames from the heat of her nakedness. Or if she moves her hips even the slightest, I claim zero responsibility for what she encounters.

Her gaze tapers onto my face, a traumatized horror taking over her expression.

"Oh my god!" she gasps. "Did I break it?"

I gingerly explore the damage with my fingers. Nothing crunches or spears me with pain, but goddamn. The overwhelming pleasure of her body molded onto mine…

Forget my crushed nose. The jolt to my dick is what worries me.

And maybe Dani feels it too because suddenly she pushes up and off me, backpedaling away, stumbling, arms windmilling before she loses her balance and ass-plants in front of me.

For five agonizing seconds, it's like the world melts away.

The sight of her … legs splayed wide like she's giving 'er for amateur night at the local strip club. Every random dot in the universe connects, forging the beam of twilight sun that slants onto her smooth pink mound like a lurid spotlight.

The gentlemanly thing to do is not fix my gaze on the sparkle.

But life as a hot-blooded male has its limitations.

And there is no denying the object of my attention: a shiny silver barbell looped in the hood of her clit, with two pink pearls on either end twinkling like Christmas presents under the tree.

Holy smokes.

Dani is completely still, quietly absorbing the devastation. Then she clamps her legs together and attempts to cover her heaving, sizeable, and fucking perfect breasts with one arm. I drag my eyes to meet hers with unbridled shame. Apologizing is out of the question. The peep show came to town, and I gawked. Guilty as charged.

So much for professional boundaries.

I finally scrape together some manners, turning my head to give her privacy from life-ending embarrassment.

After an awkward beat that seems to go on for eternity, Dani says, "We need to clean you up."

"Okay," I reply, out of my element entirely. "I'll wait here."

She's gone within seconds, scurrying inside for the safety of four walls and clothing. When the coast is clear, I sit up, the weight of what just happened pressing hard on my shoulders. What a way to make an impression, Rhys—creeper at her door.

Shit!

In the dying light of sunset, my chest is heaving as I try to catch my breath. I need a minute to recover before I can do anything about it. Blood dripping onto my t-shirt spreads into a mangled scarlet Rorschach blot, and nausea rumbles precariously in my gut. Even as a kid, injury and pain freaked me out. Dad labeled me Mr. Sensitive, and not in a loving way.

"Dani! What's going on?"

I freeze, scanning my immediate perimeter to locate the source of the shrill, disembodied voice that settles on my skin like napalm.

There. Lying face down in the grass. Dani's phone.

Another panicked *Hello???* broadcasts into the silence, prompting me to answer.

I fumble the phone to my ear and center with a calming, deep breath. "Hi. This is Dani's phone."

"Who's this?" the female voice asks, tinged with surprise.

"Uhm, Rhys?"

There's a long silence before she replies, "Oh. Hi. Is Dani okay?"

"Yeah, yeah," I snap into an easy-breezy mode, as if she and I are chilling with beers on the deck. "Do you want to talk to her?"

"Ah … she can call me later."

"Okay. I'll pass on the message. Who's this?"

Another pause, weightier, like she's debating what to say. "Her BFF," she finally says. "And tell her there's no rush. Bye."

The line goes dead in my ear. That woman was in a hurry to end the call, whoever she was. But her voice—why did it sound familiar? Some people remember faces; I'm an audio guy. Laughs, voices, songs. Sounds trigger immediate and visceral reactions, and her voice provoked a flare of goose bumps and a quickening of my heart.

My whole body is humming now. With Dani's phone unlocked in my hand, I'm tempted to cross-check the caller's name. Maybe scroll through some of her photos while I'm at it. Watch for the one of her wrapped in the arms of some slick, suited-up guy, and quietly bow out of the fruitless pursuit of my new boss. On my walk over here, I did the math. A result that didn't end up in my favor because, well, reality. Dani and I are as likely as Mother Teresa hooking up with The Joker.

But the photo on her home screen shows Dani wearing a beautiful smile and a Joey Ramone t-shirt.

That has me thinking twice.

As do her pearls.

Thank god I control my urge to poke around her business because Dani suddenly reappears in denim cut-offs and the oversized Joey shirt. Her eyes immediately travel onto the phone clutched in my hand.

My cheeks blaze. Guilt by association. Because I almost looked.

"Your friend said to call her back," I explain, thrusting the phone at her like a hot potato. "I convinced her I wasn't an ax murderer."

Dani tucks her phone into the back pocket of her shorts with a rueful half-smile. "I'm the one who almost murdered *you*."

I give a little shrug and rise to my feet, brushing dead grass off my shorts. Cool as I can be with sexy red ooze leaking from my nose.

"Next time," I say. "Hit me with your best shot."

Dani appraises me, letting her gaze run over my face. I'll take her soft eyes any day over Joey Ramone's stone-faced mug silently judging me from the front of her t-shirt.

How did you manage to create this clusterfuck in under an hour?

"Come in." Dani waves me inside. "I have a first aid kit."

I don't have to be asked twice to follow those endless tanned legs. To avoid leaving a trail of red splatters on her floor, I use my shirt as a temporary bandage. Dani rambles about the door and how the repair guy must have fixed it, but I'm only half-listening.

Compared to my extravagant villa, her crib is the equivalent of the other side of the tracks. A shack with no flair. Walls slapped with institutional beige paint. It's like a thrift store came by and dumped all the unclaimed furniture. My eyes sweep the room hunting for telltale signs of a man. Dirty white socks heaped in a corner. An Xbox. A grungy recliner that matches nothing else.

But there's none of that.

Not much of anything, to be honest.

Her place is a little hard to read, like her.

And Dani interprets my silent investigation bang on. "None of this stuff is mine," she says. "It came with the place. I moved here temporarily in June after Evelyn hired me. Vancouver is home."

"So this is a new job for you?" I ask.

"New, in terms of the wine industry," she clarifies. "But I've worked in advertising for the past eight years. Copywriter and junior creative director."

Her chin rises slightly as if daring me to question her credentials. Ha. As if. My toolbox of tricks boils down to being pretty and looking good on camera. Hardly the ammunition to throw down a challenge.

"You seem very competent," I say.

A surprised smile tugs her mouth higher. "Thank you."

I groan inwardly. *Competent?* Why don't I hand her a report card and call it a day?

Dani graciously moves on, gesturing at the strip kitchen. "I'll meet you at the sink. Otherwise known as the emergency room."

She disappears into what I guess is the bedroom, and my gaze drifts across the not-so-great room to a large picture window and the stunning vista framed within. Colin told me on the drive up that Osoyoos Lake is Canada's warmest lake. Seeing it in person, it seems to stretch on forever, glittering in the sunset like a blanket of blue-green diamonds.

The dazzling display of nature fills me with an irresistible urge to swim.

After a day without the ocean, I get antsy.

Or maybe it's the sweat prickling on my skin that feels like ants are crawling all over me. The view certainly raises the bar of this shabby hut, but how can Dani survive in this heat?

She returns seconds later carrying a small first aid kit and busies herself at the kitchen counter, opening the kit and poking through the supplies. Her skin glows with a fine mist of sweat.

"Why is your place so hot?"

Dani glances up, her face flushing a deeper shade of crimson. "My air conditioner broke. Hence…"

She trails off with a bashful smile, and I jump in with some solidarity. "I walk around my house naked too."

She levels a look at me. "But have you ever flopped nude onto a stranger?"

I pretend to think about that. "Not lately."

"By that, you mean never."

"No worries," I assure her. "Your secrets are safe with me."

Her brow rises in a question of—*can a man be trusted with secrets of that magnitude?* In the case of me, the answer is yes. My flaws are many and plentiful, but when it comes to holding on to classified information, I'm a human vault. And the more pressing question is, why are all these snappy one-liners rolling off my tongue like butter? Any woman I've ever had a speck of interest in leaves me tongue-tied and flustered, but I feel oddly protected in Dani's presence. Like I can let my guard down for once and not have it bite me in the ass.

She unravels a small roll of gauze, uses a pair of mini scissors to snip off two tidy squares, and hands both to me. "Wad one of these into each nostril."

While I stuff cotton up my nose, she inspects me from all sides, her face picture-perfect with concern. Without her glasses on, I can see flecks of blue trapped in the bottomless gray of her irises. I'm careful not to stare. I could get lost in those eyes and never find my way home.

"Why did you come over?" she asks, her quizzical gaze landing squarely on mine.

"Oh. Uhm…" She's standing so close, I can feel the heat rising from her skin, a ribbon of her sugary-sweet perfume caressing me. It short-circuits my brain. "I, uh, hoped you might have some coffee cream. There was none in my fridge."

Her brow furrows, and dammit! Can I replay that? Spin the story to be about her and not my royal neediness?

"Sorry about that." She spins to the sink, rips off two paper towels, wets them under the faucet, and motions me closer. "May I tidy you up as an apology?"

Her voice is warm, sincere, and so kind it makes me feel undeserving of her selflessness. "Yes, but please, you don't have to apologize. You've done enough. And I can survive a day without cream."

She wipes blood from my face, touching me like I'm fragile. "Which is why you're here."

"Partial survival?" I crack a smile.

Dani laughs and takes a step back. "You're funny. And you should be fine. Take a look."

She hands me a small mirror from the kit to gauge for myself. Aside from looking like a dork with gauze jammed in both nostrils, this injury is minor. But how I wish it were major if it meant more of her attention.

"Put some ice on it just in case," she recommends. "And take the supplies with you."

Light and shadows play across her face, her voice soft and final as she packs up the kit. Maybe it's the adrenaline wearing off, or her gentle compassion. Both inspire me to hunker down and get cozy, although I sense my visit is drawing to a close.

How to extend it?

I spot a tin of Folger's pre-ground on the counter next to a cheap, dollar-store plastic coffee maker.

"You steal that from a Motel 6?" I joke.

Dani cocks one thin, shaped brow. "Are you judging me?"

"Possibly."

"Says the guy with the overblown rider."

"If you can forgive me the bed, I'll overlook your taste in coffee."

She leans against the counter, studying me with a slow burn of a smile spreading on her face. "Tell me the truth," she says. "Is it worth it? Do you sleep that much better?"

"You tell me," I say. "I'm officially donating it to you when we're done."

Her eyes widen in surprise. "The plan was to send it back and eat a small restock fee."

Before I can tell her to dock the full price from my final invoice, her phone chimes. Dani tugs it out of her shorts, glances at the screen, then sends the call to voicemail.

"I should call my sister back sooner than later," she says, a hint of reluctance in her voice.

"Sister?" I tilt my head at this news. "She said she was your BFF."

Dani blinks. A blankness settles on her face. "She's both."

The niggle at the back of my mind from earlier returns. I struggled to pinpoint why that woman's voice sounded familiar. And Dani just sounded a bit wary at the mention of her.

"Oh, don't forget." Dani sets down the phone, whirls around, and opens the fridge to brandish a carton of coffee cream. She wiggles the container in her hand with a sly expression. "You probably thought I had caramel-flavored creamer, didn't you?"

I smile back. "I guess it's my lucky day."

As she hands me the cream, her fingers graze mine and linger, like they did when she took back her phone. Our eyes meet, and something else pulses in the air between us, something electric and powerful. I feel a punch of emotion in my chest, almost knocking me off my feet. All I can hear is the fan sputtering on overdrive in the other room and the frantic thrum of my own heartbeat.

"What time is brunch tomorrow?" I manage to ask.

My question slices through the loaded tension, and Dani pulls back slightly, her posture stiffening as the strange spell between us dissolves. Just like that, she slips back into official mode.

"Noon," she replies. "At Evelyn's place. Follow the path up from your villa, or text me if you get lost." She hands me the first aid kit, this time careful not to let our hands overlap. "And, speaking of texting, next time, send me one before you come over. And feel free to use the real front door."

She points to the Home Depot special next to the picture window, winks, and flashes a grin more arch than *duh, you idiot*. Feelings I have no name for churn to the surface from wherever I had them quarantined. What would it feel like to kiss that lush, lip-glossed mouth?

A thrilling sense of inevitability surges through me.

So many questions. And five full weeks to answer them.

Our goodbye doesn't feel so final.

On the short walk home through the hush of twilight, my flip-flops crunch along still-warm gravel, although the air is cooler and infused with the fruity tang of fermenting wine and a faint brininess from the nearby lake. I feel sleep dragging me down, but I'm buoyant inside. Yes, my nose got smashed, and I damn near needed the shock of a defibrillator to kickstart my heart after witnessing her jewels. But it's a known fact that women will mention a boyfriend or husband at the first opportunity.

And I gave her plenty of those.

Just before I pass out on the comfiest bed I've ever slept on, two words cradle me like welcoming arms.

Next time.

Chapter Five

DANI

After Rhys leaves, I pour myself a glass of water, ring Amelia, and mentally prepare for the barrage of questions. And the volume at which they will be shrieked. Sure enough…

"Way to keep me hanging!" Amelia shouts into my ear. "What, where, when, how? All of it. Details, puh-lease."

I wince, pulling the phone away from my ear. "Geez, Ames. Indoor voice."

"Don't you dare 'indoor voice' me," she huffs. "Spill!"

I take a deep breath and stare out the kitchen window, my eyes tracing the path that leads to his villa. The last twenty minutes feel like a pixelated blur, a whirlwind of emotions and revelations. I'm still reeling, my brain haywire from being laid bare in front of Rhys. His eyes lasered to my womanhood, and if intercourse could happen with a glance, he fucked me slow and dirty.

"Rhys came over to borrow some coffee cream."

"Cream?" Amelia's voice drips with disappointment. "That's all you've got for me?"

I nod, then remember Amelia can't see me. "What do you want me to say?"

"How about the truth? I can hear your voice," she says accusingly. "You're holding back."

We are finger-pinky swear besties and keep no secrets from each other. And who else but my sister can cherish the carnage of a near-legendary blunder that left my heart a tattered wreck? My entire world sharpened into focus in that quiet moment when all my secret spaces felt exposed under the blazing intensity of Rhys's gaze. It felt private and incredibly intimate. It left me feeling unraveled. And not unbothered. From the question that floated within his eyes, Rhys sensed it too.

And the sexy had come off him like perfume.

If I needed proof of how unprecedented this incident falls within the spectrum of my existence, Exhibit A is Amelia's concerning state when I wrap up: one of dead silence.

Then: "After a full naked takedown, with bloodshed, you nursed him in cut-offs?" Her voice leaks with disbelief. "You heroic little skank."

I wait for her to say more. In the history of the Rialto Sisters, the undisputed fact is this: Amelia will grace me with her opinion/advice/counsel whether I want it or not. Being around my baby sister turns back the clock. I become the girl who needs validation.

An old habit that defines us.

In school, I struggled to get B's. She breezed through a master's in education. I was on a mission to get fired from every waitressing gig in Vancouver. She turned down a prof gig at The University of BC to start a podcast and, eventually, make babies. She is blonde to my dark. Spunky to my steady. The Disney princess to my gnarled witch.

(Yes, sometimes it feels like that.)

She hopped from boyfriend to boyfriend like there was a never-ending supply of mesmerized men willing to fall at her feet. I wrangled my beach volleyball body into classy suits and sat alone all night at the bar, watching drunk guys fawn over petite giggling blondes in Juicy Couture sweats.

And then, cherry on the sundae of her one-upmanship, she scores an interview with Rhys for her podcast. Every word, every laugh, every thoughtful pause of that interview lives permanently in my head. Rhys sounded so sweet. So kind. I was half-certain the universe Amelia has wrapped around her finger would have sent her jetting off to Corfu to canoodle with her new Trenton Bae had she not been happily married.

So, the butterflies I'm feeling right now are not just Rhys-induced. A bit of pride is involved.

Little old me scooped my baby sister for once.

Amelia clears her throat. "So? Now what?"

"Nothing. Other than business as usual."

She snorts a laugh. "I can guarantee you he is not thinking that."

"Just because I toppled onto him naked doesn't mean I've become sexually fearless," I counter. "Or that he's even interested. It was an accident. Plain and simple."

Although, it feels like anything but. Something fundamental shifted between us during my Nurse Rialto session. A flash of emotion had moved over his face and the effect of his proximity shimmered on my skin. The question is, do I risk my newly minted career on a summer fling? With one of the most recognizable humans on the planet?

"And he lives in Greece," I say, firming it up in my mind.

"Not for the next five weeks," she flips back. "I mean, I'm not encouraging anything," she continues. "But—"

"But you are."

She heaves a sigh. "You could position it as spiritual cleansing of a former douchebag."

I squirm around a familiar feeling. Just when I think I've packed away all the debris of my crushed self-esteem.

As if she can read my mind, Amelia's voice dips. "Can I tell you my story now? I ran into him at Starbucks the other day."

Something cold blooms in my chest. "And?"

"He pretended not to recognize me until I snagged his mochaccino and confronted him."

Brett Winn is the person in reference. My ex-boyfriend, boss, and entitled loser. A cheater with a warped perspective of decency baked into his corrupt soul.

I let out a breath I didn't realize I was holding. "Tell me it ended without bloodshed."

"No literal blood spilled, but no one fucks over my sister without getting an earful." Amelia's excitement is palpable even through the phone. "I tore a strip up and down him. Mini applause from the baristas."

There is a threat to being in public with Amelia. She's the person berating a chef if the meal sucks or shrugging off dirty looks when the clerk at the supermarket has to refund the ten cents he overcharged her.

"Was his assistant there?" I'm careful not to voice Lauren's name. She's the sleek, younger model Brett traded me in for.

"Queen of the Concubines stayed camped outside in his Maserati," she says. "I spat on the sidewalk and pranced off with my latte."

I rub my forehead, imagining the scene. "Jeez, Ames."

"I believe it's, *Thank you, dear sister, for humiliating a deserving creep.* Oh, and the best part? The entire Starbucks groaned when I mentioned how he dumped you."

"You didn't?" I whisper-ask, knowing it's a futile question. I can see her holding court as if she were the main attraction at The Globe Theatre. Mind you, it is Shakespearean and fucking tragic to casually inform your girlfriend of six months that *I'm beyond your pay grade.*

That sword to the gut still bleeds. If a hot but no-name executive can mash my soul under the heel of his three-hundred-dollar Italian loafer, conventional wisdom dictates that my attraction to the fabled Rhys can only end in disaster.

But his banter, poking fun at my coffee maker, threw me off. It felt real. Normal. For an influencer heavyweight, you'd think he'd have some kind of superstar affectation. Not fierce intelligence shining deeply in his eyes. Bald curiosity too.

And my entire villa had thickened with sexual tension.

Conventional? Not in the slightest.

Rhys Trenton saw me completely naked, and damn if he didn't enjoy the view.

"By the way," Amelia says, dragging me out of my thoughts. "You haven't said anything, right?"

I take a sip of water. "Of course not."

Amelia swore me to secrecy. That I wouldn't utter a word about her podcast to Rhys, or drop a single hint that my sister, current hausfrau and milk machine, was the infamous Easy A. Not that Rhys would cobble the pieces together. Amelia transformed into a wildly different persona for her podcast, from the spiky black wig to her posh British accent.

No one but her closest allies knew who she really was.

And when she ditched the podcast two years ago after her European honeymoon with Dean, I initially assumed pending motherhood was the cause. For someone whose life MO is balls-out, shoot first and ask questions later, it struck me as odd to bail when she was on the brink of success. But Amelia danced around my questions then, and she wants to bury her alter ego for reasons she continues to dance around.

So, I'm not surprised she wraps up the conversation with a brisk "good," and we pivot to discussing our parents living their best retiree lives in the wilderness of Colombia.

Later in bed, naked and sweating through the sheets, I remind myself not to read too much into anything with Rhys. The problem with celebrities is that their attention can make you feel special. It's easy to get hooked on that fleeting warm glow. But what happens when the spotlight fades and you're left in a cold, Rhys-less world?

Better not to feel the heat at all.

Life officially changes at 10:38 on Sunday morning.

Lazing in bed with the blinds shut tight against the already fiendish heat, I power on my phone. Rhys had teased out his trip to Canada in a series of airport vignettes, and by tagging Nero Vino, our follower count had bumped up by a couple hundred. I navigate to Instagram, curious about what transpired overnight.

My private account loads first. I blink once, then twice, before a spacey feeling takes over my body. Wait. I must be hallucinating. It can't be, but there it is—a friend request icon glowing red in the right-hand corner.

From Rhys.

I feel a feathering sensation at the back of my throat.

Are you shitting me?

I suppose using my actual name as a username and a real photo made it easy for him to track me down. Am I flattered? Any woman with a pulse would be. Rhys follows mega brands or fellow influencers —accounts teeming with tens of thousands of fans and spit-shined content. For him to acknowledge Dani Rialto and her dinky private account, currently stalled out at seven hundred and sixty-one followers?

I chew on the inside of my cheek, debating the ramifications of accepting his request. Not every human seeks worship and immortality on social media, and I'm content living with @Dani_Rialto as a speck of unimportance in the Instagram handle world. Do I need the added stress of having to curate my posts? Pose in full makeup and use filters to portray a fantasy life ten times better than my regular existence?

Ignoring the request for now, I flip to his feed. Our deal with Rhys guarantees he posts a daily story or reel along with a carousel. Monday is his official start day, but the impression he left is that of a team player willing to do what it takes.

And my suspicion proves accurate.

The video story he posted last night is classic Rhys: swinging in a hammock—the one I spent two days sourcing online. But, for once, the POV is not of his face and the dramatic vista of the Ionian Sea coastline sparkling behind him. Instead, against the star-filled sky, are his crossed and beautiful feet while he holds up a glass of rosé.

The caption reads, *Pink Pearl guarantees sweet dreams.*

Winky-face emoji.

Two thousand-plus comments.

Holy shit.

Flipping to the Nero Vino account, our follower numbers have risen by over fifteen hundred. A giddiness stirs within me, radiating to my fingertips and toes. It's a known fact that brands blow up with his involvement, but to witness his Midas touch playing out in real time feels surreal.

That, however, is only half the story.

I fight back the stupid smile that's growing wider by the second.

That cheeky caption he wrote?

I will bet a million dollars he was not talking about wine.

Evelyn and Nicole Tanner are deep in conversation when I join them on the patio overlooking the vast blue waters of Lake Osoyoos.

"Hi," I say breathlessly. "Sorry I'm late."

I ran here after losing track of time, fretting over Rhys's friend request. It didn't feel right to show up without accepting it. Now we're internet buddies, for better or for worse.

"Ah, here she is." Evelyn beams, embracing me in a hug. "My secret weapon, all bright-eyed and bushy-tailed. Your timing is perfect. The caterer set everything up. All we need is our guest of honor."

Like everything Evelyn masterminds, the brunch spread looks incredible.

On a platter ringed with fat, ripe cherries, poached eggs nestle in little nests of steamed spinach. There's whipped butter, jars of peach jam, and wildflower honey. The tang of sourdough spikes the air, and toasted slices are artfully arranged in a basket, cut thick, like the crispy strips of bacon glistening in the sun. Add in the backdrop of Evelyn's dramatic modern home and the gold-plated view, and our little tableau under the shade of a pergola screams the best of wine country.

As Evelyn buzzes around the table, adjusting everything, Nicole reaches into the front pocket of her faded overalls for a stick of nicotine gum. "I heard he kept you waiting yesterday," she says, gruff and notably unimpressed as she unwraps and wads the gum into her mouth. "He better not pull that same bullshit with me."

A former fast-talking tort lawyer, Nicole reinvented herself with viticulture, finding her true calling amongst tangled vines and an industry more prone to self-importance than the law. Tall and wiry, but deceptively strong, with slate-gray hair cut short, at a distance you might mistake her for a man.

But Nicole is a passionate woman when it comes to wine.

"By the way," Evelyn says, "I had a lovely discussion with Rhys last night. So down to earth!" She removes her sunglasses, offering a pleased flicker of her eyebrow. "And he said you were *very* accommodating."

"I did my job," I say. "I'm glad he appreciated that." But the thrill of hearing that he did warms my insides.

"Oh, yes," she assures me. "He gushed on and on. How did it go with the coffee cream mission? He seemed eager to get that sorted out."

"Oh?" Nicole perks up. "Is that why you're late?"

"No!" I blush redder than the cherries. "I mean, yes, he came over. For the cream. Nothing more. I told him to reach out if he needs anything."

Evelyn and Nicole share a look. I'm rambling, filling the space like I always do. The slow-spinning floor fans on the patio feel like soldiers designated to keep my pathetic denials from floating away.

Evelyn smooths the front of her emerald caftan. "I think he's delighted to be under your watchful eyes."

Her gaze falls onto my dress, and she nods with silent approval. The dark blue sundress clings nicely before flaring into a breezy A-line. I styled my hair into two thick braids and paired it with silver hoop earrings. The overall look says casual but classy—*we are moving on from yesterday.*

Or so I hope.

"I think he's delighted to make a million dollars," I point out. "That's why he's here. Let's not fool ourselves. And, for the record, every woman knows you don't fall for man candy like Rhys. He's a guaranteed broken heart."

Nicole clears her throat and straightens in the chair, chin lifting slightly. Evelyn stills, tipping her head side to side, like a bird. Or like someone who is trying to give me a clue.

Shit.

Too late.

Just when I think Jesus has decided I have humiliated myself enough in front of this man, a deep rolling voice comes from right behind me.

"Morning."

Chapter Six

RHYS

Well, this is awkward.

I could drive a train through the tunnel of silence. Dani finds something fascinating on the patio to stare at while Evelyn, the clever old bird she is, swoops in to save the day.

"Welcome, Rhys!" she chirps, her tone slightly too bright. "You look refreshed. Did you sleep well?"

"It took a while to crash," I admit. "But I had great dreams."

The simple truth? I still haven't recovered from last night. I was in a state of near paralysis all morning, lying in bed and fantasizing about Dani's pearls—caught between torment and lack of any coping mechanism.

"Hi, I'm Nicole Tanner. Recovering lawyer." The third woman, who has been eyeing me like I'm a fraud, rises from her seat. She extends a mannish hand, dirt caked under every ragged fingernail. "I'll be schooling you on everything about rosé."

She crushes our handshake, and I'm briefly silenced by her strength. Nero's famous winemaker is more handsome than pretty, built lean, with a salt-and-pepper buzz cut and a generous mouth. She looks like a middle-aged Mick Jagger … if he were a woman.

"Nice to meet you," I say. "And I'm ready to learn." Turning to Dani, I ask, "How was your night?"

Dani has stubbornly refused to meet my eyes until now. I can see the line of tightness on her forehead, and I attempt to erase it with a wink. I'm stoked that she considers me man candy, but the heart-breaker bit?

Not so much.

"Hot," she says. "But I survived."

"I texted Zachary to get his butt in gear to repair the AC," Evelyn adds. "He did say he fixed your door yesterday. It shouldn't be sticking anymore."

Dani cracks the tiniest smile, but it vanishes quickly as Evelyn herds us into our seats.

"Please, sit and eat."

Dani and I ease into our appointed chairs, Evelyn and Nicole planted on the opposite side of the table. Feels like the perfect set-up.

"Coffee?" Evelyn asks me. "It's your favorite brand."

"Yes, please."

She pours a dark, fragrant stream from a silver carafe into my cup as birds chatter deep within the enormous willow trees flanking either side of the deck. The long tendrils sway hypnotically in the hot breeze. Not a bad way to spend a Sunday, with a killer view and surrounded by a crew of bad-ass ladies. Imperial Evelyn, tiara tucked into her beehive. What I'm guessing is a gender-fluid Nicole, country chic in dusty overalls and Birkenstocks.

And sweet Dani. Far less skin on display this morning, but she's just as hot semi-clothed.

Maybe hotter.

"I love that your winery is pro-woman, Evelyn," I say. "From what I've heard, that's rare."

A smile lights up her face. "I'm proud to be a trailblazer," she says.

"Nicole has one of the finest noses in the biz, and Dani's creative genius ups our brand game. Have you seen the labels she created?"

"She hasn't shown me anything."

Under the table, I gently nudge my knee against Dani's. It's a just-between-us move, lighthearted and meant to be imperceptible, but Dani jumps in her chair as if I'd smacked her. The table shakes, ice cubes clinking in our water glasses.

Evelyn raises an eyebrow, curious, as she and Nicole silently gauge the friction that's poked up. Dani's eyes flash on mine—a not-so-subtle message of *don't you dare go there*—before she seizes the momentum back.

"I didn't want to overload you on day one." She smiles sweetly, impressively pro.

"Well, you have to take a look," Evelyn insists. "They're utterly gorgeous. And you told me last night that you like to draw in your spare time. Why not have our two creatives gab about their respective inspirations? Start with breakfast while I grab my tablet."

Dani reaches for her arm. "They can wait. Let's eat first."

"Nonsense!" Evelyn swats Dani's hand away. "The reason you're here today is because of those labels. Tell Rhys your story. He needs to weave it into one of his videos. And remember, your success is my success."

As our eccentric host and her giant bed sheet of a dress swirl away into the house, I turn to Dani and don't try to hide my interest. "Okay, let's hear it. I'm intrigued."

Nicole settles into her chair like a movie is about to start. "This is so classic."

Dani's quiet for a few seconds, slowly succumbing to the fact she's outnumbered. After what sounds like a steadying breath, she starts, "I lost my job a few weeks ago. In the process of drowning my sorrows in a bottle of *The Emperor*—"

"That's our flagship Cabernet Sauvignon," Nicole interjects. "It's what the kids call *lit*."

"I had this vision, how to rebrand Evelyn's wines," Dani continues. "Tying everything into Nero and Rome. I fired up my laptop and got busy in Photoshop. At three in the morning, I said, 'Screw it. These look great.' I sent the labels and my resume to Evelyn in what managed to be a coherent email." She laughs at the memory. "Probably should have slept on it."

I nod, liking every word. "That's an impressive origin story."

"Necessity is the mother of invention, right?"

Dani shrugs like drunk-emailing an employer is how she rolls every day. The most my drunken nights have amounted to are sloppy hand jobs and a blistering morning hangover. But I heard how her voice hitched after admitting she lost her job. Last night's version sounded like the career pivot happened on her terms.

Evelyn rejoins us, wielding an iPad she hands off to me. "Take a gander and tell me these are not groundbreaking."

"I don't know about *groundbreaking*," Dani hedges. "They're different. But sometimes that's a good thing."

What snags my attention is the assault of color. Supersaturated pinks and dreamy blues frame a young Roman god in the clouds, casting his gaze down to the words *Pink Pearl Rosé*.

"*Rosé, for goddesses and gods*," I read the tagline aloud. "Genius. Did you come up with that?"

Dani returns my smile, hers a little shy. "I created all the images and taglines."

"Flip through the others," Evelyn encourages me. "*The Emperor* is my favorite."

Every label is a mini work of art. And the wine names riff on Nero's closest, most scandalous relationships and rumors. O, Claudia, *The Queen's Cabernet Franc* is named after his first wife, Claudia. His tutor and my man Seneca is immortalized as Seneca Syrah —*Philosophy in a glass*. Her sly reference to Nero's alleged attempt to burn down Rome so he could build a sprawling estate is reimagined as Golden House Chardonnay—*Build it and they will come*.

I side-eye Dani with a new layer of respect. Hands down, you would gravitate to these labels if you spotted them amongst a sea of regulars. But the bigger factor in my admiration? The realization that we could have an in-depth conversation about Nero. When I brought up the Roman Empire sitting in the hot tub with Myla, the only thing she knew about Rome was how to find the Prada store.

"No offense, Evelyn," I say, "but these are way better than what you have now."

She beams like a proud mother. "You're preaching to the converted. Why do you think I snapped up Dani ASAP?"

Dani leans closer to point out details, and it's profoundly unbelievable how my focus craters. A mental image of her wrapped only in her deeply sensual perfume invades my brain, all the electric and wild damage we could create. And how much longer does she plan to terrorize my arm, the warm swell of her breast languishing against it like it's no big deal?

"The first case of rebranded rosé arrived last week," Dani says. "The bottles will be front and center during the photo shoot on Friday."

She reaches for a cherry, and with the fruit trapped between her full lips, pops the stem off. I shift in my chair, feeling the effect of that more than I should.

"On that note," Evelyn says. "Have you heard from Luca? He sent some bizarre text the other day. Half Spanish gibberish. I told him to call you."

Before Dani can reply, her phone vibrates on the table. She glances at it, her features etching into a frown. "How weird is that? It's him."

"Oh, god," Evelyn mutters. "If he's calling on a Sunday, it can't be good news."

I've shot twice with Luca da Silva, the current *enfant terrible* of the fashion world. His brand consists of drama dialed up to twenty, flagrant hand gestures, and pushing the creative envelope. And last-minute changes that annoy the hell out of everyone.

Dani picks up with a friendly tone. "Hola, señor. Your ears must be burning. We were just talking about you."

The smile slowly slides off her face, and we can all hear the impassioned ranting leaking from her phone.

"What?" Dani's voice ratchets an octave higher. "You're flying in today? But the shoot isn't until..."

She's reduced to listening, eyes flicking up to meet Evelyn's in a secret discussion. "Hold on, Luca. Hold on. Evelyn's right here. Let me run this past her."

With her phone pressing tight against her shoulder, she whispers, "He says his agent double-booked him. Tomorrow is his window."

Evelyn rolls her eyes. "Ask him if he needs more money to make Friday stick."

Dani slides the phone to her ear. "Hi again. Evelyn wants to know if an increase in compensation will make any difference?"

Dani bears the brunt of another verbal tirade, nodding and repeating, "Okay, okay. And there's no way to push this? No. You're fully booked." She flashes a look of defeat at Evelyn. "Okay. It is what it is. You and Vigo arrive tonight, and we shoot tomorrow at nine a.m." Her hand tightens around the phone. "Thanks for letting us know. I better jump on this. The hotels. Yes, thanks. Ciao, ciao."

She hangs up, dumping her phone on the table with a frustrated sigh.

"That didn't sound good," I say.

"Is Yvette cool if we shoot at her house tomorrow?" Dani asks Evelyn.

"We had a shamanic practitioner booked for our rose quartz sound bath, but we'll have to cancel. Unbelievable," she grouses to no one in particular, "this happens with him all the time. What about the other model?"

Dani rockets to attention in her chair. "Oh, shit! I better email and check her availability."

"Can I help with anything?" I was secretly hoping to hit the lake with her after brunch. Mostly hoping to see her in a bikini.

"Thanks for the offer, but it's all logistics." She stands abruptly, the chair scraping across the concrete. Brain already on the unfolding disaster. "Enjoy brunch. I need to get ahead of this."

"If Luca's original model pick isn't available, you have my authority to choose someone else," Evelyn lays down the law. "We don't have time to go back and forth."

Dani turns to Nicole. "Are you cool if we reschedule you and Rhys for Tuesday?"

"Whatever works for the team," she says, calmly pouring herself a coffee.

Nicole isn't easily riled is the impression I get. If a term could define a person, she has a lock on *no-nonsense*. And I still feel her less-than-impressed look from earlier.

"I'll check in with you later, okay?" Dani touches my shoulder and excuses herself.

With the best part of brunch striding away, some shine comes off my morning. Evelyn reminds me to eat, and I help myself to the buffet, including a handful of cherries. The idea of feeding them to Dani while her tongue wraps seductively around the firm flesh becomes a disturbingly clear picture in my mind.

And here I thought her pearls were the only thing to torment me.

Evelyn helps herself to eggs and bacon with a look of relief. "Good thing Dani's on this. Nothing will fall through the cracks."

"Those labels are next level," I say. "I'm telling you right now, they're going to hit."

"Don't tell Dani I said this," Evelyn starts, her voice dropping low as she leans across the table, "but thank god she split with her jackass boyfriend. You know what they say? Heartbreak always fuels the best creativity. Just ask Taylor Swift."

I immediately feel better, and a little lighter in my soul. Dani made me suffer before she accepted my friend request this morning. As soon as she did, I skimmed through her feed to check for dudes. Not a man in sight, thankfully. Her posts were the usual random assortment of photos—her in and around Vancouver and a few snaps of her blonde sister, who, while cute, is nowhere near Dani-level beautiful.

My unspoken rule? Never post photos of the women I've dated. Number one, my phone would burst into flames from the onslaught of enraged DMs from fans. Number two, inevitably the run is short-term —me having to flee another Crazy. Why bother capturing those fleeting memories?

"By the way," Nicole waves a finger at Evelyn, "I ran into Tomas at the drugstore yesterday. He followed me like a shadow, grumbling about our 'douchebag clients who buy cliché wine.' That you and I have bribed our way to success."

Evelyn shakes her head in a way that indicates a long, painful topic she'd rather avoid. "He's a walking tragedy, bitter until the day he dies. Even though he's technically family, sometimes I wish he would drop off the face of the earth."

"Who are you talking about?" I ask.

"My first husband's brother," Evelyn says tiredly. "Tomas was the runt of the litter and lost his marbles when his family's estate was transferred to my husband, and, by default, me. The eldest child always takes over the farm. That's how it works."

"He's been on a multi-year mission to take Evelyn down," Nicole adds. "So far, unsuccessful."

"That doesn't stop him from trying." Evelyn grunts her disgust, and I can tell this is more than a sore spot. Bad blood usually is. "And how dare he suggest we're some shoestring operation hawking snake oil. Nicole," she says to me, "is a magician. When you step into her kingdom on Tuesday, you'll understand. Our wines win awards because of her."

I absorb that for a long moment. "If you don't mind me asking, why did you hire me? Sounds like you have the business under control."

Nicole takes over from here. "Pink Pearl is a newer addition to our collection. We want to make a big splash with it. Last year's vintage, what we're selling now, is a dream. The balance is exquisite. My gut says we can sweep all the awards, and a little celebrity endorsement never hurts."

Her first friendly smile lands with an understanding. "Got it. I position this as the best thing since sliced bread. Cheers to that."

Nicole and Evelyn lift their wine glasses to touch mine.

"I have a good feeling about our partnership," Evelyn says warmly. "And I'm so glad you and Dani have bonded."

Am I imagining the sparkle in the light blue of her eyes? During our meet and greet yesterday, Evelyn mentioned a third husband who had lied about wanting children and apologized by way of a massive inheritance when he passed. After a hysterectomy—a little TMI for me —the daughter she longed for remained forever a pipe dream.

When Dani emailed her out of the blue, Evelyn admitted it struck her as kismet. She felt an immediate kinship with Dani.

No matter how tough a business cookie she is, Evelyn's latent mother mode has inadvertently frothed to the surface. I suppose she sees me as a viable contender to ensure her (makeshift) daughter falls into good hands because the nugget of information she supplied about Dani's ex felt like the equivalent of her handing me the baton.

Only a fool wouldn't run with that intel.

Chapter Seven

DANI

I PULL UP TO RHYS'S VILLA THE NEXT MORNING AT SEVEN. HE'S WAITING on the porch, earbuds in, grooving to the music. A tiny hit of adrenaline hits me when I stare at him. He looks like an ad for a premium Greek vacation, skin an impossible shade of creamy mocha. All that tanned glory showcased in a mesh tank top faded to a soft violet.

He is a living, breathing example of how to glow up.

A half smile plays around his mouth as I park and lower my window. He pops out his earbuds, pockets them, and glides forward.

"Morning," I say.

He scopes out my candy-apple red Toyota Tacoma with an approving nod. "Nice ride. I didn't figure you to be a truck girl. What year is this?"

"2015."

He leans on the door without warning, poking his head in to admire the flawless interior. (I may or may not be addicted to Armor-All.)

"Vintage. Sweet. And stick, too." His laser-beam gaze slides from the stick shift onto me, and he lets out a low whistle. "Damn, girl."

His undeniable fragrance of heady spiced vanilla wafts over me, and the feeling in my chest is sharper than giddiness. Historically, I'm a pathetic mess around men this pretty. How am I not supposed to fall off the deep end with Rhys and his still-damp hair curling seductively around both ears?

"I have a present for you." His grin is more angel than devil.

A little thrill shoots up my spine. "What for?"

"I promise you'll like it." He raps his knuckles in a one-two against the sheet metal. "Sit tight."

Returning to the porch, he slings his knapsack over one shoulder and scoops up two Nero Vino-branded to-go thermoses perched on the railing. I crank open his door as he rounds the truck with full hands.

Before sliding in, he offers me one of the thermoses. "I made you a real coffee. Took a wild guess you are cream with no sugar."

"Thank you," I say, sweetly surprised.

Our fingers graze during the handoff, and a tingle of stars shoots up my arm. It's a small, stupid thing. This isn't on the scale of picking winning lottery numbers. He had a one-in-four chance of striking the right combo—black, with cream, with sugar, or with both. And yet, the kindness of his gesture feels like he handed me a million-dollar prize. Not even two days and he has me under his spell, and I haven't the slightest clue how to escape.

Rhys drops his knapsack in the back seat and parks himself in the passenger seat. He shuts the door, sealing us in with the complex, chocolatey scent of his fine coffee.

"Cheers," he raises his thermos, "for saving the photo shoot."

After ditching the gang at brunch yesterday, my afternoon became a masterclass in groveling, begging for non-existent hotel rooms and twice-oversold business-class seats. Our female model, Heather, hemmed and hawed but agreed to cut short her long weekend in exchange for a small bump in her day rate. Come seven p.m., I had pulled enough rabbits out of my ass to deserve someone else cooking me dinner.

Rhys texted just as my lasagna landed on the table at Campo Marina, the local Italian restaurant.

RT: Wanna hit the lake? Sunset looks killer.

Since arriving in June, I've spent most evenings at the lake. With kids and families packed away for the night, the tranquility worked its relaxing magic. I swam to the Nero Vino private floating raft and bobbed, stretched out on my back, while the sunset exploded in fiery oranges and reds around me.

I loved the stillness, the air alive, expectant.

So Rhys's text did tempt. The urge to dump my pasta and wine refill into my Coach bag and bolt back hovered near ninety-eight percent.

But then the other two percent took hold.

And I cursed my professionalism for holding sway over me.

DR: Sorry, tonight won't work. I just sat down for dinner.

And because I didn't want to come across as unfriendly, I followed up with:

DR: Rain check?

To which Rhys instantly replied:

RT: Sweet. Holding you to that.

And I know he will. There's an efficiency behind his casualness. Rhys is a man of his word.

I tip my Thermos against his and smile. "All in a day's work, right?"

I drink deeply, the balanced richness like liquid silk. Full-bodied and eruptive on the tongue. Heavenly.

Rhys clocks my satisfaction. "Worth it?"

"Five stars. Exactly what you should be drinking in that bed."

"Wearing a crown and ordering my servants around?" he teases.

I laugh at the image—so unlike his stripped-down vibe. "Something like that."

"Consider Café Corfu officially open for business," he says. "We also deliver."

I feel the intensity of his eye contact. I was hoping the power of his attractiveness would lessen overnight—flaws would surface, or jerk behavior—but none of those things are true. Now he's confirmed as considerate and thoughtful.

It scares the hell out of me.

I look down, heart thudding, until the feeling of being lost in our own private world passes us by.

Rhys is first to break our companionable silence. "I made a killer road trip playlist. Do you mind if I connect?"

"Did you whip together some punk rock classics just for me?"

Rhys slides his thermos between his muscled thighs and tugs out a phone from bold flamingo-print board shorts. "I like clatter as much as the next guy, but…"

"What?" I ask in mock-offense. "Furious howls and shredding jams do nothing for you?"

An air of amusement lights up his face. "I could get used to it," he stretches out the word *could*. "If someone were willing to convince me."

The unspoken innuendo makes something flip inside me. Rhys is famous for many things, chief among them being unafraid to dance on camera like no one is watching, to a steady stream of house music he adores. Would he survive if I dragged him into a mosh pit filled with punkers and their safety-pinned clothing?

But if he's willing to give it a shot, maybe he's not the music snob I am.

I snug my thermos into the cup holder and reverse down the hill.

Within seconds, Rhys has connected into my system. "Do you want me to set the GPS to Yvette's address?" he asks.

After straightening out the truck, I shift into first. My eyes flicker to his. "You read my email."

"You did hire a professional," he says without sounding arrogant. "Who plans to ease you into the beauty of house music. All you need to do is drive."

As we bump down the winery road and sultry beats start to flow out of the speakers, Rhys opens up the sunroof. Bathed in the golden glow of a new morning and his infectious mood, the tight ball of stress in my stomach that's been grinding overtime since last night slowly unwinds.

I rescued us from disaster at the eleventh hour, and my well-deserved prize is kicking back poolside at a stunning mansion while Rhys frolics in a toga.

I can already taste the chilled rosé sliding down my throat.

It all turns to shit ten minutes later.

I turn onto the highway, ready to hammer the accelerator and open up. Rhys is busy explaining the merits of DJs with très cool names like Hot Since 82, The Avener, and KiNK, when a slew of incoming texts lights up my phone. I eyeball the screen and feel my stomach sink. It's Heather, our female model. She's either pocket-dialing me endless SOS emojis or faces a real crisis.

The sharp sting in my chest tells me it's the latter.

Rhys turns down the music. He has a front-row view of my emoji-packed screen, the phone cradled in a holster on my dash.

"It's your counterpart," I say. "The other model."

"Uh-oh," he says, legitimately concerned. "If you need to pull over and deal with this, go for it."

"Hold on." I type in my password, one eye on the road, praying tragedy is not imminent. After the screen unlocks, I ask Rhys to read the texts.

He pops the phone from the holder and scans the messages. "She missed her flight. An emergency with her dog. She can't make the shoot."

"What???" I clutch the steering wheel in a death grip, blood draining from my fingers. "We start shooting in two hours!"

His liquid brown eyes sweep over me. "She says to call her ASAP."

Forget unruffled and composed—I'm immediately swallowed by a rush of chaotic thoughts. Luca needs to wrap at three to jump on a plane. And Kelowna is a far cry from New York. We are nowhere near a hotbed of replacement models who could save the day.

"You need me to navigate while you troubleshoot?" Rhys offers. "I'm here. Put me to use."

Good god. What business does he have being formidably attractive *and* helpful? Still holding his eyes, I fight to maintain calm. But my instinct tells me this might be a bag of dynamite, lit up and barrelling straight for me.

With a reluctant nod of agreement, I say, "Let me talk to her first. Hang on, I'm pulling over."

I downshift and ease onto the shoulder to park. Rhys hands over the phone, and I punch in her number, praying Heather likes a good prank.

She answers on the first ring, her voice scratchy with emotion. "I'm sooo sorry, Dani," she sniffles. "I was running out the door to catch my flight, and my dog—he hates it when I travel—bolted from the house right into the street. He got hit by a car. I'm at the vet, waiting for news after the operation." A hum of despair fills my ear before she dissolves into phlegmy tears. "I don't know what's going to happen. It doesn't look good."

A heaviness lands in my heart.

Pets are sacred. We lavish more love on them than our fellow humans at times. I still remember the empty pit in my stomach after our family dog died, and how it took weeks to fill in. How six-year-old Dani cried herself to sleep when Dad explained Chester was in doggy heaven and never coming back.

Heather has every right to flake out.

"It's okay," I assure her. "We can pivot to another solution."

She suggests calling her agent; he might have a local connection. But he's in Vancouver, and it's seven-fifteen a.m. My skin feels cold, but my insides blaze. I know how this scenario plays out. It happened with every advertising agency I worked for. Talent no-shows always boned the shoots.

After we hang up, I dump the phone in my lap, and a resounding, unladylike *fuck!* flies out before I can stop it.

Rhys glances over. "Sounds like I'm flying solo?"

I take a deep breath and try to make my voice sound confident. "The tagline is *Rosé for goddesses and gods*. A female is kind of critical. And Luca is charging Evelyn an arm and a leg for this."

I massage my temples, the beginnings of a headache creeping in.

Rhys is a master improviser on camera, but he can't conjure up another human being.

After a short silence, he lobs out what can only be described as Plan Z. "What about you?"

I stare at him for a moment, trying not to cringe. "Heather is a size two soaking wet. None of her wardrobe will fit me."

He mulls that over. "Yvette has to have a white sheet somewhere in her house. On-the-fly Roman toga?"

"These images are going worldwide," I remind him. "I'm the head of marketing. I can't be plastered on a billboard."

Cars whizz past us, and I'm seriously considering leaping into traffic. End this misery as roadkill. My sunny morning drive is now a solid hour of phone time to dig us out of a hole.

Maybe. Potentially.

"Let's run it past Luca," Rhys says, refusing to let it go. "He nailed your back against the wall. And it's not your fault Heather bailed." He runs a hand over his tousled hair, now air-dried into silky-soft waves that skim his shoulders. What it must be like to wake up and be a perfect knockout and never once battle the frizzies.

"Besides," Rhys adds, "I think we'd look good together."

I appreciate his optimism. I really do. And the reckless part of me screams, *Yes! Throw caution to the wind. Let him melt me into a puddle with just a glance and plaster my lovesick face all over Times Square.*

But I know what Luca has planned for this shoot.

Rhys and I in a vineyard acting as drunken lovers? After pussy-gate? There is no sheet large enough to shroud the violent surge of sheet-fisting animalistic vibes that thundered between us. Tempting fate feels like a bad idea.

Rhys unclicks his seatbelt and nudges me, broad-muscled shoulder to tense, in-desperate-need-of-a-massage shoulder. "C'mon. Let's swap. I'll drive, you talk."

I search my blood for some vibration, even the mildest flutter of hope. Nope.

Too overwhelmed to disagree, I unbuckle with a sigh. "Get us there in one piece, please. I can't afford to lose you too."

Chapter Eight

I CATCH GLIMPSES OF THE LAKE THAT DISAPPEAR AND REAPPEAR AS THE highway curves. It looks timeless and mighty. Familiar too, the deep blue waters unchanged from the time my family drove this highway. I was eight. Me, Sawyer and JC were crammed into the back of our Volvo station wagon, roughhousing like caged animals. Dad barked threats to dump us on the roadside until Mom swooped in, offering bribes of popsicles and donuts if we settled down.

Now I'm driving, and Dani is the person in need of settling. She's chewing so hard on her bottom lip that I fear she might draw blood.

Heather's agent offered up jack shit for a solution. Since then, Dani's left panicked voicemails with multiple modeling agencies who, like me, consider eleven a.m. a perfectly acceptable time to start the day. I'm genuinely worried about her well-being when we reach the outskirts of Kelowna. Her hundred-yard stare out the windshield smacks of defeat.

I'm desperate to help but not really sure how.

"Talk to me," I say. "Let's figure this out."

She blows out a heavy breath. "Without mincing words, we're fucked."

"Maybe not. Evelyn seemed keen to have you step in." She had, in fact, pounced all over my suggestion when Dani called her with an update.

"Keen because there is no other option."

"What are you worried about?" I ask. "Aside from the publicity? I can guide you through the motions. Happy to let you in on the secret that a monkey could pull off my entire existence."

Finally, a laugh.

"You were born to be on camera," she states. "My face is as big as a Buick. No angles. And if the camera adds ten pounds…"

She trails off, her throat bobbing with a swallow. Nerves, I can understand. But has Dani not looked in the mirror lately? If anything, Luca will drool over her untapped potential.

I float the notion a second time. "Let me talk to Luca. He is terrified of lackluster results. You are a coup," I continue, pumping her up. "A triumph of unheralded casting."

Dani raises her eyebrows ever so slightly. "Thank you for your delusionally generous view of me."

Generous? Try selfish. I badly want to understand the curious electric charge that went down between us in her place. Several hours together, in the sun, drinking rosé half-naked? I can't think of a better first date.

"Oh, shit!" Dani points frantically at the approaching off-ramp. "This is our exit!"

Tires screech on the pavement, my radical swerve just missing the barrier. We killed the GPS while Dani phoned every talent agency on planet Earth, but she navigates us from memory to a winding road littered with lakefront mansions. Yvette's multi-acre spread looms behind a stone wall and gate, the house set back from the road, entry via an intercom camouflaged within the rock. Extending my arm out the window, I press the button, and a disembodied voice—posh, welcoming, slurred—says, "Follow the driveway to the end and park."

We pass the gate onto a vast estate, the stone façade of the gothic mansion gray and imposing. To the left of a plush manicured lawn, bright green ribbons of grape vines stretch as far as the eye can see.

"Disneyland called and said they want their castle back," I joke.

Dani suppresses a laugh. "Yvette and her husband, Garth, own fifty percent of the vineyards in the Okanagan," she informs me. "They run Alameda Hills, one of the biggest producers in Canada."

"What's she like?"

Dani thinks about that. "'The Anna Wintour of Wine Country' is the nicest thing people say about her. Runner-up is 'Former model turned social climber.'"

I park in front of a five-car garage, cut the engine then turn to face her. "And your take?"

"The finest collection of filler and Chanel?"

"Ah, got it." Even if you don't specifically know a woman like Yvette, you know the type.

"I mean, honestly, she's cool," Dani repositions, perhaps feeling like she overstepped a mark. "A little high-strung, but what do I know about life as a millionaire?"

"Hello, hello!"

Our mutual gazes drift to the enthusiastic energy ball known as Evelyn marching toward us with frightening efficiency. Straight nitro.

Dani and I slide out of the truck to greet her, but I think I know what's coming based on how Evelyn sizes Dani up.

"Luca and I hashed it out," she says, confirming my speculation. "If Rhys approves and you're okay with it, let's proceed with the two of you."

"I'm down," I say without hesitation. "We talked about that possibility on the drive."

Dani shoots me a nervous look. Has she U-turned on the idea?

Evelyn quickly adds, "And whatever collective fees the model would've earned, consider them tripled."

Worldwide residuals for a print campaign can easily top ten grand. Triple that and her day rate? From Dani's expression, I can tell she's doing the math.

"If you'll be my Claudia, I promise not to murder you," I joke, even though the whole Nero-killed-his-wife thing might not be the best vibe right now. Dani looks spooked.

A dry wind whips around us as Evelyn links her arms with ours, roping us together to march across the trimmed lawn to set.

"I think this is the cat's meow," she says. "Don't you?"

Her wink is unmissable, meant only for me. This particular scheme qualifies as a win in my books, but maybe, just maybe, I'm a tiny bit nervous.

🍷

"Holy shit," Dani mutters, eyes ballooning at the display.

I know what to expect with a Luca shoot.

Dani, not so much.

Arranged in perfect rows the length of the Olympic-sized pool, a small army of wardrobe racks sprawls across the stone patio. Display tables groan under the weight of enough sandals and golden accessories to outfit the entire city of Rome. Vigo, Luca's lover, assistant, and glam squad of one, has commandeered the last of the space. Beneath a large pop-up tent, his hair and make-up emporium is open and ready for business.

"And we'll end up using, like, three things," I tell Dani. "It's crazy."

Evelyn excuses herself to round up Yvette, and part one of the Spanish Armada strides over barefoot. Dressed in skin-tight leather pants and nothing else, Luca is skinny as a coat hanger and channeling Jesus with long, loose hair.

"Ah, my Reese's Pieces!" he says in that famous bellowing baritone that switches from friendly to nasty in a snap if you dare balk at any of his batshit ideas. "Cómo estás, amigo?"

We man-hug, and I introduce him to Dani, whom he squints at, his dark eyes calculating something.

"Vigo!" he barks over his shoulder. "Vete aqui!"

Vigo, bald and bearded, hustles over. He's a small bulldog of a man, with an apron neatly tied and covering his usual shoot day ensemble: gold sparkle hotpants.

Also shoeless.

"Hola, Rhys," he lisps, batting his fake eyelashes. "And you," he clucks at Dani. "Bonita! But you are wearing far too much."

Amongst these creative freakshows, Dani sticks out like a sore thumb in her office pumps and shift dress. Hot as hell, but the more Vigo fusses around her, the less confident she looks.

Luca knits his shaggy brows together. "Will anything fit her?"

"No hay problema!" Vigo exclaims. "Everything stretches. Come, come." He tugs a wide-eyed Dani toward the collection of fabric scraps. "Vigo te hace hermosa."

When they are safely out of earshot shot, Luca asks, "You think she can handle this?"

"I'll help her out. And after a couple of glasses of wine, you know how it goes."

A Luca shoot without wine is like a company without a CEO— questionable direction. He creates his best work half-plastered. It always helps if the models are too.

He squares a makeshift frame around my face using his fingers. "I think the light and dark contrast between you will be fantastico!"

Out of the corner of my eye, Evelyn emerges from the house with whom I assume is Yvette. A skinny, angular diva with blonde hair perfectly styled and three pounds of makeup on tight, unwrinkled skin. She clearly works like hell at maintenance.

"This is Yvette Van Ness," Evelyn cheerily announces. "Hostess with the mostest."

I raise a hand in hello. "Thanks for offering up your place."

Yvette weaves slightly in her stilettos. A cigarette hangs out the side of her mouth, one eye squinting in the smoke. Already toasted at nine in the morning.

"You must be Rhys," she purrs. "Enchanté."

After a beat, I realize she expects me to kiss and not shake her outstretched hand. She certainly takes a page out of the Anna Wintour book, although I doubt Anna attends photo shoots in capri yoga pants and Canucks hockey jerseys.

"What are you drinking?" she asks me.

"Ah, nothing, yet."

Yvette drops the still-smoldering cigarette onto the patio, pulverizing it under the ball of her studded Valentino. "We start in on the wine early at Chateau Van Ness. Evie, darling," she coos, draping a hand onto her BFF's shoulder. "What is your famous saying?"

Evelyn flashes a grin and sweeps her hand theatrically from left to right. "I'd rather die drunk and defiled than sober and safe."

"Quintessential Evie," Yvette pronounces, her voice honey and smoke. "You should make that into a bumper sticker. But for now, can you check on Martha? We need refreshments pronto. With such an eventful morning ahead…" She lets the silence stretch, eyeing me with a not-so-subtle once-over. "We need all the fortification we can get."

While Vigo goes wild with Dani, Luca and I sift through my various wardrobe selects. With only so many variations of a toga with sandals, I'm dressed and ready to go in a flash, lounging poolside with Yvette and Evelyn when Vigo drags Dani out of his tent.

My brain deconstructs into a million tiny shattered pieces.

Fucking hell.

Even Luca, who's seen the hottest women on the planet half-naked, catches flies, mouth hanging open.

The safe way to describe it is that the bikini is wearing her.

Dani squirms under our collective gazes and says what we're all thinking, "It's way too small."

"What are you talking about?" Evelyn chides. "You look incredible. Doesn't she, Yvette?"

Lighting up her third cigarette, Yvette blows a stream of smoke into the endless sky. "Very vixen. *Cleopatra*, X-rated version."

Evelyn turns to me. "Do you approve? It is your shoot."

Dani flicks a nervous look in my direction. At this point, I'm not sure my heart can beat any faster and not qualify as a medical event. She is a mythical goddess, eyes huge and haunted, ringed with winged eyeliner.

And all that skin?

"I'm good if Luca is," I manage.

Luca circles Dani, humming small sounds of approval. "Drape her with that sheer toga," he instructs Vigo. "The one with the golden tassels. Add the cuffs to either arm and muss her hair. Bigger. Wilder. Sexier!" He gestures wildly, spinning around to address us in the viewing gallery. "How is everyone's wine doing?"

"I need a refill," Dani pipes up. And then, under her breath so that only I can hear: "Or an entire case."

The concept of two young, lusty Romans bonding over Pink Pearl probably sounded great in her air-conditioned office. Half-naked in the unforgiving sunlight of a morning tapped to be the hottest day of the year?

It feels like more than our acting skills are about to be tested.

Y

A European and a stickler for authenticity, Luca insists we keep drinking wine as he shoots. After two hours, Dani and I are sheened with sweat. Tipsy and touching. Her nearly transparent dress clings to her curves, and maybe it's that or the wine or the exhaustion from the jet lag, but so many feelings come out in this moment.

The heat amplifies everything.

Evelyn claps enthusiastically from the pool deck. "Bravo, you two. Love, love, love!" She unfolds herself from her sunbed and swans over to confer with Luca. "I just had a crazy idea. The invites for our gala haven't gone out yet. How do you feel about capturing something a little wilder to grace the front of them? A scandalous affair playing out amongst the grapes?"

A low sound of concern hums in Dani's throat. We're sitting on a bench, clocking time out in the shade of a willow tree. "What is she talking about?"

Luca scratches his beard with the studious expression of a vision forming. "I can shoot it long lens. Voyeuristic. Roman paparazzi style."

"Careful," Yvette warns, fanning herself under the covered daybed where she has permanently set up camp. "If this shoot gets any hotter, we will all go up in flames."

Luca strides over to huddle with us. Intense. Moody. "I want the energy to feel forbidden," he explains. "You believe you are alone, lost in time in the vineyard. Rhys, we have you sitting on a chair. Dani straddles you, a temptress with a cluster of grapes. Lust crackles. At any moment, you will rip clothes off each other. Think Romeo and Juliet. You must fuck or die."

I burst out laughing while Dani asks in a stricken voice, "Fuck or die?"

"You know the feeling, darling." Luca smiles encouragingly. "Dark magic. When the sexual tension is about to explode!"

His arms fling skyward, mimicking said explosion. Dani rises to her feet, swaying before I steady her. She looks very uncertain. And so incredibly beautiful.

"I don't know if I can fake that," she says as if talking to herself.

Me? This guy will not have to fake anything. If Luca wants sexual tension, I've got that in spades. My dick twitched earlier when Luca told us to embrace, and with resolve stronger than my lifetime of abandoned New Year's resolutions combined, I gritted my teeth and hung in there.

I was this close to dying.

Luca squeezes her shoulder, doing what he does best: getting his way. But I can tell Dani impressed him by rolling with the punches. And for all her earlier protests, she owned it in front of the camera.

In a no-turning-back tone, Luca says, "Rhys is a pro. Use him as your guide."

Dani and I drain a third bottle of rosé before Luca summons us to the vineyard. He fusses over the setup: me, ass on the chair Vigo dragged over from the pool deck. Dani, legs spread wide to straddle me.

Handing her a cluster of fat grapes, Luca reiterates the vision, "Dangle them over his mouth but deny him. You have all the power. Rhys, you strain to reach them. The grapes are a metaphor for her. You want to devour them!"

"Devour. Got it." I swipe the sweat off my forehead. "Am I touching her?"

Luca strikes a thinking pose. "Maybe your hand on her ass to start, no?"

Dani makes a small scared sound. The peace that had settled over her during the first part of the shoot has come and gone. I can smell her sweet fragrance, the coconut scent of sunscreen, and a hint of my vanilla musk woven into both. My face feels like it's on fire, flushed from the heat.

"I'm cool if you're cool," I say, lying through my teeth.

Luca struts off to get into position. Dani arranges herself over me, painstakingly careful not to press against too much flesh. Her eyes find mine, jaw set as her brows knit together.

"Do you feel self-conscious at all?" she whispers. "This is like shooting a *Playboy* centerfold."

At a less intense time, I'd tell her she makes a fine Miss August. For now, I shrug it off like this is not borderline uncensored.

"Dani!" Luca shouts from afar. "Hold the grapes higher. Use your thumb and forefinger. Dangle them like your endless charm. You hold all the power. Make him desire you!"

"Oh my god," she mumbles. "He is out of control."

He and me both. With Dani so close, I can see droplets of sweat between her cleavage, the slick dampness above her glossy lips. Her entire body glistens from the shimmer cream Vigo slathered on, and it's not even right how aroused I am. Luca takes forever, endlessly snapping, extending more than my torture.

"Yes!" Luca shouts. "You are in the throes of ecstasy. Arch into him, Dani. Use your power!"

Dani presses against me, stiff and awkward, erasing all the space. It takes one second of body contact before her eyes pop wide. A sharp intake of breath follows. She looks down at me, blinking fast, as if every flutter of her lashes can will my warmth and hardness away.

Full and vital, she was not expecting.

"Are you...?"

"Sorry." I swallow hard and manage a smile. "Workplace hazard."

"Don't move," Luca yells. "Tempt him, Dani. Seduce the helpless Rhys."

My god. The right thing, the only thing to do, is ease up. Let me and the volatile situation become flaccid. Save our dignities. And, yes, I could shrivel myself farther away, but the pleasure is immense. Her body, her hair, and her allure rivet into my soul.

"Pretend you're enjoying it."

"Are you pretending?" she whispers back.

Yeah, right. I'm glowing with heat and embarrassment and something else, something new and pulsating and unfamiliar. My eyes trace the whisper of a white cloud high in the brilliant sky.

The sun feels hotter. I feel drunker.

And Dani? She stares down at me, and I can't explain it, but something shifts in that moment. Instead of rocking her hips away from the hot wall of my dick, she starts to grind back and forth, slow and steady, like a rolling pin trying to flatten a pie crust. I can feel the pearls, the hard steel barbell raking over my flesh. Blistering white panic explodes in my chest.

"What are you doing?" I choke out the question.

Something hovers in the depths of her eyes.

Something off-limits and dark.

Blacker than this depravity.

"Nothing," she replies, an eerie confidence in her voice. Her movements.

What happened to the doubt? The hesitation? What the hell is happening?

"Bravo!" Luca calls out. "Excellent, excellent. Arch into him one more time, Dani! Bigger! Tease the grapes. Tease, tease, tease!"

She does more than tease. Dani hypnotizes me, swirling the fruit just out of reach as I strain to bite. My heart beats fast and hard. Now we're moving in unison, a slow, terrifying rhythm like I'm inside her. Her dirty grinding gets me there so fast, it becomes a hot blur. I can feel my balls tighten, the urgent need clawing into my throat. My fingers clamp onto the edge of the chair, gripping so hard they turn white.

"Is this the throes of ecstasy?" she grits out, her voice tight, on the verge.

I should have expected it. A pencil skirt or not, no woman can rock a pierced clit, bow down to Joey Ramone and drink roadside coffee while claiming to be a prude.

"The grapes," I plead, my voice a pathetic rasp. "Don't hang me out to dry."

The taut grape flesh finally skims my lips. With a vicious bite, I rupture the skin, juice squirting over my face as stars burst behind my eyes and liquid warmth erupts under my toga. A guttural cry buried deep in my chest aches for release, but I'm a shell of a man whimpering through the hot, agonized pulses.

And dammit, how is Dani still holding on?

Not fair.

Not when she fucking ruins me.

Chapter Nine

DANI

ALCOHOL AND BAD DECISIONS. A MARRIAGE MADE IN HELL. AND I'M DEEP in purgatory, locked in the poolside bathroom. Face red and hot from shame and sun. A sloshed Roman tramp perched on a toilet seat, unable to herd my thoughts into anything coherent.

Dear god.

Looking back, none of it feels real. But now I have to brave a table full of actual people waiting for me to join them for lunch. I stagger to the sink and stare in the mirror at my messy, mediocre self. Since when has Dani Rialto acted like an outlaw?

I dry-humped Rhys like a common tart.

Even worse, I liked it.

The control.

His lack of it.

My mind starts caving in on itself again. I hear Rhys's urgent words. See that beautiful face scrunch up before the tension flooded out of him. How do I explain my behavior away? That Luca screaming about power cracked open the memory vault and plunged me into darkness. Into the black hole better known as Brett Winn, who had promised me the moon—a pay raise, an upgrade to our most exclusive client account, to be his plus-one at the prestigious Cannes Lions advertising event—with the small caveat of blowing him at his every whim.

I run cold water and splash my face, buying time to think. Can I claim a rosé blackout as my defense? Blame the wine for fueling every reckless grind onto a helpless and confused Rhys?

Sorry for the twisted vengeance! You know how it goes…

My brows pull together in a fraught *now-what-have-I-done* look. The truth is, I allowed the dark souvenir of Brett's manipulative behavior to cloud my judgment. How can Rhys look at me and not think I'm a first-rate psycho?

I fantasize about reversing course, running to my truck, and peeling out of here, but five stressed-out minutes later, I creep out to face my council of judgment. On the patio, several sun umbrellas shade a long table heaving with colorful Spanish tapas. Evelyn and Yvette have claimed the king and queen seats on either end. A besotted Vigo has camped beside Rhys. The lone seat is mercifully next to Luca.

With traces of Rhys's DNA clinging to my skin, how much closer do we need to be?

Evelyn tracks my approach with a critical eye. All the light chatter trails off, and the uneasy silence wraps around me like a blanket. I'm still vibrantly and vividly out of sorts.

"There you are," she says. "We were just discussing who should check in on you."

I tuck a lock of hair nervously behind one ear and plant myself beside Luca. "I, uh, I just needed to cool down."

Yvette smirks, reaching for her bottomless wine glass. "I bet."

The air feels thick and heavy. I can sense Rhys's eyes across the table, scanning me through my core. And me, Textbook Drunk, too ashamed to look at him.

Vigo pushes a bowl piled high with fragrant saffron rice in my direction. Something in his face tells me I'm being pitied. "Eat, darling. You'll feel better."

Despite a grumbling stomach and a glorious feast, I have zero appetite. But I go through the motions, spooning rice onto my plate while Luca scrubs through photos on his camera.

"Magnifico!" he beams. "You two nailed it."

He angles the viewfinder to me, and my throat thickens to the point that swallowing becomes impossible. Luca captured the moment when Rhys's fingers clamped against the chair, the world collapsed into a pinhole of black, and I left reality, entering a heightened state, oblivious to everything.

But I cannot show my face anywhere if that photo goes public.

I smile through the terror. "Powerful stuff."

"Can I see?" Rhys asks.

Luca hands off the Leica to Rhys, who studies the photo, magnifies it, and scrolls onward. If our lack of communication is a red flag, no one has the bad manners to address it.

"Well?" Evelyn prods after a few seconds of focused silence. "How would you describe those photos?"

Rhys glances up to lock eyes with me in a wordless exchange. I feel my chest tighten like it did as I battled the big O and every instinct to melt into bliss.

Does he know? Was it that obvious?

Something like a shadow passes over his face before he returns the camera to Luca and says, "*In vino veritas.*"

Evelyn squeals her appreciation. "Eloquently said, Rhys! And may I suggest a toast to that ancient wisdom?" She lifts her wine glass, and we all follow suit. Well, I reach for my water glass. Any more wine and I'll slide off this chair into a puddle of regret.

"What exactly are we toasting?" Yvette asks. "I'm horrible with languages."

Rhys is the first to clink my glass, the unmistakable sound of a challenge in his voice when he says, "*In wine, there is truth.*"

My hope of Rhys hopping a ride back with Evelyn dies on the vine because she and Yvette have a function tonight in Kelowna. After a flurry of air kisses and promises to *absolutely* connect in Marbella over Christmas, Rhys untangles himself from the Luca and Vigo hug fest to join me in the truck.

He slams the door shut, and my stomach flips with anxiety. Welcome to the waking nightmare.

"Did you need any groceries?" I ask. "I can stop on the way."

"I'm good." He grips the handle above the window, silent and motionless as a tombstone. He gives me nothing, no indication of how far I dug my own grave.

I start the truck, if only to drown out the unpleasant stillness.

On the short drive to the highway, out of the corner of my eye, I clock Rhys's jaw and how it grinds back and forth. His right leg shimmies up and down like it has a pulse all its own. I dream of a painless packing up of this afternoon, storing it deep in a locked basement.

But what can I say to fix this, aside from nothing?

On the highway, I gun the engine. The momentum feels liberating, and Rhys lets out a deep breath that sounds like it's been brewing for half a century.

"I don't know how you process stuff," he says, "but I need to talk this out."

My heart starts to race, triggered by his words. I've never had to deal with anything like this.

"I'm sorry," my voice is small, "I get a little adventurous after drinking."

He glances over, an eyebrow cocked to high heaven. "A little?"

"That is not who I am in real life."

"Interesting. What would the real Dani have done differently?"

"Found a legit model and spared myself a lifetime of embarrassment?" The question squeaks out, and I ignore the twist in my stomach that says this could all blow up because of me. "I'm not unbothered by what happened," I add, pitifully aware of how lame that sounds.

He snorts a laugh. "Could have fooled me."

The way he locks eyes with me says it all—my lunchtime avoidance didn't win me any favors. Rhys tried hard to turn our fleeting eye contact into something lasting, and his ability to act unfazed while my insides raged? Tragic.

I gather my breath and what's left of my pride. "Look, I want to do a great job for Evelyn. This collaboration with you is important. Can we just…"

"Pretend it never happened?" he finishes.

I crack the tiniest remorseful smile. "Is that okay?"

In my mind, amiable Rhys replies with, *No sweat.* The next five weeks fly by, uncomplicated. I spend every morning power-meditating on how I never thought it was possible to hate Brett Winn more. But the longer Rhys says nothing, the more I think he might not answer.

Then, "Only if you promise never to pull a stunt like that again. Guys can also have their hearts broken."

He searches my face, and I can see the naked truth of his words playing out in the tremor around his mouth. Heaviness settles in my stomach—fathomless, ceaseless guilt. I'm mortified it's come to this.

"Understood." There is no point begging forgiveness in a broken voice and making matters worse.

It's a struggle to keep the speedometer under a hundred and twenty clicks per hour. My skin feels too tight. My mind is a disordered wreck. I try to focus on the orange sun and the blue sky without a single cloud, the light brown hills covered in scrub. This job was supposed to be my second coming. A reboot of my life. Are the wine gods working against me? Is it cruel fate that Heather bailed today? How did I allow this to happen? Because what went down today is not what I'd call taking the initiative.

The road winds and dips and climbs again.

Out of the blue, Rhys asks, "Did that turn you on?"

I go very still, while every second of that aching moment rushes through me. I can taste every beat of my heart, see his lips full and softly parted, and hear the heaviness of his breathing.

Why has Rhys asked an impossible question, kickstarting a conversation I'm not ready to have? Pressure builds in my lungs, all of me blowing up, doing everything in my power not to admit it. Despite my runaway drunken revenge train, being close to him felt natural.

It felt right.

But if I utter those words, then what?

"Do you need me to repeat the question?" he nudges.

No, actually. What I'd like is for this commute to be something other than a cringeworthy reminder that a wine-fueled woman knows no bounds.

Or boundaries.

"Even if it did," I say, careful not to admit to anything, "that doesn't make it right."

"Then why go there if you know it's wrong?"

I blow out a breath. Jesus. Why won't he drop it? Why push harder on a darkening bruise? *Because sometimes life is a dumpster fire of bad decisions* is what I want to scream. Because I fell hard for my ex-boss, smug in his Armani suits and swaths of Paco Rabanne cologne. And because Brett abused his power, I sank to his dubious level and snagged the opportunity to lean into mine.

Of course it wasn't right.

I momentarily lost my bearings in the vineyard because it felt fucking great to be in charge. Because charismatic and elusive men are my weakness, Rhys, and you are the gold standard.

"Can we talk about something else?" My voice is more cutting than intended.

After a very, very long silence, he asks, "How about those Canucks?"

Chapter Ten

RHYS

Fᴜᴄᴋ!

My heart twists in my chest, and I can't manage a deep breath. I slam the fridge door shut so hard, the jolt rattles my teeth. I should have hit the liquor store. Rosé won't cut it at a time like this. Shooters of flaming eighty-proof rum are what this guy needs to settle down.

Way to ease us in, Dani.

Like, how about a lakeside sunset together before making my body scream? Am I supposed to pretend that away?

She dropped me off a minute ago, and we both said polite good-byes after suffering through silence darker than deep space on the ride home. And now a zillion strange emotions swirl inside me. A wild ache. Unexplainable shit.

It's just a little early for moves this intense, and for feelings like this.

Going through the motions of idle chit-chat during lunch while the knot in my chest refused to untangle was brutal. I tried to silently connect with her, to help me perform some mental arithmetic, to figure out what it all meant, because something untold fuelled her. Instead of a playful manhandling, she rode me into wasteland territory with six guns blazing.

To prove a point is what it felt like.

I pace around my expensive kitchen that smells like lemons, feeling caged in, trapped in an endless loop. I can still smell her, feel her skin beneath my fingers, her voluptuous body pinned needily against mine.

The explosion of need in my blood caught me off guard.

Me shutting her down on the way home didn't pave the path to resolution, but the need to protect my heart kicked in automatically. The rumors about me are partly true, told spectacularly to my face last month by one of the countless women who have chased me.

"Everyone knows you don't fall for Rhys because you cannot fall for anyone."

And for the record, "countless women" is not a humble brag. I'd trade quality over quantity in a heartbeat. Especially when, every other week, some Crazy sets her sights on me.

Feeling hollowed out and a little lost, I crash onto the sofa. I stare off into space, my hands clenched into fists before I even realize it. The whole *No Man is an Island* thing suddenly hits hard.

I might have lost touch with reality while camped out on Corfu, keeping everything—family, the idea of love, my insecurities—at bay. That's what hurt little boys do after a lifetime of searching for a father figure: they numb themselves by leaving home, talking to an inanimate object, and embracing the adoration of strangers because the alternative—being unwanted—sucks.

The trouble is, the more I realized fans always want something from me, the less I gave of myself, to the point where my inability to fall for someone is an actual thing.

Oh sure, you can drop me into any party, and I'll light it up. Golden, sunny Rhys. Quick to make you laugh. Ready to pose in a selfie. I can be the guy you think I am. The truth is, I don't even know who I am anymore. A façade? A fucking hologram?

Virtual reality Rhys.

There, but not real.

In the dense silence of my hot, airless villa, I replay everything in my mind from the minute I arrived here. Dani gave me the impression that she might be different. Or at least see beyond the veneer of a pretty boy influencer. Why I stubbornly cling to that notion after two days of knowing her is ludicrous, especially after she wielded those goddamned grapes like a temptress overjoyed to witness the fall of a feeble, weakened man.

That doesn't change the weight of what happened. And her guilt-ridden aura during lunch speaks to a deeper, stormier motivation.

I gnaw on my thumb, mind racing.

Now what?

I have a five-week commitment to honor. There is no island to hide on. Unlike a perfectly curated post, I can't edit out the morning and pretend it never happened.

This mess with Dani needs to get sorted.

Recent events say showing up uninvited at Dani's place spells all kinds of trouble. But giving her a heads-up might mean she ghosts me. The only play is a sniper attack. And now that I know where her front door is, I plan to stay glued to the welcome mat until we erase this tiny hill of weirdness.

I knock on her door, not aggressively, but with an intensity that rings through the wood. If Dani views me as a six-foot-one piece of ass who can't keep it in his pants, not only will Sawyer have a leg up, but this powerful feeling rattling my heart might eat me alive.

I sense this is something bigger than me, but I don't understand it.

I don't know what follows this.

Ten seconds pass. No answer. I knock again, louder. Despite all my positive self-talk on the way over, there is a chance of being told to fuck right off.

If she's home, that is.

I took a long cold shower, napped, and scarfed down a microwaved burrito before I summoned the courage for this mission impossible. Is Dani out on the town? Raging with the seniors? Restless thoughts ricochet in my brain as I stare at the lake, inhaling and trying to let nature calm me. The still green water feels trapped, confined by the dusty hills. On Corfu, the turquoise sea stretches forever, a never-ending horizon.

"Hi."

I spin around to find Dani hovering in the doorway, a purple robe wrapped tight around her. Domestic goddess. And the current threat to my emotional well being.

"Hey there." I smile even as I feel my throat go a little tight.

A moment of silence passes. Dani angles her head, waiting for me to go on. I can sense the smile slipping from my face, but an emotion lurks in her expression, enough to make me brave the nerves.

"You know, today ended a bit weird, and I'm not great with weird, so I thought maybe I could cash in the rain check? To watch the sunset together," I clarify because it's apparent she has no clue what I'm talking about. "It doesn't have to be anything other than two people watching the sunset," I'm quick to add before she shuts me down.

She raises her eyebrows ever so slightly. I had no clue how she'd react when she saw me, and I half-expected her eyes to glare holes into me. But those light gray wonders skim over me with interest and make my body come alive.

"I'm still trying to recover from today," she admits, hands suddenly fidgety, twining and untwining.

"You and me both."

Dani studies me for a beat. We both know none of today had to do with me. But her actions were not small and meaningless. Am I here to hold her feet to the fire or grill her about motives? No. Do I want to understand what was behind that fine coat of hurt in her eyes as she broke me? Yes, but that can wait.

All I want is to smash the bullshit simmering between us from earlier.

The longer Dani says nothing, the more I feel the moment slipping away. So, I tell myself not to be too excited with her crinkle of a smile.

"Give me a minute," she says. "I'll throw on my bikini and grab some towels. It's still a goddamn furnace in here."

"One hundred and ten stairs." Dani directs my attention to the clearing at the cliff's edge. "Trust me when I say you'll feel them on the way back up."

What I feel is a sharp jab of arousal in my chest. Holy smokes. Her crochet cover-up covers very little. The deep plunge of her red bikini top reveals an overflowing amount of touchable flesh.

"Let me carry that." I reach for her canvas bag stuffed with two beach towels. It weighs nothing, but I would carry her down to the lake if it meant my fertilization of Yvette's prized Chardonnay terroir becomes a distant memory.

"There's a raft we can swim to if you want," she says.

"Perfect. I could use a cooldown."

Dani takes the lead down slatted stairs that are so camouflaged that they seem to sprout naturally from the sand-colored landscape. As we descend, the town comes into view, glowing softly with lights, while the lake stretches out vast and glittering, tranquil before dusk settles. But another view has me equally captivated: her ass cheeks jiggling in the high-cut bottoms of her bikini, bouncing along in silent rhythm with the smacking sound of our flip-flops.

Dear lord. That is a fine rear view.

The stairs end on a strip of fine sand dividing the land from the lake. All the magical sounds and scents of Eau de Summer hit me at once—water lapping on the shore, air spiked with the smoky tang of grilled burgers and charcoal briquettes from a distant campground. Rowdy voices echo across the water, their crispness tricking me into thinking they're closer than they are.

But this end of the lake is deserted—a moonscape.

"Is this all part of Evelyn's property?" I ask.

"If she had her way, Evelyn would own the entire town." Dani shoots me a cryptic smile. "But, yeah, everything up until to that marker is Nero Vino."

She indicates a small sign hammered deep into the sand and marked with PRIVATE PROPERTY.

"Not exactly the great wall of Trump," I say with a smile.

"I run into the odd person," she admits. "Dog walkers mostly. But tonight, we have it all to ourselves."

I meet her eyes, wrestling with the idea that she's acknowledged we need privacy to hash things out. Then she pops her cover-up off in one smooth motion, and, goddamn, I can't acknowledge shit. *Sports Illustrated Swimsuit Edition* missed the boat with her.

I drop the bag and kick my flip-flops off, dragging my eyes from her to the lake. "Is that our destination?"

Twenty meters offshore, a raft bobs in the gentle current. It's twelve by twelve, give or take, with a handrail mounted on one side and supported on rusted-out oil drums.

"Do you want to race?" she asks.

"Is there a prize if I win?"

Dani stands there, hair flowing in the breeze, a challenging glint in her eyes. "What makes you so sure you'll win?"

"I swim every day." I'm not trying to sound obnoxiously superior. But also, fair warning.

"Are you willing to wager your glory?" She bites back a smile, no denying she enjoys teasing me. Not that I had much to begin with, but she throws me so completely off my game.

I peel off my t-shirt and toss it onto the sand, feeling a tiny hit of pride as she drinks me in. "On the count of three?"

"I'm ready when you are."

Dani sways from side to side with a smile I'll recognize later as downright duplicitous. I should have seen it coming. She bolts before my countdown ends, crashing through the water with a *whoop* before disappearing beneath the surface in a smooth, clean dive.

So much for following the rules.

I give her a small head start, then surge for the gold, my feet sinking into the soft mud of the lakebed before I plunge into the shallows. Without ocean currents to battle, I reach the colder depths in record time.

Up ahead of me, she's focused on only one thing: beating my ass.

Not a chance.

With wheels and the engine to swim all day, I power past her. Seconds later, I hoist myself onto the raft and strike a victory pose.

Dani pauses to tread water and watch me preen. "You're such a guy," she says, laughing. "Can't handle a woman beating you."

"I'd say my inability to handle you was made pretty clear," I correct. "I had to redeem myself."

Dani's expression doesn't change, but her eyes cloud, and she breaststrokes the remaining distance to the handrail in silence. Silhouetted against the hot-pink sunset that stains the sky, the outline of her glistening curves rising out of the water takes my breath away. All that damp, dark hair clinging to her like a wetsuit, her body designed, so it seems, to test my personal weaknesses.

Dani squeezes water from her hair, scouring me with a look that storms through my blood.

"Speaking of redemption," she says, "what I did today was wrong and stupid. I fucked up, pardon my French. I'm sorry."

Wow. Straight up owning it. But the look on her face conveys the effort it took to get there.

I bow my head a touch to acknowledge her endeavor. "Apology accepted."

"And I called you a heartbreaker," she adds, biting her lip in a way that distracts me. "Which implies you're a womanizing shit, when I really know nothing about you."

Much to the chagrin of every female who has tried to worm their way into my life, Rhys the player is the furthest thing from the truth. But I don't miss the opportunity to steer this conversation to where I think it needs to go.

"Did someone break your heart recently?" I ask.

Her eyes flick to the raft with a little wrinkle forming between her brows, and am I too rapt, waiting for that *yes?*

"It happens to everyone, right?"

"True," I admit. "But it still sucks."

We regard each other openly, and I fight the urge to fill the silence. At one point yesterday, before things got crazy, Dani said she started following my Insta in June once she learned Evelyn had hired me. That alone ramped up my interest in her.

A beauty like her who is not a built-in Crazy?

What are the odds?

"What about you?" she asks. "Any recent calamities of the heart?"

Myla qualifies as a calamity, but not in the way Dani implies. And no way in hell am I bringing the topic of her up. "I'm too busy for heartbreak."

Dani stays silent, but I can feel her sizing me up. Maybe she's wondering how someone like me could be single. Whatever the case, we sink into the quiet connection of the moment, watching the sun's final rays dance on the rippling surface of the lake. The half-bright moon climbs above the willow trees scattered along the shore, and a breeze kicks in, carrying a sweet fragrance that hits high in the nose.

Dani glances my way, a shy smile tugging at her lips.

We are perfectly isolated out here.

Am I reading her right? Is this my time to bust a move?

The answer comes in the form of a rogue gust of wind. The force of it churns the lake, the raft surging beneath us, canting to one side. We pitch forward, gripping the nearest things to steady ourselves, which happens to be each other.

"Whoa!" Dani yelps, reeling, unsteady on her feet.

I hold her tight to ride out the upheaval, me with a newfound appreciation for all things immaculate timing. Because when the raft levels out, Dani and I remain close.

Touching.

"I swear I didn't plan that," I say, battling the temptation to let my hands wander beyond their resting place on her waist.

She looks up at me from under her fringe of wet, dark lashes. Eyes soft as a whisper.

"You're warm," she murmurs.

"Is now the time for a lame hot-blooded male joke?"

After a low, sexy laugh, she asks, "Is that all you got?"

I feel a fizzy sort of scrambling in my brain. I've heard of chemistry and felt a lick of it here and there, but never like this: middle-earth and elemental. Dangerous as the dusk contouring her beautiful face.

Awareness hums between our damp bodies.

And those damn roaming fingers of hers make it impossible to stay casual and in control. I don't think she knows how much she's affecting me.

"If you're trying to turn me off you," I say, my voice thick, "you're doing a spectacularly bad job."

For five long seconds, it's just us and the weight of everything unspoken while the undulating water creates this dream-like sensation. My skin, every part of me, tingles with desire. I think I know what's about to happen, and I'm shaking ever so slightly when I draw her closer. But right before our mouths connect for that first, forbidden time, she twists her face away.

"I don't think kissing me is a good idea," she says, a high note in her voice that wasn't there before.

"Do you have a better idea?" I ask, refusing to let her go.

She glances at the shoreline, fading into dusk. I silently beg her to take me down, but she slips free of my grip instead.

"How about another race back?" she suggests.

I try to keep cool, masking my disappointment. We were on the verge. I know Dani felt it—she had to, what with my erection the size of a torpedo and pulsing hard against her bare thigh. So why are we still talking? We should be a hot, breathless blur of grasping hands, mouths, and tongues. Lost in a primal frenzy to devour each other.

Seriously, how did I screw this up?

"Glutton for punishment?" I ask with a pumped-up smile.

Dani ponders the question briefly. "Maybe I need to be punished."

"I can arrange that," I quip, out of fucking nowhere. Out of desperation, really, because punishment is not part of my contract, nor am I skilled at inflicting physical pain.

Her eyes dart to the sand and, okay, I get it. This, again—the race fake-out. It's not the punishment I envisioned, but if you can't devour the woman, you might as well beat her at her own game. I brace myself for her move, my twitching muscles ready to dive right after her.

But I guess she dupes me, times two.

With a wily grin, she plants her hands against my chest and shoves hard. I stumble backward, time and space frozen into a singular moment, my body tight with the urgency to steady itself. Then I'm falling, and the cool grip of the lake clamps around my lungs. I thrash to the surface, gasping for air, struggling at this precise moment to locate my dignity after being unceremoniously dumped.

And my manhood has already shriveled and surrendered, appalled at the betrayal.

Retreat! False alarm.

And Dani? She's *laughing*—full-throated and unapologetic—as she sprints off the raft, launching herself into the air. Tucked into a deadly cannonball, she plunges into the depths beside me with a joyous holler. The spray peppers my eyes, but the sting is peanuts compared to the chaos pounding beneath my skin and ribcage like a second, competing heartbeat.

So full of feelings.

Chapter Eleven

DANI

"Dani?"

Evelyn's voice snaps me out of my daydream. I sit up in my desk chair, blinking fast. "Yes?"

Hands parked at her waist, Evelyn assesses my face and the signs of puppy love written all over it. "Dear, dear," she clucks, her voice gentle. "Someone's in a fog."

"Sorry." I crack a sheepish grin. "So much going on."

She lifts a micro-bladed brow and why, why, why am I blushing? Because Evelyn has a way of finding cracks in your armor you never knew existed.

And because my brain is far away.

Lost in a summer's night, bodies this close to letting go.

Out on the raft, in the fading light, I could feel my entire being responding to just a flicker of his brown eyes. There was nothing else I wanted at that moment but to kiss Rhys. Know the taste of his mouth and skin. But my heart went arrhythmic with fear. He is so out of my league.

How do I not end up hurt?

"What time does Sawyer arrive today?" Evelyn prods me back into the moment, reminding me of the upcoming meeting with Rhys's older brother.

Sawyer reached out last week, angling for a tour of the amphitheater. Trenton Talent Management doesn't just represent internet personalities like Rhys—they have actors and bands under their wing. Sawyer teased a couple of acts we should check out and slotted himself into my schedule for a meet and greet. He also pushed for my cell number, and I now regret caving. I eye my phone, bracing for another text to pile onto the five others Sawyer fired off since leaving Vancouver. The hourly barrage kicked off at eight this morning, which means Rhys wasn't the first Trenton to light up my phone.

But the one text I keep re-reading came from him at nine-thirty, the dignified waking hour of an influencer.

RT: Thanks for last night. Official reboot?

With the goofiest smile spreading across my face, I replied,

DR: Sold.

And he responded with a photo of a barista-level cappuccino, complete with a heart drawn in the milky froth.

This mutual attraction can only end in disaster, but tell that to my brain. I'd lain wide awake in bed last night with my mind and body on fire. After Rhys raced me back to shore, no contest, I braced for a time-trial stair challenge. Maybe the desert night calmed his competitive edge because he insisted on walking behind me, the darkened pathway illuminated by his phone flashlight. Twice, his hand caught me when I stumbled.

The journey back felt three times longer than our meandering trip down.

On the doorstep of my villa, my heart thundered as he asked about the morning debrief with Nicole and the visit with Sawyer. He stood close. Too close. The warmth emanating from his body felt stronger than the heat of the day.

And then his lips pressed against my cheek, soft and chaste. "Peace out," he'd said before the night swallowed him whole.

I looked upward into the cathedral of the universe, a rush of heat where his mouth grazed my skin.

No wonder it took hours for my pulse to power down and my eyelids to shut.

I was properly scandalized for one day.

Evelyn clears her throat and observes me with a knowing smile.

Shit.

"Oh, uh," I stammer, cheeks aflame. "His last update said two. I can give you a shout once he arrives."

"You kick things off first. We can enjoy a tipple in the tasting room aprés."

Evelyn smooths her immaculate hair, cutting a fine figure in her tailored Italian tennis dress and diamond statement earrings. Up before sunrise to make her bi-weekly doubles tennis match and happily working until sunset every day, she makes every other entrepreneur look like a freeloading sloth.

"And how is Rhys faring this morning?" she inquires. "Is he with Nicole?"

"Yes, they started at ten. So far, so good. They're getting along like a house on fire."

Her brow rises again. "Privy to a play-by-play, are you?"

"No. I mean, yes, he's keeping me in the loop."

"That's the beauty of working with a professional," she beams. "They know the little things matter." But it's something altogether more complicated than that. And Evelyn is all over it, judging from her lingering stare. "Is it today or tomorrow that the film crew arrives?"

"Later tonight," I say. "I checked in with them earlier."

Sixty-plus crew lurk on your average film set, but our tight setup consists of a duo—a camera operator ambitiously named Francis Shutter, and Rita, a sound/lighting/jack-of-all-trades. Sawyer told me Rhys balked at the idea of the crew—he favored the run-and-gun approach. But Evelyn wanted properly lit footage to repurpose, so Bettina, bless her dragon soul, insisted on it.

"Pity," Evelyn murmurs. "I thought it might be a kind gesture to offer Sawyer a complimentary evening in their cabin."

"I believe he drives back to Vancouver tonight." Or I hope he is because good luck trying to find accommodations.

"He must be very keen on this concert arrangement. Such a long trip for a simple tour."

We hold each other's gazes for four little heartbeats. Evelyn smiles fondly at me, but it's as if she knows I know something critical and am not sharing it with her, which is partly true.

She strolls to the far wall, wiping a finger along the top of the framed map of Osoyoos, inspecting it for dust. Satisfied the cleaners are earning their keep, she asks, "Tell me, dear, has Luca sent the proofs from yesterday?"

Guilt spirals in my stomach at the solid wall of emails still to read, including one from Shania Twain's manager. And, as of five minutes ago, Luca.

I blaze a smile. "Not yet."

"Be a love and forward them ASAP. I need to select one to grace the cover of our invitations." She moves to the door and pauses to scan my face. "Are you okay with that? You seemed a little out of sorts after the shoot yesterday. Did my enthusiasm for the extra creative push you beyond your comfort zone?"

Push beyond? More like smashed it through a concrete barrier. And I am nervous as hell about the pictures. How can I forget what I did when a constant reminder lives on in perpetuity?

And what will Dad think?

Instead of dwelling on those questions, I lie through my teeth, telling Evelyn I was proud to represent her brand. Then I bury myself in work for the rest of the morning, refusing to consider my imminent fame as a wine hussy.

🍷

Unlike his brother, Sawyer arrives early.

My office window overlooks the parking lot, and I know it's him before he steps out of his Beemer. It's one of those sleek matte ones with custom rims and blackout windows. The sort of car Iron Man would drive. And Sawyer exits this glorified spaceship as if he's Robert Downey Jr. about to walk the red carpet.

Graceful, alert, owning the space.

He's handsome in a fireman way—square-jawed and gym-jacked. Dark hair cut short. Unsmiling and so pale. What a contrast to Rhys and his golden shine.

He struts across the gravel and pushes inside the tasting room. I touch up my lip gloss, text Rhys his brother has arrived, and make my way to the land of free-flowing wine. Early afternoon is the busiest time for tastings, and the room is thick with tourists and drunken chatter, our smartly dressed staff pouring with a heavy hand. Everyone looks happy and glowing, their crystal glasses filled with crimson or amber wine, the liquids catching the light like jewels.

The room exudes understated opulence: a rustic yet modern vibe that cost Evelyn a small fortune. Her vision started with heavy terracotta floor tiles and walls sponged the same warm yellow as the outside of the building. Priceless Basquiats from her private art collection hang impressively amongst the scarred antiques imported from Europe, and the arched windows set deep into the thick walls allow just the right amount of dappled sunlight in.

Add in the hidden diffusers that waft in a lemony-lavender scent while Vivaldi violins serenade quietly from the Sonos, it is dreamy and perfectly on point.

All designed to drain your wallet faster than you can say boo.

Draped in a beautifully cut suit, Sawyer is custom-made for this room, but he sticks out like a sore thumb amongst the sunburnt shorts-and-sandals crowd. I approach him while he scopes out a magnum of our flagship Cabernet Sauvignon priced to move at nine hundred dollars.

"Sawyer?"

He looks up, startled, and the tight set of his jaw relaxes when I smile and introduce myself. Whipping off his Matrix-style sunglasses, two piercing eyes the shade of ultramarine sweep over me.

"Dani," he repeats like he's trying out the sound of my name. "Nice to meet you."

We shake hands, his grip firm, commanding, and appropriate for someone wearing a watch that can tell time, temperature, and if the water in the Maldives will irritate his skin. If money and power needed a single visual, he is it.

"Likewise. Welcome to Nero Vino. How was the drive up?"

"On the phone the entire time," he says, a little tiredly. "This is an escape for me, so thank you."

"Evelyn will join us for a wine tasting later if you have time. And Rhys should be here soon. He asked to come along."

His brow furrows as if that is the last thing he wants to hear. "How are things going with him?" he asks but talks over me before I reply. "I gave him an earful about the airport situation. It is unacceptable to leave you in a lurch like that."

From his tone, I gather he wants me to align with him—jump on the bandwagon and trash Rhys. He looks like the kind of guy who demands a lot of things.

"No complaints," I say. "Rhys is very accommodating."

Sawyer slowly nods as if waiting for the punch line. His skin is smooth and dewy like he mists himself with Evian. Or maybe stem cells.

"In that case," he says, "bring on the wine. My assistant wrangled a room for tonight, but since when does a glorified broom closet in a motel go for five hundred dollars?"

I stifle a laugh, trying to imagine the grand figure of Sawyer huddled in budget accommodations, where the glasses come wrapped in plastic and mysterious rashes sprout after contact with the bedspread.

"Consider yourself lucky. Rooms are tough to come by at this time of year."

I fleetingly wonder why Rhys did not offer his sofa bed to Sawyer, but when he strolls into the tasting room, the answer might lie in how his sunny warmth noticeably shrivels as he approaches us.

Or how his chin nod in Sawyer's direction reads more belligerent than bro. "I take it that Batmobile outside is yours?"

Sawyer stares Rhys down, unblinking. "Are you jealous of the doors?"

Rhys had a Jeep Wrangler shipped from Canada to Corfu, and he famously navigates the narrow hillsides with the doors off and house music cranking.

"I'm not jealous of anything you own."

Rhys smiles, although it doesn't reach his eyes. With no hug, fist bump, or even a hello, my head is on a swivel, assessing their dynamic. Rhys's stance is pure fire, but Sawyer, taller by a couple of inches, uses that slight advantage to peer down at his brother.

"I thought you were filming today, and now I hear you're crashing our party."

"We wrapped early." Rhys shrugs then gives Sawyer the cold shoulder to address me. "I love Nicole, by the way. Super chill and knowledgeable. And the vineyard looks sweet on camera. I already have the vignette planned for later."

"Great! Our follower count jumped another thousand after your post yesterday. It's amazing how people are responding." I beam at him, aware that I'm gushing, but whatever. His body felt so warm against mine last night. The memory of it got me through most of the morning.

"The amazing thing is that my introverted baby brother makes a fortune by shoving his face in front of a camera," Sawyer chimes in with decidedly less enthusiasm.

It's cold in here. The central air clutches my bones. But it just got one a hell of a lot cooler.

Rhys crosses both arms over his chest. "What can I say? Some of us are naturals in the spotlight. And some of us were born to push paper."

Along with irritation, something eternal and unmoveable hangs in his voice. This is not the picture of brotherly warm and fuzzies I imagined. This is a conversation that feels like it will need a fast exit.

"Dani and I plan to push lots of paper while we discuss the bands and talk shop. Nothing that ever interested you before," Sawyer replies, a bit testily if I'm not mistaken.

"What interests me is the amphitheater," Rhys emphasizes. "Becoming intimate with every inch of this place."

I lift my chin, shaking off the strange hot-cold rush that's come over me from Rhys's steady stare. "Why don't we make it a family affair?" I suggest. "Any extra exposure Rhys gives us is a win."

After a beat, Sawyer says, "Sure," like it's the least interesting thing I've said so far. Then he levels an uncompromising gaze at Rhys, whose smirk brims with triumph.

Very suddenly, I see the problem.

These two are at war.

Chapter Twelve

RHYS

It's one of two things. Either Sawyer has managed real change, or he found a way to override his natural tendency to be an uptight douche. Did not expect him to rock the rizz. But he's still reaching in that bougie suit and square-toed loafers that crunch annoyingly on the pea gravel.

Did he think a winery had paved pathways?

"Evelyn speaks very highly of you," he says to Dani. "'A rare and revolutionary talent' is how she phrased it."

She laughs, and here's another unprecedented angle to process: my brother and comedic flair, together in the same body.

"Take that with a grain of salt," she says. "Evelyn has a taste for the theatrical."

"Nero Vino is the Valley's biggest success story. To pull that off requires a competent village."

"And your rebranding is next-level," I add, inserting myself into Sawyer's shameless schmoozing. "Those labels are works of art."

Dani shoots me a look. Something about her in those glasses fuels a perverse school teacher fantasy I didn't even know I had. "Don't pump me up too much," she warns. "The market tells the ultimate tale."

"You took a risk, which ninety-nine percent of the world never does. And look what happened."

"You reached for the stars too. Leaving home at fifteen, creating an empire from nothing."

Four sentences exchanged, with Sawyer not uttering any of them? Of course, he butts back in. "I'd like to see your rebrand ideas," he says. "If you're free tonight, we can discuss how all this might come together over dinner."

Hold on. Vibe check. Dani and I are technically on the fringes of a situationship. I've seen her naked. My DNA marked her skin. She's living rent-free in my head. All that and Sawyer is first to corral her into a dinner date?

"I thought you were driving home tonight?" If I say it, maybe it becomes the truth.

"Nope." Sawyer fishes a business card from his blazer, handing it to Dani like it's the key to heaven. "And next time you're in the city, give me a call. I'll return the favor and give you a tour of our offices."

Dani studies the embossed cardstock. I glance down at the simple black-on-white and feel this formless pressure on my brain. Sawyer Trenton, CEO. He drives a luxury rocket ship. Has an investment portfolio and actually knows what's inside of it. Instead of draining money from Nero Vino like I am, he can pump up their bottom line. The sky suddenly feels very big and very bright, and I feel like the younger brother again, smaller and needing to prove myself.

"They're like any other office," I say. "Not what I'd call appointment-viewing."

"And how would you know?" Sawyer scoffs. "You've never set foot inside them."

Dani side-eyes me with a quizzical expression. Any chance Sawyer gets, he treats me like I'm a cold sore on date night. Our clashes stem from what Mom used to call our *unique dispositions*, if that means fighting in the yard over nothing, hating each other irrationally, and arguing just because.

But our verbal sparring hits pause as we round a massive Ponderosa pine. My initial impression of the winery felt small; I barely saw past the tasting room and my villa (blame Dani for stealing my focus). But this morning, Nicole gave me the grand tour: a tank farm packed with gleaming silver tanks holding future vintages, the bottling line, her so-called "wizard lab," and a warehouse stacked with a cool million in inventory.

And now this.

The pathway peters out onto the ridge of a grassy knoll terraced into steps that funnel down to a stage framed by a killer view of the lake.

"Wow," I say. "Pretty sweet venue for a concert."

Sawyer lowers his sunglasses. His gaze sweeps across the vista, and I can practically hear the cash register tallying ticket sales in his head. "What's the capacity?"

"Six hundred," Dani replies. "Tickets run from twenty to thirty bucks."

"So a band might clear four or five grand." Sawyer, the numbers guy, knows the math inside out.

"Is this where Shania plays for Divine Debauchery?" I ask.

Dani nods. "Evelyn transforms this place into a majestic Roman ruin. From the photos I've seen, it looks incredible."

"What's Divine Debauchery?" Sawyer asks. "And are you talking Shania Twain?"

"It's a private party held on Labor Day weekend. And, yes," Dani adds, "that Shania."

"You have her booked?" Sawyer looks impressed, and that happens once a century. At one point, Trenton Talent Management tried to woo her into the fold with no luck. Even magical Peter had a few busts here and there.

"Maybe," Dani hedges. "We're still in negotiation."

"That's cutting it close."

She blows out a breath. "Tell me about it."

Sawyer and I fill in the blanks at the same time.

"If you need help…" he offers, while I say, "I know all the top DJs."

Dani tilts her head at the proposals flying in from either side. "Let me ask Evelyn. It's been a delicate situation so far."

"Negotiation is my strong suit," Sawyer adds, which feels like a dig at me and to reaffirm (to himself) he doesn't take shit from anybody anymore. I'm not a betting man, but I guarantee the Istanbul incident from our childhood still haunts him. Our dad went ballistic on Sawyer, shaming him publicly for not bargaining harder with the huckster selling trinkets in the bazaar. Sawyer, fifteen, had just stood there, on the verge of tears, while I mentally egged him on—*don't let him railroad you. Stick up for yourself.*

But he didn't.

He stood down.

Later, in the steam room, he admitted to me that it felt wrong to grind the shoeless vendor for a few cents when we were living it up in the lap of luxury at the Four Seasons hotel.

Something about that argument changed Sawyer. He became even more rigid and dispassionate. If he wasn't dragged into the business and pursued engineering like he wanted to, I wonder if he'd be less of a prick.

Firstborns bear the responsibility of family legacy in a specific way.

"*If* Shania books," Sawyer continues, always with another play, "do you need an opening act?"

"Who do you have in mind?" I hope it's some mediocre ankle-biter outfit she can say no to without thinking.

"Have either of you heard of Gia Barlow?"

Dani's mouth drops. I hate how her face lights up and that Sawyer is the cause.

"Really?" she asks with starstruck wonder. "Pop My Cherry is my new favorite band."

Sawyer puffs his chest out like a proud rooster. "They're ready to cut a new EP. She shared a couple of tracks, and, I swear, they're the next Nirvana."

"You've signed them?" Even across the pond, the buzz is out on Gia. Part Italian, all ripper performer, and notoriously uncensored, she's blasting through life powered by zero fucks.

Before he can answer, Dani's phone jingles. She glances at the screen and excuses herself, Sawyer's gaze firmly on her ass as she walks away to take the call. Her dress is something else—black and snug with a hem just shy of appropriate. I wish I could stop staring, but the problem is, I know what's underneath it.

"Damn, she's hot," Sawyer mutters. "Any scoop?"

"Ah, shit, you know what?" I smack my palm against my forehead, playing it up. "Evelyn mentioned a boyfriend."

"Long-term?"

I shrug, one lie following another. "No idea."

He continues to scope her out, dispensing the sage wisdom of a career agent who knows everyone has a price. "Nothing lasts forever, right?"

"That's inspirational," I snort. "With two marriages dead in the water, you're angling for a third?"

"Who said anything about marriage? I'm happy with playdates in between eighteen holes with my crew."

"Worst-case scenario, you can always marry your golf clubs."

It's been so long since I heard Sawyer laugh that I forget what it sounded like. A deep, rolling belly laugh that is at complete odds with his dry-as-dust personality.

"There's an idea," he says. "Save a ton on the backend, right?"

He smiles, and it takes me a few seconds to name the strange sensation dancing on my skin. Camaraderie? Nah, it can't be. The earth still rotates eastward.

"JC said Tara came after you hard for alimony."

"Like a wrecking ball. I never heard the end of it from Dad." He shakes his head, and I do, at this moment, sympathize. Peter had game in all arenas save for fatherhood. "What about you?" he shifts gears. "Still living the bachelor dream?"

I pretend to stare out at the lake while watching Dani. "More like a nightmare. Fame sucks. Even behind locked gates on an island, my privacy gets violated."

After a brief silence, Sawyer says, "You never had an easy time bonding with people."

And just like that, the ghosts crowd in. I overcame my introverted tendencies, but fame has intensified my struggle with relationships.

For all the freewheeling spontaneity I project, put me on a raft with a woman I like, and I become thick-tongued and useless.

"That Gia deal legit?" I shift the focus off me. "She's a huge score."

Sawyer draws a circle on the grass with his dumb-ass shoe tip. "Between you and me, they haven't signed yet. But they will," he insists. "Gia's a huge fan of JC."

As soon as he utters the name, all the tiny hairs on the back of my neck bristle to attention. "What does that mean?"

Sawyer drums his fingers when he's nervous, and he's only nervous when he's working up the courage to do something out of his comfort zone. "She's looking for a new guitarist."

It takes a lot to forget about Dani and her curves hovering nearby. But my focus dissolves into a pinhole of sharp white rage lasered onto Sawyer.

Is he fucking serious?

"Have you forgotten JC doesn't play live anymore?" Not that I have to tell him that our middle brother had a breakdown from the excesses of touring life. He swore never to go on the road again. And these days, the only way bands make serious money is by touring.

"I know," Sawyer says, irritation creeping into his voice because he's busted. "Nothing is set in stone. Just floating ideas around at this stage. And don't screw it up by saying anything, okay?"

"You'd throw your own brother under the bus for a deal? Have you even asked him?" My voice rises, enough to catch Dani's attention. She looks over and signals that her call will wrap up soon.

Sawyer angles closer, his voice tight and low. "We sign her, and it could mean millions. While you're off in Grecian La La Land, the company's taken a hit. Covid. SAG strikes. Any scrap on the table and there's a bloodbath to secure it. This is what I do. And who do you think it was who negotiated your million? I stepped in to hammer Evelyn. Bettina was willing to walk away at seven hundred thousand."

My brow furrows. "She never told me that."

"Of course she didn't. I always look out for you. Family first. Something you might want to consider."

I take the hit, ignoring the twinge in my stomach. "Family first, huh? You know better than to get JC mixed up in this shit. Unemployed guitarists make up half of LA's population. Tap into that."

Dani returns, her smile ticking down a notch as our ugly energy smacks into her. But for all she knows, Sawyer's sour expression is more a default mode than a reflection of his actual mood. Me? I've been moonlighting at the school of make-believe and acing every class. I can pretend with the best of them.

"Sorry about that," she says. "Let's walk down to the point. The view only gets better."

Sawyer and I fall on either side of her again, and this time, I jump in. "Like I said, if you need help with entertainment, give me a holler. I have all the top guys on speed dial."

"Calvin Harris?" She drops one of the biggest names in what feels like a test.

"Just partied with him last month."

My gaze lands on Sawyer, hard and unforgiving. Fine if he wants to muck around in my deals. But I will cut off an arm before I witness JC sink back into the bleakness he almost suffocated in.

Chapter Thirteen

DANI

Four hours later, Sawyer and I are seated at an outdoor table overlooking Lake Osoyoos. The evening blazes August-hot. I take a sip of water, scoping out the trendy steakhouse. Furnished in dark wood and posturing, it's as sleek and polished as Sawyer. His lustrous dress shirt reeks expensive, diamonds twinkling on the pristine white cuffs. Slacks pressed just so.

With his probing questions on the ride over, I'm picking up on a date vibe.

A tall, fresh-faced waitress hustles over, smiling brightly through her frazzle. The restaurant is packed and buzzing like game seven in the Stanley Cup Finals is about to unfold.

"Good evening," she says. "My name is Elaine. I'll be your server tonight. Wine to start, by the looks of it?"

Deeply engrossed in a wine menu thicker than a September issue of *Vogue*, Sawyer slides his eyes to meet mine. "Do you prefer white or red?"

"I'm a red girl, but I'm happy with any color."

Sawyer snaps the wine list shut. "A bottle of the Oculus, please."

Elaine hesitates and glances at me for some unknown reason. "That one is five hundred dollars a bottle."

Sawyer pins her with a look. "If I order something," he says, "it means I can pay for it."

Sawyer flaunted his extensive wine knowledge all afternoon, dropping the big names out of Napa and France. But our well-meaning server does not deserve a dress down in a tone reserved for bitches of the highest order.

Elaine smiles charitably, as you do with a fussy a-hole guest. "Of course. I double-check to be on the safe side, what with the prices being unlisted." She reaches for the wine menu and comically battles with Sawyer over who retains possession of it.

Sawyer wins, yanking it out of her grip. "I'll hold on to this for later."

I dig deep inside myself not to panic. Later? How long does he plan to be here? We knocked back wine with Evelyn in the tasting room for two hours with most of the selling points discussed. She seemed quite taken with Sawyer and his grand schemes. The idea of replacing Shania with Pop My Cherry tickled her pink.

While we quaffed every Nero Vino varietal, Rhys dropped several hints about joining us for dinner that Sawyer flatly ignored. My guess? It tied back to the weird tension that flared between them on our walk earlier.

But I hold on to the small spark of hope that Rhys will appear.

If a window of opportunity arises, I'll text him our location.

"I guess they're not used to the high-rolling crowd," I say after Elaine moves on.

"Amateur," Sawyer mutters, flicking a crumb off the tablecloth. "Anyway…" His gaze settles on me. "Tell me about you. Is your relocation here permanent? You mentioned at the wine tasting that you might work part-time in Vancouver."

Subtle as a sledgehammer, that Sawyer. And I was right. A woman always knows.

"I'm playing it by ear," I say.

We cruised here in the luxury of his BMW 8 series, top down, warm wind gusting through my hair. His cologne smelled spicy and spendy, and the whip-stitched leather seats cradled me like a cocoon. An attractive, high-powered man whisking me to dinner?

Funny, how all that once mattered.

Tonight, it plain irritated me when Sawyer asked if I owned my condo. Qualifying me, the little snot! Did he think my humble abode worth a measly eight hundred grand could ever measure up to his gated mansion next to Lululemon mastermind Chip Wilson, with the Pacific Ocean as his backyard? (Yes, he dropped all of those details.)

My neighbor is a sixty-year-old pensioner who loves opera at full blast and cooking everything with garlic.

"But will you be…"

A hush settles over the restaurant, halting Sawyer mid-sentence. Like every other set of eyes in here, we turn toward the shift in vibration.

Rhys.

Scanning the restaurant from the hostess stand. A guy who lights up the room merely by being in it.

I don't miss the way his expression brightens when he finds my face in the crowd. He holds up a hand in a gesture of *hey there*. I wave back with a genuine case of the flutters.

My rescuer, in all his dreamy glory.

Rhys cuts past the crowded tables, oblivious to, or pretending not to notice, the stares and whispers. Sawyer, mouth drawn into a thin, hard line, oozes annoyance. Rhys and his carefree ease only amplify that whatever makes him cool and hip somehow bypassed the rigid and world-weary Sawyer.

Tableside, Rhys knocks his elbow playfully against my shoulder. "Small world, huh? Nicole recommended this place for dinner. You mind if I join in?"

"Sure." I throw a look at Sawyer.

He smiles, but it's tight. "Pull up a chair."

Rhys asks the couple one table over whether he can swipe their extra seat. Much to the chagrin of her balding date, the woman, wearing a tie-dye muumuu, gushes, "Of course!"

She practically throws the chair and herself at Rhys, who is deeply sexy draped in a lilac t-shirt stamped with HANG LOOSE and his simple Seneca pendant. In comparison, the one-million-thread-count shirt and gold link Gucci necklace Sawyer wears scream *trying too hard!*

Rhys settles beside me, glowing serenely for someone who just lied. Nicole pointedly told me to avoid the crowd here—nothing but wannabe tourists and Albertan cowboys throwing around their dirty oil sands money.

Eyes darting back and forth between us, Rhys asks innocently, "Am I interrupting anything?"

"No," Sawyer answers, although his flat tone says otherwise. "But thrilled you can pick up the tab."

Rhys laughs and helps himself to Sawyer's glass of water. "Nice try, See Saw. This is a write-off for you, business and all."

I feel the tension rise. That *business* had a bite to it. Will this turn into a full-blown pissing match? Then Rhys slides his arm around the back of my chair, cementing whatever power play is going down. He leans in, our faces almost touching. His warmth, all that vanilla-scented goodness, sends my brain spinning, heartbeat in my ears.

Whispering loud enough for Sawyer to hear, he says, "I told you he was chintzy."

🍷

Before Rhys dropped in, Sawyer seemed intent on stretching out the evening. But he waves off Elaine's inquiry about a second bottle of wine. Then he inhales his spiced duck breast and signals for the check the second I swallow my last bite of salmon.

"What's the rush?" Rhys soaks up the last vestiges of balsamic and oil with a heel of crusty bread.

"I need to be fresh." Sawyer signals Elaine again for the check. "Six a.m. leave."

Rhys rolls his eyes and turns to me. "Did you want dessert or coffee?"

"I'm fine." I'm happy to blow this joint and all the eyes that pretended not to stare at us as Rhys shared colorful stories about their childhood, Sawyer constantly interrupting to correct his version of events.

Elaine scurries to our table with the payment terminal and a nervous expression. Sawyer glares at Rhys, dumps his napkin on the table, and excuses himself.

Meow.

"Typical," Rhys mutters.

He whips out his credit card to pay, making friends with Elaine along the way. She giggles a little too loud at his friendly banter.

I sit up straighter, aware of the flush on her cheeks, and Rhys seemingly pleased to be the architect of it. Okay, wait. I'm not supposed to feel territorial and protective. But during dinner, our knees touched more than once under the table.

And this time, I didn't jump.

Elaine finally glides away on cloud nine, and Rhys leans both elbows on the table, his eyes slowly skating across my face. "Hey," he says in that smooth, suave voice. "Nice night, minus you-know-who."

The bubbles fizz in my chest again. He's beautiful, in a poetic way. And he exudes an air of mystery beneath his happy-go-lucky persona. Like I have only scratched the surface of him.

"If you don't mind me asking, what's up with you and him?"

I wait for his shoulders to clench or the smile to slip, but he only shrugs. "Quality time with Sawyer is an oxymoron."

"Is that why he doesn't manage you?"

He reaches for Sawyer's glass of wine, drains the remains, then spins the empty glass on the tablecloth. "One of the reasons," he finally says. "Maybe you can tell him I'm a dream to work with. Aside from the workplace hazards."

His eyes snap to mine, and a rush of fire comes with his wink, one that has me reaching for my water to drown out the chaotic rhythm of my heartbeats.

"Hazard is the perfect word to describe you," I say.

Rhys chuckles, once more nudging his knee against mine. He's done a lot of that tonight—finding ways to touch me. "I'm the wrong brother if you want safe and square."

"In that case," I say, "I'll tell Evelyn she made the right choice."

Rhys searches my eyes. The lights in here dimmed at some point, and the glow softens every edge like the wine has softened my resolve. I smile through the mounting pressure coming over me with every flicker of his lashes.

"I'm not talking about Evelyn," he says.

I'm silent, grasping for something to say. Rhys waits patiently, and the way he looks at me, with that simmering charisma—it eats me alive. Where is the clever comeback at the tip of my tongue? And how many more times can I resist him?

After wishing all night for Sawyer to disappear, his return saves me from falling into the black hole of Rhys, where time has no meaning and words elude me.

He yanks on his Hugo Boss blazer, blunt and businesslike. "Did you pay?" he asks Rhys.

Rhys stands and beats Sawyer to the draw, pulling back my chair with a gallant flourish. "Consider it your fee for my ride home."

❦

"Is this normal traffic?" Sawyer asks.

Like Vegas, Osoyoos also has a strip—a far less glamorous stretch of asphalt known as Highway 3. You have to time it right on peak summer days to avoid bumper-to-bumper traffic, but the road clogged with cars at eight thirty on a Tuesday night?

"Not really," I reply.

Sawyer aggressively noses in front of a dusty old Chevy truck, flipping the bird to whoever honks in displeasure. The sky is molten yellow, and shadows are starting to stretch longer. It's still deadly hot.

"Can anyone see in through your windows?" Rhys pipes up from the back seat.

Sawyer glances at him in the rearview mirror. "No. I had them all tinted. Why?"

"Just curious."

Concern has leaked into his voice, and when I glance back, Rhys is eyeing the Corollas and Civics cruising past—windows rolled down, sharp-eyed females locked on the Beemer. Suddenly, I feel very conspicuous. We are the equivalent of the Hope Diamond in a sea of dime-store knockoffs.

Minutes later, we veer off the highway onto the back road leading to Nero Vino, and my spidey sense kicks into overdrive. Several cars tail us, but where are they headed? All the wineries along this lonely stretch have shuttered for the night.

The answer becomes clear as we crest the final hill before the winery. A bottleneck of cars parked helter-skelter blocks the entrance, headlights spraying eerie yellow beams across the desert. A cluster of young women in shorts and tank tops camped out front swivel in unison to zone in on us.

"Can you pin it, bro?" Rhys mutters anxiously from the back seat. "Get past this."

"I can't run them over," Sawyer replies as the pack forms a semi-circle barricade on the road.

Hungry looks and unstable energy.

On the hunt.

"Fuck!" Rhys slides to the floorboard like we're in a zombie invasion and he's the last brain standing.

"What's going on?" I squint at a splinter-thin guy with a shock of orange hair, arguing with a girl draped over the hood of his Cross Trek like some car mechanic calendar pin-up. She looks ready to leap up and feast on his throat at any minute.

"Piss off, okay?" he shouts. "I have no clue where Rhys is. And can you please get off my car?"

Ah, now I understand who he is. The appropriately named Francis Shutter looks exactly like his Facebook profile picture—eighty percent freckles and twenty percent geek.

"What the heck?" I mutter. "Stop the car, please. That's our camera guy."

"Don't leave your door open," Rhys warns. "I'm telling you, this could get weird."

Sawyer pulls onto the shoulder and parks. I hop out and hear the soft *clunk* of all the door locks engaging. Smart move, considering the herd of females surging forward to descend on the Beemer.

"Is he in there?" one cries.

"Is that him?"

A buxom redhead in a tube top mashes her face against the window and coos, "Rhys! I love yooou."

Like an ant infestation at a picnic, they crawl around the car leaving sticky fingerprints and Revlon blusher streaked on Sawyer's immaculate windows. Not wanting to miss any action, the females in the cars that followed us stampede out to join their brethren, eyes wide with wonder. My quick head count ends at twenty-five.

"Dani!" Francis recognizes me from our Zoom call and storms over. "I've been trying to get up, but they won't let me pass."

Shit. He said my name. I was hoping to fly under the radar.

"Hi," I say. "Let me handle this. Is Rita here?"

"Not yet." He keeps a firm eye on the gum-snapping girls. "But I warned her about this zoo."

With his weak chin and science nerd vibe, it's safe to say Francis is not a teenage girl's wet dream. But the girl he was clashing with stink-eyes me in a judgy head-to-toe sweep.

"Who are you?" she asks, all winged eyeliner and attitude.

"I work for the winery. This is a private road, and whoever owns these cars needs to move them. Now."

None of them budge. If anything, they band tighter together in lip-glossed solidarity until a stout ponytailed girl steps forward. In a bright yellow onesie and combat boots laced tight mid-calf, she carries herself with the air of someone who runs the show.

"Is Rhys staying up there?" she asks. "We saw his posts about this place."

Filled with families and retirees, Osoyoos is the most unlikely hub of celebrity stalking. And Rhys doesn't court fame. He keeps a safe distance from it. But I recall the woman in the corner of the restaurant holding up her phone in our direction. After a long, hard stare from me, she set it down. Who knows if she, or Ponytail, contributed one of the hundreds of slightly deranged comments on his recent posts? All I know is that I need to protect Rhys. And brush these divas-in-training out of our hair.

"He's doing some promotional work with us," I admit because they know the truth. "But I have no idea where he's staying."

The group exchanges wary glances of the *Can she be trusted?* variety. Being suspicious of adults never goes out of vogue if you're a teenager.

Ponytail takes a hit of her vape. "Will he be here tomorrow?"

"Not sure. It's all very hush-hush. And," I add, taking a stab at their ages while knowing the enforcement of this is loose, "anyone under nineteen has to be accompanied by an adult at all times. You can't come up there otherwise."

As they digest that news in pouty silence, the heavily tinted driver's window of the Beemer rolls down. I can hear the collective drawing of breaths, followed by slightly disappointed ones. But only slightly. While Sawyer is not Rhys, he is easy on the eyes.

"Hey, babe," he says to me. "We need to go. Sorry, ladies." He flashes a confident smile at the group. "My girlfriend and I need to Netflix and chill. It's been a long day."

Fake dating to get out of a pickle? Brilliant. But will they buy it? They huddle together and debate in low-level murmuring. I glance at Sawyer, who signals with his eyes that he's ready to take them on if necessary.

Jesus. Is this how tonight ends? In a rumble?

The council of teeny boppers separates, and Ponytail addresses them in the determined tone of a bounty hunter. "Let's get some food and call every hotel. This place is tiny. We'll find him. Or come back tomorrow."

"The owner lives up on the property, and she's old-school tough," I warn her. "One thousand percent she will not tolerate a bunch of minors hanging around. Stay away, unless you want the cops involved."

Ponytail snorts a laugh. The threat of police? Bring it on, sister. But she rallies her crew for departure, and they disperse, blue smoke blowing out of the tailpipes as they convoy away.

After they clear out, Francis brushes off dust from his garden-variety film-set wardrobe of Dickie's and Doc Martens. "Nice work and all," he says, "but if we need to deal with that for the next few weeks, forget any clean sound takes. You should look into crowd control."

I sigh, watching the dust plumes from the mob's departure settle in the twilight. "I'll talk to Evelyn tomorrow. We may need to hire security."

In the car, Sawyer asks Rhys, "Is it always like this?"

Very slowly, the rear window slides lower. Rhys has unfolded himself from the floor, his face pale beneath the tan. "Only a few times. But once is enough never to forget."

"Oh shit, man!" Francis exclaims. "You were in there the whole time? You play the dangerous game."

Rhys and I lock eyes, his flecked with doubt. Damage control never came up with Bettina, and she left no stone unturned. Or so I thought.

But here we are, not even a week in, and a fangirl squad is already on alert, ready to pounce. Small numbers now, but if even a fraction of his thirty million fans descend on Osoyoos, we're screwed.

Chapter Fourteen

RHYS

HERE'S THE PROBLEM WITH BEING FAMOUS: FANS APPROACH ME WITH WHAT they believe is a genuine level playing field. The reality? Hardwired expectations hum dangerously beneath their smiles and sincerity. Interaction with enough Crazies has proved their uncanny ability to memorize every minuscule detail of my life, and they hold on to them like religion.

They speculate and fictionalize.

Create this entire narrative in their minds.

Inevitably, I disappoint them when they realize hologram Rhys is just another guy. Not magic. Not mythical. And not available at their disposal twenty-four-seven. And they act bruised and disappointed if I wave them off, when all I want is to buy some fucking bananas in peace.

Witnessing a revamped opinion of me take over their faces is a weird hit. Like I somehow let them down.

I stare up at the bedroom ceiling with a grave realization settling over me. This Nero Vino gig felt safe. Five weeks in small-town Cana-da? Sold. The most aggro Canadians get is walking into a parking meter and saying *sorry.*

Or so I thought.

Now I'm stuck at a winery in a half-a-horse town, population five thousand and change, with Crazies hitting me from all sides. Anxiety crests, and I shut my eyes, breathing through the tension locking my shoulders and jaw. Myla texted me last night, and I'll spare you the details other than stating the obvious: she is certifiable. I stupidly replied to her X-rated video with all the outrage I could muster and prayed her radio silence meant the end of it.

Wishful thinking.

My screen lit up like a firework display with a cascade of heart emojis and smiley faces.

MB: Sooorrrryyy! Just miiis you! When are u back?

Honestly? I'm beginning to worry in real time. Myla is crossing a line, and I don't have the energy to deal with Interpol or whoever handles the weirdos. After blocking her number, I feel better, but a lingering sense of unease remains.

Fans used to be chill once upon a time. There's a hysteria to them now that unsettles me. From my vantage point last night—crammed onto the floorboard of the Beemer—I saw no faces but heard the shrill desperation in their voices. A demand that I somehow owed them an appearance in exchange for stalking me.

Not a chance.

Not after that scene from London two years ago.

A group of us influencers scored VIP invites to a Wimbledon after-party hosted by Drake. The tunes rocked, and we partied hard, but the mob we got caught up in after—it was scary shit. I walked out of the club at midnight with some legit stars, and a screaming horde of fangirls stormed past the unprepared security-for-hire squeezed into their Suit Warehouse specials. They closed around us with the frenzy of vultures descending on a carcass.

It felt surreal, like being in the eye of a storm.

A cluster of humanity ebbing and flowing.

Hands grabbing at me.

A favorite t-shirt got ripped, and my scalp throbbed for days where a chunk of hair got yanked out.

I camped out in Corfu doing a month of solitary after that debacle.

And still, one of the Crazies stalked me there.

I roll onto my side, tucking a pillow between my legs, mind revving in overdrive. This racket—the internet race to the bottom—cannot continue. It is that simple. I need to pursue something different, but I can't put my finger on the *how-to*. And what other skills do I have? Real acting? Not a chance, unless Brazzers is hiring.

Jizz in the vineyard? You got it!

Fuck me.

As I ruminate on paths and possibilities, my phone buzzes on the side table. I grab it, paranoia creeping in, half-expecting more Myla harassment. But it's Sawyer, trying me for the third time. I send him to the outer space of voicemail, knowing it will infuriate him. Yeah, I should be the bigger person and thank him for stepping up last night, but his ridiculous comment pissed me off.

My girlfriend and I need to Netflix and chill.

Is there anything worse than cowering on the floorboards of your brother's pimpmobile, and then, hey, he decides to emasculate you?! What a jerk. Am I surprised? Not after I crashed his party last night. Concerned that his limited charms might sway Dani, I called every restaurant, knowing Sawyer, like Dad, would rather take a bullet than show up without a reservation.

Waiting for a table is what commoners do.

Was it my imagination, or did Dani look downright relieved to see my face?

She looked hot and sharp, flawlessly dressed. I own nothing that needs a hanger, but is it time to invest in a blazer? Hard to picture me and Dani hitting the town when her effortless dazzle outshines my best wrinkle-free tee times infinity.

Is my idle vibe holding her back? Or the five-week expiration date stamped on my forehead? She strikes me as the tactical type, risk-averse to messing around with a stranger who plans to hightail it home, paycheck cashed. The thing is, I don't know how jazzed I am to head home. All that awaits is more of the same, as the world turns and another year of mindlessness drifts by.

But where do I go?

More importantly, how do Dani and I kick back with a glass of wine and work up to first base when she home-runned me on day three? I've never ping-ponged between the extremes of Nude Encounters of the First Kind and Dry Hump 101. Never felt this weird glow, like I'm radioactive. My mind and soul lit up. Thirty-six hours in each other's orbits, and I'm flailing like a man lost at sea.

I need to get a grip. Organize my thoughts, my life, and how to tranquilize the desperate urge to claim Dani's mouth. And somehow escape these fangirls.

I check the time on my phone. Dani lands in an hour, along with Francis and Rita, to talk filming around a fleet of Ccrazies. I'm praying to God, this time, shit doesn't get weird.

Dani arrives first, hair twirled into a high bun. A weird tension crackles around her, like a whole other atmosphere. The very definition of preoccupied.

"Morning," I say. "Come in. It looks like you could use a coffee."

She throws me a relieved look. "That would be great."

Dani glides past me, curves wrapped tight in a purple dress and rocking nude heels with zippers on the back. Booty high and swinging. My heart goes a little nuts. Every time I see her, I feel this breathless high.

"Latte or cappuccino?" I ask.

"Whatever's easiest," she says distractedly.

I find her eyes. "Everything cool?"

"Uhm, I came early so we could talk in private." She clocks my open laptop on the kitchen island. "Am I interrupting anything?"

She would have, thirty minutes ago. Drawing is how I whiled away the hours of loneliness after landing solo in Europe. Dani has a leg up on me with design, but I can convincingly render real life. Enough that, after I captured her creamy pink folds studded with silver in my journal, it set off a chain reaction.

"I was in the middle of a PowerPoint to solve world hunger. But that can wait."

I flash a smile hoping to enable one of hers. Bingo. Dani perches on a kitchen stool, and now I have the good fortune of not only making her laugh but the weight of her gaze warming my skin.

"You're underrated as a comedian," she says.

I join her at the island, ass on a stool, smacking the lid of my laptop shut. "Overrated in every other department."

Her brow furrows. "Why would you say that?"

Why indeed did I shine a light into my dark interior world? Because it's haunted me all morning. Not my cleverest comeback, but it rolled off my tongue before I could stop it.

"It looked like you needed a laugh," is how I position it. "And what did you want to talk about?"

Dani pauses just long enough to make me nervous. "Your brother," she finally says.

My jaw clenches. Earlier, my stress level had dipped considerably thanks to a vision of Dani on the raft, fingers working between her legs, while my hand worked overtime under the duvet.

But it's back, racing to new highs.

She cannot be into Sawyer. Give me this one thing, Higher Power. You owe me.

I cross both arms over my chest, if only to stop it from exploding. "What about him?"

"Did he say anything to you about me? What I mean is," she quickly adds, "I picked up on a more-than-business vibe. On the off chance he mentioned something..."

The opportunity to roast Sawyer is tantalizing. Twice divorced. A hopeless workaholic she might see on the weekends, gliding bored and stiff through some high society function. As much fun as the plague.

But I don't.

And I also dance around the truth.

"I can't speak for him. We aren't super tight in that way."

She searches my face, earnest and unguarded. I feel a little destroyed. Did it cross her mind to ask about me? Does she not feel the sexual tension crackling between us? The purchase of a thousand blazers suddenly feels hopeless.

"Thanks," she says. "I didn't mean to put you on the spot." A shaft of morning sunlight cuts though the kitchen, forcing Dani to shield her eyes. "I liked the stories you told last night. I get the whole sibling drama angle. It's the same with me and my sister. Minus the vomit."

We share a little laugh. The tale of Sawyer having to collect the drunk asses of his two younger brothers from the copshop at one in the morning is a classic. On the drive home, I threw up in the back seat of his 3 Series, and the damn thing reeked of stale puke until he sold it.

One of the many reasons why Sawyer tried to cockblock me last night.

But even he managed a grin when I imitated Dad in conniption mode, the bright lights of the kitchen shining on his delinquent sons as he declared JC and me grounded "for-fucking-ever."

"I was a little shit, to be fair," I admit.

"Speaking of little shits." Dani repositions herself on the stool. "I gave Evelyn the rundown from last night. She asked me to hire security. Two guys at the front entrance twenty-four-seven starting today at noon."

"Uh-oh." This feels like the beginning of something bad. "Tell me what you need. I can stick around here if that makes your life easier. Me and the team can improvise. And thank you for last night." I tap my foot against her bare calf. "You were fierce."

Her cheeks pink ever so slightly. "I appreciate that."

I would appreciate more than a respectful smile. What is it going to take to break her barrier?

"We're in this together," I say, making it clear she can count on me. "Aside from our swimming wager, of course." I wink. "Think you can beat me to the raft? Because we still have to play that fair and square."

That does it. Her eyes light up, the spark I was aiming for. "Are we putting money on that?" she shoots back.

"We could bet on a few different outcomes."

I smile, short of fixing her with admiring eyes. Timeless idiocy, me being King Obvious, but whatever. The Sawyer obstacle toppled has me screaming for the finish line.

And who ruins the moment but the duo I wanted nothing to do with?

Francis and Rita stroll in, assuming an open door means they can forgo the courtesy of knocking.

"Hey, man," Francis says in that chummy way of film folk who approximate their hiring with Insta-friend status. I already know his reedy voice will get under my skin within minutes. "This is Rita."

He gestures at the unsmiling lump beside him who radiates all the charm of Charles Manson crossed with a troll. Her butch stance suggests perpetual conflict or an incoming headlock with one of her heavily tattooed arms. Hardcore bee-yotch brims in eyes cold and brown as coffee stains, in case her t-shirt printed with THIS SHIT IS EXTRA didn't tip you off. The only thing missing is a rifle slung across her shoulders.

"Who do I talk to about getting some oat milk in our cabin?" is the first thing she demands. "I don't do dairy."

Dani's eyes snap to mine with an uncertain stare. Did she expect some polite witticism to fly out of that scowling mouth? Welcome to Charm School.

I knew I should have pushed harder for no film crew.

Chapter Fifteen

DANI

I CUT THROUGH THE PARKING LOT, GREETING THE FIRST WAVE OF winetasters crawling out of their Carreras and Cadillacs. My head throbs. The irritation that crept over my skin has yet to disappear. The Francis and Rita show. Talk about a lesson in tediousness.

I felt my eyes cross as Francis painstakingly mapped out focal lengths, shutter speeds and filters, forgetting entirely the purpose of our meeting was not about him. Rhys thankfully cut him off, but then his waif sidekick Rita chimed in, all gloom and doom about capturing sound while battling groupies.

God, what a piece of work.

I found her morbidly fascinating. Young and dogged, all clothes made from hemp, because, well … earth. Five-feet-nothing of global activist lecturing Rhys on his dismal carbon footprint, flying halfway around the world to hawk booze.

When I gently reminded her about manners, she scowled at me like I clubbed baby seals for fun.

I feel for Rhys stuck with those two all day.

I swing into my office and decide to give it an hour before I call Bettina and ask what the hell she was thinking. I need my murderous thoughts about Rita to subside. If she pulls any warrior shit with Nicole, the firm plant of a Croc on her ass will be the next thing she feels.

And speaking of feeling…

Rhys posts shirtless all the time—who wouldn't with those abs? But dayum. He made it impossible to concentrate. Board shorts slung low on his slim hips. A band of thick elastic stitched with POLO RALPH LAUREN snugged tight against his muscles tanned gold. Sitting two feet away from him in the kitchen, I could count the soft blond hairs guarding his nipples.

I've never felt emotions like that before, never felt that … covetous.

And here I thought his fangirls would be the death of me.

Barely a minute after I plunk behind the desk to collect my unpure thoughts, the office phone rings. An unknown number. My intuition says *do not pick up*. Trouble always comes in threes.

Fangirls. Francis and Rita. Is the universe saving the worst for last?

I chew the inside of my cheek before picking up on the fifth ring. "Marketing, this is Dani."

"Miss Rialto?" a drawling male voice asks.

Right away, from his tone, I know this isn't good. I clear my throat. "This is she."

"Constable Davidson from the Royal Canadian Mounted Police calling," he says, pausing after for dramatic effect. Law enforcement prides itself on intimidating you with title alone. And it's working, judging from the bloom of sweat on my lower back.

"What can I do for you?" Even over the phone, he sounds like a big dude on a mission. I power on my computer and load my email program.

"We had an incident last night by the lake," he starts. "A group of young women acting drunk and disorderly. Apparently, a certain celebrity is in town doing some work for your winery?"

I feel my mouth go dry. An email from Shania's agent claims the pole position of my email inbox, a frowny face emoji in the subject line.

"Yes, we've hired an influencer to promote one of our wines," I say, giving him the basics and nothing else.

And because I'm an impatient masochist, I open the email.

"Influencer," Davidson says in that slow, languid way of someone twirling a toothpick back and forth in his mouth. "I heard of those. And he warrants you hiring some security?"

I skim the email, my stomach sinking.

Deeply sorry!

Clashes with her holiday dates.

Next time?

I blink, re-reading in case I missed the *Just kidding!* Nope. Shania is out. The rejection feels personal, even though it should be completely impersonal.

"Miss Rialto?" The constable's heavy baritone rings in my ear.

"Yes," I say, shaking off the Shania distraction. "We had some fans at the winery last night, and they dispersed peacefully. But it felt prudent to hire security. As a safeguard."

After a long silence, he asks, "Should we be concerned? This is our busy season. Not the time for any ruckus. And your winery already creates enough hubbub with that event."

He says *event* like someone might say *cancer*.

"With security, I think we're good."

No sooner do those words leave my lips when my iPhone vibrates on the desk.

AR: CALL ME ASAP!!!!

AR: LIKE, NOW!!!!

As usual, my sister and her remarkable restraint with all caps and exclamation points.

I quickly text her back, hoping to calm her down.

DR: I'm on a call. What's up?

AR: Uhm, hello??? The reel he just posted?

I feel a pinch in both temples. Now what?

"Can you give me this fellow's name?" the constable asks. "Behooves me to do some research."

A forceful swallow works my throat. Shit. Hard to sell a guy as harmless with a social media handle of @thetrentontroublemaker. "Rhys Trenton. You can find him on Instagram."

If you even know what that is, I don't say. Mr. Davidson sounds north of age sixty, and if he's on Facebook, I'll eat my desk. In the pause that follows, I quickly navigate to Rhys's Insta account.

He threw together a behind-the-scenes vignette from the photo shoot. Snippets of Luca and Vigo. Yvette's house. The lunch I barely touched. But the three thousand-plus comments are aimed square at the shot of me that made the cut.

A profile shot of me flaunting enough side boob to feed a small family. He snapped it covertly, but the light was perfect. My skin looks flawless. And it was well before my soul-gutting moment, so my smile is relaxed.

The caption? *Our Roman Queen.* Five flame emojis underneath.

A nugget of angst pings my lungs. I'm flattered he snuck the pic, but talk about the wrong post at the wrong time. If any of the girls from last night see this, they'll put two and two together. The only saving grace is that Rhys didn't tag me.

"You sure you have things under control up there, Miss Rialto?" the constable presses.

No, I'm not sure. In fact, I'm one thousand percent certain this whole project is flying off the rails.

"Absolutely. We have all our filming permits, and everything's by the book. You could do me one favor though."

His tone shifts into something less friendly. "What's that?"

"We'd like to keep it on the down low that Rhys is at the winery. Your help is appreciated."

Silence. My ballsy assumption that he will help hangs precariously in the air.

Finally: "You around later today? I might mosey my way up there to take a look around."

Great. First whiff of a celebrity in town and everyone wants a look.

"Of course." I fake a smile he can hear across the phone. "We're open until six p.m. Come by any time."

I hang up, feeling the walls close in. Shania's out. The RCMP now has a shiny boot in our affairs. A gang of fangirls waits to sink their talons into Rhys, and our media team thinks they walk on water.

Can the day get any better?

My phone buzzes again.

AR: It's been five. Just sayin'

In the interest of getting her off my back, I call Amelia right away.

"Since when did you get so hot?" she demands. "And you said nothing to me about this photo shoot."

"It all happened in the blink of an eye. I can't front-run every detail with you."

"Have you read any of the comments?"

"A couple," I admit. Who knew there were so many variations of *Who's that ho?*

After a brief silence, Amelia says, "You're handling this remarkably well."

On another day, that comment might have rolled off my back. But the truth is, I'm on edge and uncertain where this is all heading. And lying underneath her observation is that I should be a wreck—that I can't handle pressure like she can. I exhale sharply. Jesus. Does it always have to be a competition? She even one-upped my birthday by a day. June fourth to my June fifth. It's like she started her scorecard with me from the womb.

Before I say something I regret, Evelyn appears in the doorway.

"I'll check in later, Ames. Gotta run. Hello," I say to Evelyn with a ready smile.

"Hello, dear. You look a little stressed."

She scans my palatial office, and I feel the weight of her scrutiny. My heart skips away, double tempo. I can't unload all of this right now. I need to process.

"Just one of those mornings."

Evelyn stares at me for three seconds before giving me the benefit of the doubt. "If the situation gets dire with those girls, let me know ASAP. Gail Stafford from Osoyoos Tourism texted me this morning saying it was important. Do you mind giving her a ring? I have a feeling she wants to stick her nose into this too."

Oh god. Gail is the local chatterbox. Another prying local. "Will do."

"So you know," she continues, "Tomas plans to attend the Wine Grower's meeting tonight. Don the armor. He will go off on Divine Debauchery and a million other things."

Tomas Sato. A bitter black cloud with a vendetta against nearly every winery in the Valley. But especially Nero Vino. It's a feud that stretches back to the seventies, after Evelyn married his brother, Hugo. They had a falling out, and things got worse when Evelyn had the nerve to step into the business Tomas thought was no place for a woman.

Evelyn knew little about winemaking, but with entrepreneurial parents, she knew how to make money. She pushed Hugo to snap up property right, left and center, establishing one of the biggest landholdings in the Valley.

Land she still owns.

Land Tomas believes he should profit from.

"Maybe I should talk to him," I suggest. "If he hears things from a different perspective, that might calm him down."

"His problem is that he needs to get laid," Evelyn says with her usual shameless flair. "Not enough women young or foolish enough in this town for his liking. But, yes, try to walk him off his soapbox. And please remind Gail of Nero Vino's generous support. Without my funding, half of this town wouldn't exist."

"By the way," I add, "Shania just bailed. Am I good to run with plan B?"

"Really?" Evelyn's brows lift in surprise. "You can't rely on anyone these days. Except you, of course. Yes, please talk to Sawyer and Rhys about their backups. The purse strings are wide open. We need entertainment. Work your negotiating charms."

The last thing I want to lay on Sawyer is charm. He purred goodbye to me last night with intention. Elbow on the console, leaning in. Shania on the bill meant less contact with him— a chance to avoid the tricky *It's not you, it's me* conversation.

Or rather, *It's your brother.*

Evelyn is halfway out the door when she stops and smiles at me over her shoulder.

"I'd say Rhys is turning out to be your savior. Be sure to let him know how grateful you are."

Chapter Sixteen

I AM OFFICIALLY IN HELL WITH NONE OF THE PERKS, STRANDED ALONGSIDE a near-catatonic Nicole, who will kick Francis in the ass sooner than I will if he continues at his glacial rate. These union film guys can't function beyond airtight.

"I need to reset," Francis mutters, to no one's surprise. "Lost focus at the end. How was the sound take, Reets?"

"I can still hear the refrigerator," she claims, thrusting her chin upward in diva disgust.

A shadow of misery touches Nicole's features. Today is our Q and A about her winemaking process. She's been good with delivery and keeping things light between takes, but the lack of takes has taken a toll. Francis has postured around all morning acting like a true titan of tech, but I could have captured a week's worth of content in the time it took him to get set up.

And Rita? Don't even get me started.

"Why don't we break for lunch early?" I suggest. "Meet back here in an hour?"

"It's only eleven," Rita blithely states, as if I can't read the giant clock above Nicole's workstation. As if eating before noon carries the threat of her turning into a pumpkin.

"Right. So, we'll see you at twelve."

Nicole and I wait out the thick silence as Lucifer and his wife pack up. Once our dynamic duo has left the building, Nicole blows out an exasperated sigh that could send a sailboat to Fiji.

"Pardon me, but can I face a firing squad instead?"

"Having fun yet?" I joke back.

"I thought the law was painful. Those two are needles jammed into my skull." She pushes out of her chair, heaving a sigh. "I have an extra egg salad sandwich. And we can sneak in some wine. Numb ourselves for the second act."

"Sold," I say.

Nicole fetches the grub from her cubbyhole kitchen and returns with a bottle of The Emperor and two glasses. It's that kind of day when the pour reaches the rim.

"Cheers," she says, careful not to spill as we clink glasses. "Because you…" Her eyes soften, crinkling at the corners. "You're okay."

"Is that a compliment?" I ask, just to be sure. I knew from our inaugural first meeting, she considered me ick for whatever reason. But I felt her thaw on Tuesday. Have we reached full melt?

Nicole swirls her glass, releasing a cascade of fragrant scents that tickle my nose—ripe berries, a hint of spice. She inhales deeply and looks drunk with love. "What I expected was attitude and aviators. Not a hair out of place. Dumb as a stick."

"Wow. Tell me how you really feel."

When Nicole smiles, her whole face changes, and she leans back, happy to indulge my request that she's clearly put some thought into. "A pinhead princeling who wouldn't know the difference between rosé or rotgut if it slapped him in the face."

I absorb the hit. Take it like a man, Rhys. "Appreciate the honesty. Although, ouch."

Her grin widens. "Be happy someone around here appreciates you."

Okay. Rita and I *might* have gotten off on the wrong foot. In my defense, I was trying to do both of them a solid, offering pointers—angles I previously sussed out, where the light worked best, and dead spots for sound. As soon as I dipped a toe into her craft, Rita turned on me, fully and completely.

"Dude," she'd bristled in a classic *fuck you* tone, "just because you're the 'star,'" air quotes around that, "doesn't mean you're the boss of us."

Both of Nicole's eyebrows had shot skyward.

Me? I backed off.

Only a fool wages war with this new breed of righteous warrior. And Rita is a specific brand of hater. The bitter, jealous ones who diss me as a talentless overnight sensation, and I'm like, you idiots, I've been at this for sixteen years. I early-adopted Instagram when you were bawling in diapers. Sure, I fumbled around at the beginning, like everyone. Niche and content and metrics? Those meant nothing when I started. Yes, I rode the wave to the top through timing and sheer luck. Yes, I make it look easy, swinging in my hammock every night, rambling on about life. Post the video and, presto, ten new companies beg me to flog their products for ridiculous sums.

Any chimpanzee, right?

Not that I need her undying devotion to feel better about myself, but seriously.

If it's so fucking easy, you do it.

As Nicole and I munch sandwiches and swill wine, we replay the "best of" Rita lines. Sound-bites that I grudgingly admit were hilarious, if they weren't so damn pompous.

"What did she say to you in your villa this morning?" Nicole asks.

"That I was no better than a Russian oligarch who floated around on a yacht worth more than Africa's GDP while feasting on the last lobsters dragged off the ocean floor."

Nicole laughs so hard, wine squirts out of her nose. She clears her throat, banging a fist against her chest to halt the laughing coughs. "I cannot believe those words left her mouth."

I side-eye her. "Is it me or you who tells Evelyn she should be ashamed for aggrandizing a Roman emperor who was the showpiece for degeneracy?"

Nicole shakes her head, at a loss. "Can't you fire her?"

"I hope so. Dani's looking into it." Nothing would please me more than to have Rita stare poverty in the face. I take another sip of wine, addicted to the velvety texture that coats my tongue, flavors of dark cherry and cacao unfolding with a shimmer of tobacco. No wonder this inspired Dani to create her incredible labels.

"Maybe we should offer her some wine," Nicole suggests. "Calm her the hell down."

"She probably drinks Yellow Tail," I say, damning Rita forever. "Or wine coolers."

Nicole mulls me over with a warm, wistful smile. "Where were you when I was straight and twenty years younger?"

At six p.m., I am done. Depleted. In need of a beer, or ten, and some quiet time in my hammock. If the clock-puncher life means dealing with the human equivalents of sixty-grit sandpaper, maybe I'll stick to influencing after all.

The lone bright spot of the day was Dani. She dropped by after lunch to share two pieces of news. One, we were stuck with Rita. It turns out she's the daughter of Bettina's sister and needs this gig. No real surprise that Rita has burned a few bridges in the biz. Given that, you'd think she might try and sand down her caustic personality.

The scarier notion? Maybe what we witnessed *was* her trying.

Newsflash number two hit me like a curveball. With Shania out and Sawyer charging off to scoop Gia, was I cool looping in Dani with Calvin's people? I said, "No problem" when I should have said, "Stop the goddamned presses." Calvin was one thing, but Sawyer unleashed with JC's wellbeing on the line? A big and bad idea. But it wasn't the time and place to bring that up, so I asked if Dani was around later to talk details. She had a meeting with Evelyn but floated tomorrow instead. I mentioned another swim at the lake, and

Nicole's head snapped around so fast, that I half-expected it to fly off.

She caught that *another.*

And she displayed remarkable restraint waiting until Dani left before she sidled up to me with a smirk bigger than the moon. "Well, well, well," she said. "Anything you'd like to share?"

I kept my mouth shut. The truth is, there is nothing to share unless I can make shit happen. For sure Nicole could offer up womanly advice, but only one person on the planet can guide me through this.

The guy who knows me better than I know myself.

Back in the safety of my villa, I grab a beer, crack it open, and sink into the hammock before hitting FaceTime. JC's easy smile fills the screen, warm and comforting, as always.

"Hey, little buddy," he says. "How's life in wine world?"

"You know—drunken mayhem and chaos. The usual."

JC chuckles. "Still flying the Troublemaker flag for the rest of us. Atta boy."

He flops onto the couch in his Hollywood rental, socked feet up on the armrest. Since January, he's been living the LA dream—booked solid as a hotshot session musician and scoring films. It's been nearly a year since I last saw him, but whenever we talk, our trashy teenage rebellion inevitably pops up.

"I got into trouble because of you," I remind him. "But you had the skills to talk your way out of anything."

My brother's silver tongue wooed women, law enforcement, and, most importantly, our father. Effortless charm is JC's hallmark. At thirty-three, he's still boyishly handsome. Athletic and lean. His gunmetal-blue eyes permanently sparkle with mischief, and he's a super kind dude for someone legit famous. Even his name is the coolest thing ever—Jameson Chevalier. He never gelled with it—considered it froufrou—and rebranded himself as JC on his thirteenth birthday.

Determined resolve is yet another thing my brother owns in spades.

"Whoops," he says, shifting on the couch, his attention momentarily snagged. "Look what I found."

Between two fingers dangles a very expensive-looking bra, JC grinning like the cat who ate the canary.

"Are you still dating Kerry?" I ask, latching on to the name I last recall.

He shrugs and sets the bra down. "In her mind we are. But you know how it goes at the House of JC." I sure do. JC slips in and out of relationships like I do pairs of shorts. "And when are you going to take the plunge?" he asks. "All those chicks dive-bombing you and not a single one worthy of your heart? Your meat can only take so much personal abuse."

"Actually…" I take a deep pull of my frosty lager then clear out the thickness in my throat. "I met someone."

This news shocks him into a sitting position. "Is the sex any good?"

"Uhm …. we haven't made it that far."

"Does she live in Greece?"

"No. She works for a winery."

He peers at me straight on. "Winery, as in Nero Vino?"

"Yup."

"Wait." He tilts his head in the manner of someone calculating. "Today is Thursday and you got there … Saturday?"

"That's why we haven't made it that far."

He breaks into howling laughter. "Jesus, Rhys. Does she know you like her? Or are you still hiding out in the dark corners silently pining?"

I feel my cheeks go hot. JC tried hard to wrench me out of my shy shell. But after one too many parties where I hovered in the corner, too scared to talk to any woman, he stopped dragging me out.

"She's the head of marketing," I say. "My boss, effectively."

His eyes light up as he bites back a smirk. "Are you still mesmerized by women in authority?"

As expected, JC roughs me up whenever he can. Although I admit there is something alluring about powerful females in a suit. "How about instead of taking the piss out of me, you give me some advice?"

He leans back to get comfy, running a hand through hair that a music reporter (female, of course) once described as the color of melted dark chocolate. For reals. "Lay it on me, buddy. The doctor is in."

I can count the number of times JC has paid full attention to any of my stories on one hand. This time, he is dialed in. Laser-focused. Not a single interruption. When I wrap up my summary of what's transpired, his mouth hangs near his knees.

"Holy shit, bro," he says, stunned, and a little in awe. "I mean, hot stuff, but not very professional taking you down during a photo shoot."

"You had to be there." Defensiveness creeps in because the weird, private bubble moment defied explanation.

"Not that I need to point out the obvious, but action speaks louder than words. No woman grinds you into oblivion just because. You're sure she's single?"

I nod. That much, I'm sure of.

"And nothing since the almost-kiss on the raft."

I shake my head.

JC thinks about that, arranging himself cross-legged on the couch. Getting settled to offer up the advice I asked for. "It sounds like she needs the right fire lit under her. No woman wants a limp-dick lying there letting her do all the work. You need to be the aggressor."

I pick at the beer label, knowing he's right. I need to bust a move, but the thought leaves me cold. "You know that's not my style."

"Christ, buddy," JC groans. "You're too goddamned pretty to be single. Step up to the plate and swing. It's like that guy complaining he never wins the lottery but refuses to buy a ticket."

"Yeah, but—" The sound of another call interrupts my protest. JC scans the details on his screen. "You need to take that?"

"It's Sawyer." He sends our big brother to voicemail. "I'll catch up with him after."

Huh. I bet I know why Sawyer is calling. Do I say something or stand down? Under ordinary circumstances, I would spill the beans. But now Dani and Nero Vino are involved, and the tangled knot of family business, brotherhood, and my own motivations are too extreme for me to untangle.

And when it comes to JC, he'll do what he wants. Every single time.

But can I claim I knew nothing if I have to live through the damage and debris of a decimated JC for a second time?

"Listen, bro," he says. "Still early days, but I've never seen you this invested. It sounds like Dani might be the one you can finally let down your walls for. Walk me through your plan, and I'll help you tweak it. Or if you don't have a clue, let me shed some light on how you seduce a woman."

I feel a wave of relief, and that's the magic of JC.

Not only does he understand me, he wants the best for me.

And will do whatever it takes.

Chapter Seventeen

DANI

"How will you fix this?"

Gail Stafford levels an arctic stare at me. She has too many teeth, her pale spring coloring does not support an orange blazer, and she is mighty pious for a civil servant. Unfortunately, bad news has done what it does best: spread. And in a town this size, where you have to leave to change your mind, her mind is made up: I better clean up this mess, pronto.

"We'll restrict filming to the property," I remind her for the second time. "Until the buzz dies down."

"And if it doesn't?"

The longer she stares at me, the more I think she's trying to conjure a new me into existence.

One who will bend to her will.

"It isn't a crime to hire an influencer," I say. "Evelyn paid for his time, and we need to honor the contract."

Gail smiles, although nothing changes in her cold blue eyes.

"Osoyoos is more than one business. And Nero Vino has had plenty of concessions. Divine Debauchery already puts a massive strain on the community."

"By strain, do you mean all the businesses making fortunes from the celebrities dropping cash? Or are you put off by all the media attention you become the face of?"

My sweetly delivered questions douse the room in silence. Her office is all corporate spartan, with tidy stacks of brochures, mandated furniture from Staples, and zero temptation of running wild. Gail squints at me, pressing her fingers to her temples, holding back a tide of righteous fury. As much as she wants to notch a black mark beside the Nero Vino name, she knows the gala adds a significant bump to the local coffers.

Rhys in town, however, offers no uptick in revenue. Only more glory, esteem, and press for Evelyn, who, in her opinion, has enough of all three, thank you very much.

"Miss Rialto," she says, nixing the friendly *Dani* she started with, "I hoped you would be a team player. Evelyn has operated as a lone wolf for too long. She can only push her luck so far."

I clasp my hands together on my lap. Words cannot express how little I am enjoying this exchange. After Constable Davidson poked around yesterday, searching for invisible reasons to flag Rhys as an issue, I'm about done with locals sticking their noses into our affairs.

But there is no upshot to letting my frustration get the better of me.

Anger isn't smart.

Still, that doesn't make a witch hunt right. Vilifying Evelyn is just plain lame.

"Evelyn contributes over two hundred thousand dollars a year to the community," I say, primed with the numbers. "She offers the locals free entrance to the amphitheater so they can enjoy the entertainment. When other wineries are desperate for more hands, she gladly shares her seasonal workers, no questions asked or hands out for compensation."

Her coral-stained lips purse as if she sucked on a lemon. I half-expect her to drop mention of a kickback—would not put it past her pantsuit.

"Some might call that buying votes," she finally says.

"And some might call it giving back."

Gail studies me, rifling through the options: Friend? Foe? Another pain in the ass?

"Look," I say, pleasantly agreeable now that I've got her cornered and squirming. "You and I both know the wheels need to keep turning. The wildfires hit all the wineries hard, and last year's freak winter weather didn't help. A boost in tourism benefits everyone."

Gail opens her mouth to interrupt, but I silence her with a raised hand. "I understand your concerns. His fans are being invasive—calling hotels and prowling the campgrounds. But from my experience managing spin, this dies down when there's no fuel. So we will do our best to keep his exposure in the community to a minimum. But he's here to promote the winery. Unless someone coughs up a million dollars for him to leave, it's business as usual."

She glares at me like I'm a defective cog in her wheel. No one is bringing ten times her annual salary to the table to send Rhys packing.

And we both know it.

Underneath the milky skin of her throat, a spidery blue vein pulses her discontent. "I'll speak with the hotels and businesses, sand down their concerns, and mention this could all die sooner rather than later. However," she adds in her sternest you-won-this round-but-the-fight-is-still-on voice, "if anything involving Rhys brings shame to this town, Evelyn better be prepared to face the consequences."

Disaster magnet is the term that keeps running through my mind. Gail, that is. She'd mistaken me for a pushover, and my pushing back rattled her. Granted, small sitcom troubles are the extent of her domain. A few drunken yahoos. Kids with contraband fireworks. The odd misdemeanor.

A rowdy battalion disrupting her idyllic Osoyoos summer?

Not on her watch.

So, her threat against Evelyn wasn't idle. Bureaucrats love wielding their limited power, and triggering Gail's wrath is too easy in the dog days of summer. Deadly wildfires have been a serious threat in the past decade, torching vineyards, homes, and, most devastatingly, hopes and dreams. This summer has been quiet, but with the hottest August on record, the Valley is a bone-dry tinderbox, one spark away from catastrophe.

But that doesn't give Gail a free pass to be a snarky bitch.

Back in the office, I'm scrolling through a dense wall of emails when one stops me cold, freezing the blood in my veins.

From: Bwinn@winnmediainc.com

Subject line: Did you create those labels on my time???

My shoulders slump with defeat, and for a long minute, I stare at his accusation. His pettiness knows no bounds. Brett is in a league of his own, a completely different species. Not a homo sapiens, more like a homo schmuck. Prince fuck face. I force myself to open the email, my stomach shrinking in on itself while I skim his latest attempt to tear me down.

Lawyer. Breach of Non-Compete. Sue.

Disbelief spills out of me in a sharp exhale. In a sea of negative words, those appear triple-sized. And more menacing because of it.

I know what's happened.

The only thing he and I still have in common is a love of wine. He subscribes to *Wine Spectator* and follows several wine bloggers. The *Vancouver Sun* wine critic wrote a glowing feature on Nero Vino, and Evelyn insisted he show my labels in the article.

It was published three days ago.

Something breaks inside of me. A single tear escapes, and I swipe angrily at it. Yes, Brett ticks every douche cliché box on the list, but I will not give him the satisfaction. Screw him and his antics.

"Hey. Everything cool?"

I glance up to find Rhys in the doorway, eyebrows pinched together. Something sparks in his expression, a quick flare that fades before I can grasp it. Shit. Did he see me cry? When I set them down, my glasses hit the desktop with a loud clatter.

"Of course," I say, too bright, clamping my emotions down. "Come in."

Rhys ambles in, taking in all the old money nonchalance with a curious look. How many winery offices have an original Frida Kahlo on the wall? Or Italian marble desks with a vintage Tiffany lamp to highlight just how much money grapes can make?

"So this is where all the magic happens," he says.

I power on a phony smile. "Some days."

He perches on the corner of my desk. Our gazes meet, and then we both look away. I fidget—tilting my monitor, rearranging loose papers —anything to ignore the pounding inside my chest.

"How are things going with Rita and Francis today?" I ask.

"Better," he says, "in that I've only wanted to strangle them twice."

"Are you on lunch break?"

"Yeah." He scuffs the floor with the toe of his flip-flop. "I wanted to check in to see if you're still down for a swim later."

Dammit. I'd spaced on that. And by the way Rhys tilts his head at me, I can tell he knows I did.

"A swim sounds perfect." My voice wavers and I hold on to my plastic smile for dear life. All I can hear is his silence. My chest feels like a washcloth wringing tight.

"Anything you want to talk about?" he asks, solemn as a priest.

His eyes are bright and full of caring. My breath comes out in shorter and shorter gusts, the freefall into emotion imminent.

Don't lose it.

"How much time do you have?" I ask.

He pretends to look at a watch on his wrist. "Four weeks."

A half-laugh, half-choking sound escapes my throat. For him to find humor at my lowest moment is nothing short of incredible.

"Have you considered a comedy career?" I ask, in all seriousness.

"Not this week." His expression transitions from mild amusement back to concern. "But this," he says, his finger circling in front of me to indicate what he means, "has to do with me, right?"

"No." I bite my lip and gaze up at him from under my lashes, debating if honesty is the best course of action. "And yes."

"Tell me about the no part," he says, his voice quiet.

His compassion, the unvarnished sincerity of it, steadies my battered heart. I could do a one-eighty and brush him off, but the improbability of that likely speaks for itself. My body feels heavy as I lean back into the chair and his attention remains entirely fixed on me.

Bit by bit, I reveal the Brett files, minus the degrading sex and the correlation to what happened at the vineyard. And because embarrassment isn't enough, I move on to Gail and Constable Davidson, ending with the shitshow of last night's Wine Growers meeting, where Tomas threatened to run Evelyn out of town for being nothing more than a competent businesswoman to his drunken, saggy ass.

Rhys listens without interrupting, drumming his fingers across the square line of his jaw. I imagine it's too much for a random drop-in to confirm tonight's social agenda.

Then something dark flashes in his eyes.

And his voice sounds equally black when he says, "Your ex sounds like an idiot."

I'm not going to lie. How Brett immediately becomes his enemy warms me. "Then I've presented him fairly."

"How does it work with Photoshop?" he asks. "Is there a time-stamp to prove you created those after the fact?"

"You can add a timestamp. It gets prepended to the filename. I don't know if that holds up as sufficient in the eye of the law."

"If you need any help," Rhys offers, "I have a SWAT team of lawyers. I try not to talk to them, but if you need an introduction…"

"Thank you," I say, unsure if diving deeper into Brett's pit of piranhas is the way to go. "I appreciate that. And sorry for dumping." I give a shaky laugh and try to lighten the atmosphere. "I shouldn't be telling you all these things."

"Sometimes it's good to vent," he says, his voice softer, lower, as he crouches beside me. "People do weird things when they feel threatened. Your talent probably scares him."

His eyes skate across my face. I shiver slightly at how it feels to have him watch me like this. Like he has secrets. And I do too, because I've watched him just as intently for years. How many times did I trace his features in my mind's eye since then?

"Please don't worry about all the other stuff," I say. "It will sort itself out."

"Hey. We're in this together."

He touches my arm with a smile so endearing that my heart does a little flip in my chest. I feel the same way I did the first time I saw Rhys in the flesh—like my world has suddenly gotten a bit bigger and brighter.

I take a deep breath. "So, tonight…."

"How does eight sound?"

"Remind me again. Is it a swim or a race?"

He rises back to standing and offers a slight grin. "Both?"

"And we're putting money on it this time?"

"I'm happy to win for free," he says, and why not be carefree in his dismissal of me even standing a chance? I felt the water surge as he effortlessly passed me with his efficient, clean strokes and perfect flutter kicks. What rookie fool bets against an Olympian?

This one, apparently.

"Five dollars," I suggest. "Just for the fun of it."

He crosses his arms and chuckles, finding humor in what's sure to be a losing proposition for me. "Wow. You're the big league. I was going to order some pizza for dinner. We can make that the bet. Loser pays for pizza?"

I chew on the end of my pen, as good an outlet as any for my spiking nerves. "Deal."

"What's your favorite?" he asks, eyes skimming my office as if looking for clues.

I stop myself just before I say *Greek*. It is my go-to, but it feels too preciously on point. "Hawaiian."

He snaps his fingers and points at me in a gesture of—*Called it!* No smugness or macho overkill, though. And I like him even more for that.

"You got it. Meet you at your place at eight, pizzas in hand."

"The weather is supposed to turn this afternoon," I warn him. "They're predicting thunder and lightning."

"I'm willing to risk it if you are."

His smile deepens, crinkles at the corners of his light brown eyes. It shouldn't be so devastating, this whole sexy-sweet thing he's got going on, but it is. Nothing about Rhys Trenton coming into my life is quite the way I imagined it would be.

Chapter Eighteen

RHYS

BUILD IT, AND THEY WILL COME.

Or in my case, *draw it into existence.*

Either way, here's hoping this manifestation stuff works.

I snap my journal shut and let the nerves flutter through me. The past two hours were a whirlwind of carnal inspiration. Closing my eyes, the sketches of me and Dani in every possible variation of sin flicker to life in my mind with graphic detail. Dani on all fours in this very bedroom, with me holding on to her hair like reins, buried deep and losing it. On my hammock in Greece, her legs spread wide for me to pray at her altar. And the sensory bits? Vivid to the extreme. The *clink* of her barbell against my teeth when I suck her clit. What damage her slippery, satin tongue might inflict on my dick.

I lie back on the bed, struggling to process it all. In my world, the quiet stuff, the little things, resonate more than grand displays. After Dani shared the Brett trauma, we relaxed into what felt like a genuine connection. We were speaking the same language—or at least I hope we were—because my mind has already flash-forwarded to heavy trembling sighs and bodies melting together.

And then there's one other problem.

The operative word being "one."

Some idiot forgot to check his supplies—or lack thereof. I fished through my travel kit and found a single condom, ragged and forgotten. Expired by well over a year, and now burdened with the task of holding back a mother lode of Trenton DNA. And I missed the boat to ask the taxi driver for a drugstore detour. It's almost eight, and the pizzas are on their way. Is it premature to assume condom usage? Maybe. But JC was right. I need to man up and try because everything about Dani feels fated.

And I knew, one day, no matter what everyone said, I would fall for someone.

I think I know who she is.

And this time, I'm ready.

We charge down the stairs to the beach, Dani juggling towels and wine. I'm carrying two pizzas and enough anxiety to fill the lake twice over. The plan of action solidified earlier in my mind only to now scatter with every jackrabbit beat of my heart.

"What do you think?" I ask. "Do we beat the storm?"

Dani shouts over her shoulder, "Maybe!"

The sprawling gray storm clouds slowly engulf the bright blue sky of this afternoon, the moisture in the air making all the smells more prominent. There's a distinct earthy scent of pine and sun-baked minerals. The spritz of cologne I added earlier now feels pointless against the fresh, raw scents of nature.

When we spill onto the sand, Dani stares in awe at the chop waiting for us. "Wow! Look at the waves!"

The raft is rollicking, the air heavy and filled with the thick, wet slurping sounds of water sucked up against and released against the oil cans. Not exactly a calm dinner party platform.

No wonder the beach is deserted as far as the eye can see.

"I think we should leave the wine and pizzas here," I say.

Dani drops her bag into the sand. "But we still swim, right?"

"Are we playing fair this time?"

"How much were the pizzas?" she asks with a smile.

"A million, plus tip."

She laughs, wriggling out of her cut-offs, her tight body on display in a bright yellow bikini splashed with flowers. I whip off my shirt, dropping it next to our dinner. A towering column of angry cumulus clouds swirls closer, and I can feel the static in the air, the drop of barometric pressure that precedes a howler.

"We better move it before the storm hits," I say.

But my feet stay planted on the sand. Is this beyond stupid? A lightning strike on water is dangerous. It travels along the surface in all directions. The raft is essentially open season for electrocution. And, yes, JC said no woman wants a limp dick.

But I'd rather have a dick than none at all.

"Are you ready?" Dani's eyes hold a dangerous glint that promise me my life will never be the same after tonight.

Every molecule in my body tingles hot. If anticipation is catching, I'm running a fever.

"Three, two..." I start.

"Try and catch me!" Dani hollers, crashing into the chop with wild abandon. Childlike. Like the storm has possessed her. No intention of playing fair.

Immediately I know: time to risk life and limb in the pursuit of her.

I'm in the water, then under it, all silence and space, gliding like a fish until my arms and legs kick into high gear, propelling me straight to Dani. My hands clamp around her ankle, and she squeals, thrashing to break free, but I hold tight.

"Are you going to drag me to the raft?" she asks, like she's daring me to.

Despite being jostled in the waves with the muddy ground untouchable, I feel grounded and brave, alive with determination.

You need to be the aggressor.

"Nope!" I shout over the wind. "I'm dragging you to me."

Invigorated by a sense of purpose, I tug her closer. I don't know how it happens—if I divine her arms to wrap around me—but our bodies collide, and the air leaves my lungs in a rush. Then, everything goes still. The seconds tick by. Lake water splashes into my face. The warm sun from three hours ago is like a memory from a distant world.

"Are you okay?" Dani sounds a little nervous. The trill in her laugh wasn't there before.

"Absolutely."

My arms circle her slim waist, and I soak in how safe and secure I feel holding her, our legs churning beneath the surface to keep us afloat. The wind whistles through the narrow gap between our damp bodies, and it feels like the temperature dropped by ten degrees. Dani clings to me, and I watch the silver in her irises darken into charcoal. Her lips part, and my heart lurches in my chest.

"Do it," she whispers.

I want to. I really, really do. I'm ninety-nine percent sure I'll self-destruct if she refuses my kiss, but that awful sense of being adrift is finally gone, and if that's not the inspiration I need, I don't know what is.

My mouth crashes against hers, and Dani opens up for me, just as ready. Our first bruising, ravenous kiss, and my pent-up frustration dissolves into a soft, aching groan. She swallows my sounds, twirling her tongue to claim mine. She tastes like cherries and sin. I feel her warmth spreading through me, and then I feel her everywhere. Breasts pushed against my pecs. Fingers digging into my hair. In the greedy blur of roaming mouths and tongues, I barely register the first fat drops of rain splattering onto my skin.

Then a blinding flash of white illuminates the sky.

We tear off each other's mouths, and I pull Dani tighter against my body as thunder rumbles like a thousand stomping feet above us.

"Holy fuck," I mutter.

Dani glances skyward at the dome of midnight blue darkening to black. "Let's get to the raft."

"It'll be safer on shore," I tell her.

She tugs on my hand, her touch blazing through me. "But this is closer."

I nod, mute. I guess we're doing this.

We swim to the raft, the warm wind slapping water into my eyes. I haul myself up first, offer Dani my hand, and hoist her out of the lake with one sturdy yank. Roiling waves tip the raft at crazy angles.

It feels wild. Electric. Daring and violent. My heart is beating like crazy.

"This is incredible!" Dani shouts, laughing, half-crazed as she twirls on the dock like a kid, arms splayed wide and face tilted to the sky.

I'm caught in a crossfire of too many conflicting emotions. My entire body is still processing our kiss—the heaviness of it.

I need more.

"C'mere," I say, and seal her in my arms.

Our kiss is dirtier this time, wickedly addictive, fingers buried in each other's hair. We ravage each other without finesse, without game. Lost in the whiplash of the storm and each other, Dani moans, rolling her hips against my erection and devouring my mouth with naked hunger. I want her so bad it feels like nothing else matters.

Nothing exists except us.

And then another bolt of lightning splits the sky, turning it violet as a spike of adrenaline burns a trail of stardust into my lungs. Our kiss fumbles, my breath sharp, ragged bursts, Dani's body trembling against mine. We are nose to nose, forehead to forehead, no space between us. I'm reeling, feeling almost too much. She pins me with a look that makes my pulse climb a notch. It's not the look from the photo shoot. This one is a little nutso.

"What are you thinking?" It's a scary question for any man to ask a woman.

Her long, tanned fingers anchor onto my waist. "I think we ride out the storm on the raft."

I swallow hard, getting the gist of what she's saying. But this untamed environment feels wrong. Not for our first time.

"Are you sure?"

That question is out before I realize what a stupid thing it is to ask. Her eyes are fever-bright, no illusions. And the sky opens up before she can answer, rain sleeting down, the thunderclap like a sonic boom. I cradle her protectively against my shoulder, hearts pounding together. She palms my belly and then slides her hand under the band of my shorts.

Waits. Hovers.

My eyes shutter closed.

The heat of her hand so close to *there* is borderline agony.

"You can touch me," I whisper into the wet tangle of her hair. "Anywhere."

Her hand dips, traveling far enough to find me warm and full and brutally ready.

"I was thinking," she says, her breath warming my skin. "It would be a shame to miss out on that ridiculous bed. How do you feel about a sixty-nine?"

The constricted feeling in my chest tightens into a hard ball of disbelief. As I said, I'm not the numbers guy.

But that one?

I know it.

Every guy knows it.

"Is that a trick question?" I ask, just to be sure. Before I really lose my shit.

The velvety grip of her hand sends my brain spinning, and she lifts her eyes to mine in silent response. The jury's out whether I self-implode before the storm takes me out.

"Dani," I mutter. "Jesus."

"Is that a yes?" she murmurs, voice thick like warm honey.

A wave crashes into the raft, spraying us with a fine mist. I steady her, feeling the tension in her limbs holding on to us. We're exposed out here, taking a risk in more ways than one. But darkness is falling fast. Will anyone notice us? And can we track anything other than the torment about to obliterate us?

Mere trivialities.

The fierce throb of my pulse is the only thing I can hear, the shit-storm of emotions coursing through me nothing short of exhilarating. Never before have I felt so unsure yet completely sure about every-thing. If I go down going down on her, so be it.

I cannot wait to taste her.

Hang the fuck on.

Chapter Nineteen

DANI

HE SMELLS DELICIOUS—OF DAMPNESS AND SUMMER, VANILLA AND SPICE.
Like clichéd heaven. Or the finest version of perdition. My skin is on
fire, blood burning from the feel of him beneath my fingers. All that
huge warmth, so eager.

Ready to be savored.

Rhys rocks tight against me, trailing soft kisses down my throat.
"I'll lie on my back," he murmurs. "You sit on top of me. Better me
than you to get a splinter."

He unties and shucks off his shorts. Little by little, I process the
erotic onslaught. Standing tall and proud, he satisfies all of my curiosity. Rhys is beautifully endowed, from shaft to glistening crown. But on
his face, wet with the slow, steady rain, a question lingers.

How reckless are we to sixty-nine in the middle of an electrical
storm on a raft rocking tenuously on metal oil cans?

Too late now.

The wild waiting for me is right here—the danger is in leaving.

Rhys sinks his fingers into my biceps and pulls me down with him. His dark irises flare as he gazes at me with outrageous want. "Can I take your bikini off?"

"Yes," I whisper back.

His hands reach around me, fingers fumbling to untie the knot. I can hear his breath catch when the weight of my breasts tumbles free. He holds them in both hands, running his thumbs over the swollen nipples.

His breath reduces to a hitch. "Dani. You are perfect."

I'm not immune to him either. And it's downright shameful how my eyes scour every inch of him.

"We chose the right guy for a rosé of the gods."

He smiles and closes his mouth over a nipple, sucking it as waves of rapture shudder through me. I gasp, arching my back, face upturned to draw air into my quaking lungs. Raindrops ping against my flesh like a hundred fingertips coaxing my arousal from the inside out.

It's impossible to think beyond this moment.

My body screams for his.

Rhys frees my nipple and helps me shimmy out of my bottoms. It takes a bit to get us situated. The raft is slick and cold from the rain, but his warm hands are everywhere, running down the length of my body before they settle on my hips. He tilts them just so, exposing all of my quivering pink privates to the heavens.

His soft hands trace the curves of my ass and slide lower.

The warmth between my legs slowly turns into a desperate throbbing.

Slowly, like he's unwrapping a gift, he spreads my wet folds.

I can't speak. I can barely register the fathomless lake stretching out in front of me. It's so different in the dark. And it feels like something magic is about to happen. Something more powerful than the storm. And then he drags his tongue south to north along my seam in a single sensuous stroke, decimating me with a cascade of pleasure that floods through me like a tsunami.

I see stars. The moon. Fucking Pluto. Then nothing but the blackness of annihilation.

"Jesus," I breathe.

He kisses and nips my trembling thighs, and I press back to encourage more.

"Don't forget about me," he mumbles as his teeth skate over my barbell in a wrathful tease.

I wrap my hand around his satin skin, and his groan vibrates through every inch of him. I can smell the spike of his need curling up from his thicket of blond hair. Angling properly to engulf him, I draw his impossibly lovely sex into the warmth and willingness of my mouth. And when I suck the crown of him, he whimpers and writhes beneath me.

"Yes," he groans. "Take all of me."

Buffeted by wind and waves, the raft rocks and rolls, aiding my rhythm, but I lose my will to do anything but moan as he circles my clit and starts sucking. It's paralyzing how good it feels.

And then another blinding flash of ultra-white turns night into day. Breath lodges deep in my throat as charged air ripples over my skin, nipples tightening in response. The air is damp and smells of ozone, the sky thick with swirling clouds. My toes clench with excitement, and I grin myself stupid.

The threat, the thrill. Surrounded by the crack and sizzle of lightning. Honest-to-God destruction this close, and we both know it.

Is that why Rhys surges as if struck by lightning? He pushes his tongue into me all the way, an equilibrium of force and singlemindedness that evaporates any remaining shred of my misgivings. A cry escapes my throat, the rain turns into sideways end-of-the-world damnation sleet, and I blink through the rivulets of water pouring down my forehead as Rhys tortures me with his mouth and fingers, easily familiar in my innermost spaces. He makes tight, hungry sounds, growling like the thunder.

No man has eaten me out like this.

Commanding. Determined. Invading my secret center with insatiable intensity.

It's too much, too soon, and I'm panting *please, please, please.*

But his momentum never wavers.

His pace quickens, and I spiral higher as the rapture builds. He's taking me to a place of animalistic need, all of it black and smothering.

In the part of my brain that rules primal instinct, I suddenly understand the storm, the beat of its rhythm. A ribbon of release curls tighter and tighter, funneling lower until it snaps, and I can't hold the ache back any longer. Pleasure and pain, equally composed, surge within me, and I time the gap between the next blast of light and sound to scream his name into the thunder's roar. For a moment, I feel as weightless as the rain I can no longer feel on my skin.

In the hands of forces bigger than myself.

Bliss for fucking ever.

Shudders rip through me, my eyes struggling to see straight, to see anything. My brain is an irretrievable mess, my heart near bursting, but Rhys and his body, his need, calls to me and draws me back in. Under the rationed light of dusk, I take him deep, as far as I can. His moan becomes one with the howling wind and the thrum of it sends a shockwave through my being, burning through me to the curling toes of both feet. I intensify my efforts, using one hand in tandem with my mouth to wrap around his dick.

"Christ, Dani!" he cries.

I feel the clench of his body beneath my still spasming one, bearing the final savage thrusting of his hips. Then he groans, his salted warmth spilling deep into my mouth, and I savor the taste of his sweet surrender.

🍷

I dreamed of this—two celestial beings under a blanket of stars. But in all my fantasies, Rhys and I swung together in his hammock overlooking the Ionian Sea during a golden sunset. We are not two drenched rats on a raft in Osoyoos bathed in moonlight, the air still and heavy. Undone by orgasms so violent, our breaths remain shallow and labored.

Hearts thundering.

Beneath the weight of my head, his chest rises and falls. Rhys runs his hand through the matted mess of my hair, pressing a kiss against my forehead.

"That was mind-blowing," he says. "Thank you."

Weaving my fingers into his, I bring our joined hands to meet my lips. "I think we guilt-tripped the storm into leaving. Try and match our force, sucker."

I feel his smile spread against the back of my head. "But what we did was crazy."

"I tried not to think about that."

"That was a thinking-optional moment," he concurs, snugging me closer, needier, like he wants me to be inside of him. Such a gentle soul.

I feel utterly euphoric, brain flying on equal parts adrenaline and dopamine. Danger thwarted and aglow with triumph. I don't question for a single second that he feels less impacted than me.

"Have you ever been to Greece?" Rhys asks.

My body stills, lungs not far behind. I feel the finely sculpted muscles of his chest tense in response. I breathe into the darkness, allowing the intention of his question to reverberate through me.

"I'm embarrassed to admit that my biggest globe-trotting adventure is an all-inclusive in Mazatlán."

Rhys chuckles, the sound rumbling deep in his chest. "We can easily change that."

My heart contracts with a feeling so intense, I'm almost afraid of it.

We?

He shifts beneath me, eyes tracking over my face, searching with a focused awareness.

"What do you think?"

I swallow—or try to. My throat has thickened to the point of closure. But me in his gilded world? Hanging out with the social media elite and European trust-fund sucklings? Would they view me as another disposable fan girl? Would he?

I speak up to not evade the subject. "I'd like to visit."

Rhys tips my chin higher with his index finger. He drags it back and forth over my lips, waiting, smiling. It's a small, tender move that makes my heart flip, but for reasons I can't explain, I think of him alone on Corfu, separated from his family by miles and years. His easy charm and affability are virtually trademarked, but how can someone be estranged from their family and not have it affect them?

And he should have a million girlfriends and doesn't. Or none that

I know of. Why me, of all people? And I hate it that my self-sabotage creeps in. That it feels impossible for Rhys to like me when I'm here with him, moonlight dancing on our skin after he made magic between my legs.

Charmingly assertive and deliciously insistent, he kisses me, one hand cupping my naked breast. All at once, that giddy feeling is back, swelling so fast in me, I feel like my body might explode. When we're connected, nothing else matters. I lose myself a little.

He pulls off my mouth with a deep, contended-sounding sigh. I rest against his fast-beating heart and let the gentle rocking of the raft quiet my racing mind. Visions of me in Greece set alight. The thrill leaves me feeling like the whole world is in sync with my excitement.

"By the way," he says, his foot nudging mine, "you have great feet."

"Are you joking?" My quivering body tightens with utter disbelief. "I hate my feet."

"Why?" He strokes the top of one with his buttery sole. "They're wide and well-formed. Straight toes. Not arched and wiry like mine."

I twist my face up to his and register he is, in fact, not joking. "I'm sorry, but your feet are perfect. This is coming from the daughter of a podiatrist. Trust me, I've seen some gnarly feet."

"Is that what your dad does?"

"Did," I correct. "He retired last year. He and my mom are on this wild South American adventure."

"That sounds cool." He wipes a slick band of hair off my forehead and smiles a little tentatively. "I'd love to travel with you." He kisses the crown of my head with such tenderness, I feel an ache in my chest. In the darkness, the sense of intimacy only increases, and a silence descends, heavier than before. "But only if you're up for it," he adds, his quietest words so far.

I don't trust myself to say anything. The gamble of blurting out something impulsive seems too great. I'd revealed too much in my office. Or not enough? Perhaps the right amount. We had wandered off track, but bonded. If this is the diversion, I'll happily wander down the path to see where it leads.

Spent but sated, I curl into his warmth. I don't know how late it is.

Don't really care. At some point, we will make our way back. So I lie crooked in the safety of his arms, where I feel the most incredible sense of belonging, being exactly where I'm supposed to be, content to bask under the sky thick with stars for just a while longer.

Chapter Twenty

RHYS

"LOOKS LIKE I'M COOKING DINNER."

Dani squints at the tangled undergrowth lit up with my phone's flashlight. Four sets of eyes glow red. A pack of opportunistic raccoons, busted. Waterlogged crusts hang from their claws, the remnants of our two ransacked pizzas lying mangled in front of them.

"What a bunch of scavengers!" Dani exclaims. "Look at them, all smug."

The beasts of the wild are indeed radiating vibes of *give 'em a reason to stare.*

Our laughter seems to run up and down the lake.

We don our clothing, reclaim the wine, towels, and soggy pizza boxes, and head out. Ten minutes later, lungs ablaze from the steps, we slink past Dani's villa, both of us walking quickly, head down, the pulse of blood blushing my cheeks, darkness our safe harbor.

I doubt Evelyn runs around this late, but Nicole mentioned she has the sleep schedule of a coked-up vampire and regularly wanders the moonlit vineyards. After I braved my nerves and asked Dani to come back to my place, her *yes* became my new mission.

No chance encounters to slow us down, please.

Only an embarrassing fumble for my key card that the underside of the welcome mat seems to have swallowed. My hand finds its way to the small of Dani's back, guiding her inside. I flick on the lights, dimming them into a less attacking glare. The silence of the villa stretches my nerves tight. It feels strange that everything looks the same, that nothing has changed except me. I feel like a different person entirely.

Dani looks over, and the emotion rushing through me has no name. I've never quite mastered the game of ushering a woman straight into my bedroom, so I stand there waiting for her to say something.

"I'm not super hungry," she admits, her long lashes fluttering against flushed cheeks.

Oh, right, the dinner I promised. Already forgotten.

No surprise, really. Not after how she destroyed me on the raft.

I crossed galaxies and event horizons and crashed into nothingness before Dani worked me into the finale, and I slowly floated back to earth a spent husk, the minutes behind me fogging into nothing.

I am weak for her.

How it feels to want to touch and to be touched.

The heat and prickle of it, the fire.

"I do a mean charcuterie board," I say. "Why don't you jump in the shower, and I'll get busy?"

Dani stares blank-faced at the darkened bedroom I'm pointing at. I take in her expression. Nerves, maybe, entering my personal domain.

"I have nothing to hide," I assure her, mentally cataloging the toilet seat left down, towels neatly hung, and my La Mer toiletries lined up like soldiers on the counter. (I'm not an animal, even if she makes me feel like one.) "And feel free to use my body wash," I add. "You can rock Alpine Apex."

Her mouth quirks into a smile. "Then we'll both smell terrific."

"*Wild and untamed*," I quote the brand tagline, adopting an over-the-top announcer's voice as I strike a macho adventurer pose.

Dani follows up with her version of posturing. *"Powerful as an avalanche."*

I feel a surge of pure connection, so intense it wobbles my kneecaps. In a single, unbroken gesture, I pull Dani close and rock us back and forth. The same current that hummed between us in her kitchen kicks in. Bolder and more powerful.

"You should be writing their ad copy, Miss Pink Pearl."

"One day," she says. "I'll have my own agency."

"Is that your dream?"

She hesitates a moment. Then, "One of them."

"Based solely on your crisis management skills, I'd bet a small fortune on your success. You slayed during the model fiasco. You shit-kicked those fangirls outta here, and never once lost your cool. You were polite. You were bloody *determined.*"

She laughs a little, like my assessment of her was the upshot she needs. "Thanks for the props. But I'm not Wonder Woman."

"Says who? You proved clutch in the tough times. And look at how creative you are. People like you move mountains, given the chance." I capture her chin with my thumb and forefinger and lever those beautiful strange irises back to mine. For some unknown reason, the tagline of *Are they real, or are they Maybelline?* fills my head. "What would it take to open your own agency?"

"Money. And moxie." She looks away for a beat and then back to me. "Mostly the latter. The belief in myself."

"You do not lack gumption," I say. "Not from what I've seen."

She's the type to embrace fear, unafraid to make a decision, a head full of ideas. This can only mean a jerk like Brett probably shredded her self-confidence—to the point where she's second-guessing herself. Suddenly, an idea pops into my head.

The *how-to* that eluded me.

"Maybe I can help you."

Her forehead crinkles with confusion. "What do you mean?"

Did not expect us to land here. Funny how it all crystalizes into this actual thing. But before I can explain what I'm thinking, my phone vibrates in the beach bag.

"Hold on," I tell her. "I need to turn that damn thing off."

Instead of blindly shutting it down, I skim the message first.

MT: Hi Rhys. Any news??? Love you. Mom.

Tension climbs my spine, both shoulders square, and my eyes dart briefly to Dani. We're both quiet, but the air doesn't feel empty.

"If you need to text or talk, go right ahead," she says. "I can hang out in the bedroom."

A shallow breath escapes my lips, and I keep my voice steady. "It's cool. Nothing pressing."

Nothing, unless you count the guilt weighing down on me. I owe Mom. I know that much. My disappearing act messed her up, and she's been begging for a visit since I got back, texting me every day. Dad weaponized his authority by denying Mom the chance to visit me in Greece, proof positive that he and I are more alike than I realized. Two goats, stubborn as hell. The fact that we have anything in common is a miracle, though that has no bearing on the real issue: this is still my mess to fix.

But it's like needing a root canal, and you procrastinate scheduling it for months.

Then you wonder why your teeth rot and fall out.

I shut the phone off, swallow past the knot in my throat, and tell Dani I'm not hungry either—not for food. She studies me, sensing there's something, but recognizing now is not the time to lean in. And while I like to spend my Friday nights marinating in family drama as much as the next guy, my thoughts have drifted to her tanned legs poking through the artfully frayed denim and how they would feel wrapped around my face.

She smiles. I smile back. Vibing without words.

Needless to say, I tug her across the villa into my bedroom.

No limp dicks here.

Not anymore.

Dani can love me with her mouth all night, and it would almost be enough.

But this... Damn.

We're making out under the downpour of the rain shower, and I have her pressed against the wall, gripping her ass, lost in the rush. We move in a synchronized dirty rhythm just like I plan to do when I flex inside her pussy.

"Oh, Jesus, Rhys," she mutters into my mouth. "You feel so good."

Sweet, sweet Dani. My name on her lips is the hottest thing I've heard. And talk about feeling it. She's taken me to the edge of orgasm and backed off. Slowed down only to speed back up again. Now I'm grinding her double time, and I can feel the pulse beat of my throat, hammering like hers.

"If you don't fuck me now," she pants, "I will personally fire you."

The urgency in her voice, her demand, the *threat*. What has happened to buttoned-up Dani?

I press another groaning kiss to her mouth. "Oh, I plan to, but remember the bed?"

"Oh yeah." She giggles, eyes hooded and sexy. "Time to get our money's worth."

We towel each other off, me rubbing circles on her ass with the thick terry. She slaps my bare butt, then her hands are everywhere, making my temperature skyrocket in every place that needs attention. We stagger out of the bathroom and topple backward onto the bed in a tangle of limbs. I cage her in with my body, pinning her with a bruising kiss. Every contact with her tongue is like a shot of euphoria in my veins. My heart feels ready to burst.

Somehow, I find the wherewithal to disentangle myself and reach for my discarded shorts on the floor. I hold up the dull silver packet as evidence of the dusty relic it is.

"Do I get the honors?" she asks with a mischievous smile.

"Sure, but be careful. I only have one. Rookie move," I add, owning it. "Unless you have a stash?"

She throws me a look. "Osoyoos isn't exactly the epicenter of dating."

"Then this guy will be first in line at the drugstore tomorrow morning," I assure her.

"I think the plan is neither of us gets up early."

Her eyes fall to my smooth naked flesh, brutally swollen. She gestures for the goods and, hot damn, she rips the package open with her teeth. I sound like a man on the edge of defeat when she grips me, rolling on the condom. I've never felt this desire to consume someone, to dig in and never let go.

"Let's try and go slow, okay?" My voice is a pathetic plea.

"I don't care if you're fast."

"But *I* care. This is our first time."

She gazes up at me with a forlorn, bewildered expression. "That's such a sweet thing to say."

"Lie back," I whisper. "This will be anything but sweet."

Her head sinks into the puffy pillows, and I kiss her again—deep and searching—before sitting back on my haunches to admire the view. She wets a finger and draws slow circles over her hardware, her clit. My breathing turns ragged, all that glistening pink flesh ready and waiting.

"You're the first to see this," she confesses, toying with the barbell. "I got the piercing a week before I started here."

My hands move along her legs, seeking skin and softness. Lord knows, I become that guy—possessive and selfish. A need to claim my territory.

"I want to be the only person to see it."

I hoist her legs, yanking her flush against me as a squeal of surprise escapes her lips. I position an ankle on either side of my shoulders, and when her eyes meet mine, she swallows hard.

"I, I thought you said slow."

"I changed my mind."

"What are you going to do?" It comes out slight, husky, and possibly nervous.

I could torture her pussy with soft suction and send her careening to the edge. Drill her like a blunt instrument with my tongue until she begged for mercy. Maybe later, when I'm not powerless to her pull.

And there is no answer, none that will satisfy her like I plan to.

I angle myself onto her wetness, dip my crown in, and the adrenaline spike bathes my brain in an endless sea of light. She's molten, and I'm teetering on the edge, unable to tolerate the feeling in my heart. How will I ever get this right?

"Rhys," Dani calls out, soft as a song, her voice a million miles away.

There's only one remedy here.

In one wild and violent thrust, we're joined and consummated.

She gasps at the uncertainty. The unknown. And maybe, the size of me. The shifting of her hips to absorb me transforms my longing into a staggering shock of lust.

This is what I've been aching for.

Dani looks up at me with wide, unblinking, soft eyes. We're on the threshold. Our connection is blossoming, taking shape in our minds. With my gaze on her face, hands holding her hips tight, I fuck her deep and hard, stoking her impossible deep spot. She fists the sheets, face agonized, her rising moans releasing my own. The lust flows beyond my capacity to rein it in. It's sitting at the end of everything building between us, me thinking, Christ, how will I ever recover from the wonders of her body because nothing has ever felt like this?

"Please," Dani whimpers.

"Please what?" I dictate her moans with every thrust.

"Please don't let this end."

It feels like hours pass because we don't hurry but tease each other to the razor-sharp edge of bliss and pain. Chasing the fire before we succumb to it. Suddenly, I'm aware of how fast my breaths are coming, the painful squeeze in my heart. Dani tips closer to the abyss, and I plunge deeper and deeper until she peaks. Then I fuck her through the shudders with ferocious strokes, and she wails, "Oh, shiiit," her nails scratching up and down my back, digging into the taut muscles of my ass. My blood is burning inside me, and I feel my control slipping out of my grip.

Somehow, I knew it would be like this.

Earth-shattering mayhem.

And then I'm coming undone, one agonized molecule at a time.

Chapter Twenty-One

DANI

I WAKE UP WITH HIS ARMS BANDED AROUND ME. I FEEL RADIANT. Dreamily wonderful. The bedroom seems alive with warmth, and from my angle of view, with Rhys bathed in the dappled morning light, tiny hairs of copper and gold frame his jaw like a stubbled halo.

"Hi," I say, my voice scratchy from sleep.

His eyes roam over the morning mess of me. "Howdy. Triple orgasm hair looks great on you, FYI."

A throaty laugh spills from my lips. "Is that where I capped out?"

"And all these years," he says with a widening smile, "my family has considered me an underachiever."

"Somehow I doubt that," I flirt back, light-hearted, assuming his sarcasm also falls into that category. What child becomes a self-made multi-millionaire without full respect? "And my body votes for over-achiever."

"Speaking of your body…" Rhys nuzzles closer, groping under the duvet to interlace his hand with mine. "Beneath your firm, lady boss exterior lies a very pliant woman."

I blush from the pleasure of remembering and embarrassment of the sounds that leaked out of me. His whispered filth and stolen kisses. There was no right or wrong, just hips and rhythm, shudder and surrender. The wreckage of the bed says it all. Pillows chucked around the room, and sheets untucked from my vicious fisting of them when Rhys sank into me with a plunderous thrust.

"There is zero chance now of exchanging this mattress for a partial refund," I say in a mock solemn tone.

He laughs and leans in to kiss my raw and swollen lips. I feel guilty for the blooming purple bruise on the side of his throat. My teeth did that. But it's his fault for shattering me. And he continues to tease my inner fire, rubbing our conjoined hands against the frisky throb of his erection.

"I need to replenish the supplies," he says. "And make you a coffee. Hang here. I'll be back in a few, K?"

"No!" I protest as he disentangles himself from our nested bodies. I feel warm, soothed, and safe. Still lost in the pleasure of newfound intimacy. "Stay with me."

"The longer I lie next to you, unable to do a thing about it, the greater the torture," he explains. "But I have a plan."

He rolls out of bed and slips into his shorts while I watch, taking in the lines of his muscled back and shoulders. I think of how he dominated me, his hands firm and warm, the devastation pinching his features when he let go.

I don't know what I expected.

Something very Rhys-like. Sweetly sexy. Gentle.

Not lights-out, boundary-pushing fucking.

Not decimating spikes of pleasures that liquified me.

Or Rhys howling something in what I think was Greek but would sound dirty in any language.

And how he studied me after, like he wanted to read me for every reaction from his handiwork, made my insides blaze even hotter.

I prop myself up on both elbows and level my gaze at him. "And what does your plan entail? Other than a dash to the drugstore."

"Not spilling the details. But we'll both need the power of caffeine to survive what I have in mind."

Rhys's eyes flash with victory as he steals another kiss, hands supporting him on the bed, our mouths crashing together. Goddamn. He still tastes like me. After a seductive tongue twirl that leaves me whimpering for more, he pulls back with a winsome smile.

He is thoroughly adorable in his transparency on how much he enjoys having an evil plan.

But I still deliver a pillow to his face.

"Hurry up then, barista. And make mine a triple shot."

He waltzes out of the bedroom, whistling some unfamiliar tune. A minute later, the crackle of beans ground into the finest espresso granules floats through the door. An ear-to-ear grin takes over my face. Nestled against his shoulder last night, when we were in that drifting space of near sleep, drained and raw from end-of-the-world sex, he'd kissed me and said I was perfect except for my taste in coffee.

And we both laughed as hard as our spent energies could allow.

But whatever is doing the happy jig in my stomach this morning feels kind of perfect. I slept like the dead thanks to a functioning air-conditioner. Or was it the bed? Or a certain someone who tipped me over the edge of surrender?

The answer is all three and not necessarily in that order.

I curl up like a snail and let out a contented sigh, savoring the morning sunlight streaming through the window, and the promise of a day spent together. The air smells faintly of fresh linen and us. I'm somewhere else entirely—replaying moments from last night—when my eyes latch onto a journal that lies closed on his nightstand. It's not one of those spiral-bound cheapies, either. The leather looks expensive, the rich brown worn to a luster like a cowboy's saddle.

A generic clicker pen branded with *Miko's Taverna* rests on top, and a ribbon bookmark pokes out like a quiet invitation.

My mind rewinds, spinning back through time. Was it there last night? Half-blind with lust and the lights dimmed, I can't say for sure. And in the umpteen Rhys videos I've watched, not once has he referred to a journal on camera.

But at lunch the other day, Evelyn asked him about his drawings.

All the tiny hairs on the back of my neck rocket to attention.

What's inside? Notes of inspiration? Memories? Secrets? What if he's drawn me? The possibilities are giddy and heavy all at once. I glance at the wide-open door. My ears perk. I can hear Rhys humming while he preps our coffee. Adrenaline crackles on my skin, and I feel a rise of something sneaky and wrong in my soul.

God, it's so tempting.

No, Dani. That is a violation of privacy.

When Amelia snapped the lock open to my eighth-grade diary, she sobbed for a full week, devastated that I didn't secretly worship her as everyone else did. Worse, I resented her for how easy she made it all look.

And we didn't talk for weeks until she forgave me. (Never mind that she crossed the line. I was only too happy to be back in her good books.)

Point is, do I need to know his innermost thoughts? He just made love to me like we invented sex. Do I need the ego boost of seeing our names written together with pretty hearts drawn around them?

Maybe I do.

Rhys and I have come together so quickly. What do I know about him, aside from what he reveals on Instagram? A peek into the journal mind of the least attainable man on Earth could reveal so much. The air in the room shifts, suddenly charged, as if the journal itself is holding its breath, waiting to see what I do.

I reach for it, the pad of my finger skimming the soft leather.

Just one quick look…

"Hey, Dani," Rhys calls out.

I snatch my hand away a millisecond before he appears in the doorway. Red-faced with guilt, my heart hammering in both ears, the pressure in my chest eases when I realize he's on the phone. It's pressed against his shoulder to muffle his question from whomever he's talking to.

"Yes?" The word squeaks out.

"Do you need anything from the drugstore?" he asks.

"Who are you talking to?"

"The taxi company," he whispers back.

My eyes widen with the realization. "You're having *them* buy condoms?"

He smiles shyly and shrugs. His eyes are bright as the day. "It saves me from having to go out. And I'm happy to pay a premium for 911 delivery."

I open my mouth to say something, but nothing comes out. If Gail finds out about this, I'll never hear the end of it. Next, she'll accuse Rhys of orchestrating orgies with the locals.

"Is that okay?" Rhys asks, low-voiced, clocking the concern written all over my face. "I can blast into town with your truck instead if you want."

Jesus. I can see it now. The bustling Saturday morning drugstore with the local peanut gallery weighing in on the giant box of Ultra-thins and Rhys bouncing from foot to foot, eager to have the cashier ring up the purchase.

"No, the taxi is fine," I say. "I'll text the security guy at the gate. That way the driver can breeze in without the third degree."

I insisted the security company provide the contact details of every guard as part of the control process to keep the lines of communication open. And so far, no hiccups. Our hired-by-the-hour muscle men have kept the fans at bay. But I don't trust them to keep tight-lipped when the friendly neighborhood taxi driver rolls up and jokes about condoms coming in hot.

Rhys blows me a smooch and U-turns back into the kitchen. I hear him pouring on the charm over the phone, offering a tidy bonus for expedited delivery.

Me? My focus drills back onto his journal.

I like to think I have morals and standards, but I've already told him one tiny white lie. About how long I've been a follower of his. Will he even care once I tell him the truth? If anything, he might find my pathetic crush kind of sweet.

But snooping is a lie compounded.

And betraying trust is a slippery slope. Carrie Bradshaw from *Sex in the City* once ripped into her boyfriend's secret box, convinced he was withholding something, and that relationship bit the dust.

Rhys has said and done nothing to warrant such an intrusion. And,

I remind myself, he is the antithesis of Brett. Rhys is not an inhumane lizard of foulness. And maybe this can be more than a summer fling, so why jam a fledgling us under a microscope and look for cracks before we're fully formed?

Enough already! My my inner voice blasts. *Enjoy the moment without second-guessing everything.*

Relationships flourish with trust, patience, effort, and, most importantly, time.

And my bubble of positivity shrinks just a little, because time is the one thing Rhys and I don't have.

Chapter Twenty-Two

RHYS

How do I describe the most amazing sex of my life? The list virtually writes itself: Life-altering. Seventh heaven. Better than oxygen.

Dani is all killer, no filler.

No wonder I'm humming like a love-struck fool.

While I silently thank everyone from Santa to Santeria for last night's miracle, my morning espresso ritual unfolds. Dani brings the fuzziness of my interior world into sharp focus, as precise as the burr grinder pulverizes the beans. Tamping down the grounds recalls my assault and her beautiful gray eyes, blurry and fevered from the damage. The rich scent of brewing java warms me like she's melting the protective shell around my heart.

Even the milk bubbling in the frother is a scandalous reminder of how she took all of me on the raft, blowing my mind while she blew me. It was over in a heartbeat, and I never had a minute to process how perfectly I fit into her mouth. Can it be this real, this early on?

It has to be. My usual instinct—to flee or crowbar a woman out of my bed—is nowhere to be found. And the physical reactions always tell the true tale. Her touch makes my pulse go haywire. I felt enormous and magnificent sliding deep into her fire, and the greedy response of her hips welcomed every inch of me.

And I could see the shift in her eyes the moment she released.

She let go.

Forgot about real life and remembered only me.

Lost in the enchanted memory, a loud, growling sound snaps my attention back to the here and now.

The bright light filtering in through the front blinds suddenly darkens. Is that a car? Strange. There's no way the taxi driver made it here that fast. Suddenly my heartbeat sounds too loud in my ears.

I pad silently on bare feet to the window, slot two fingers into the blinds and spread them to view just enough of what can only be described as a pending catastrophe. Sawyer slides out of a monstrous SUV, rocking Dita sunglasses that I almost bought and gripping an enormous bouquet of red roses.

My stomach drops.

And not because I'm a peony guy.

For Sawyer, there is a correct way to do everything—from business deals to transactional dating to spontaneous visits. No way in hell he shows up here for no reason. He must have texted me multiple times about this surprise visit. But my phone battery was dying last night before Dani and I tilted the world off its axis. And I forgot to charge it.

I forgot a lot of things last night.

I'd like to forget this nightmare too. Because I think I know why my brother is here.

A chill settles over my bones as I dash for the door, swinging it wide before Sawyer knocks and alerts Dani.

"Hi," I say. "Wasn't expecting you."

"Last-minute trip," he explains. "I flew into Kelowna this morning." That explains the rental GMC. Sawyer would rather eat deep-fried spiders than roll in a domestic. "I'm looking for Dani," he continues. "Any idea where she might be?"

Shit, I knew it. He's decked out in Tommy Hilfiger weekend warrior duds. Looking all spiffy for a reason.

"Is she not at her villa?"

He tilts his head in that irritated Sawyer way. "Would I be here if she was?"

"Was *she* expecting you?"

I need to deflect because my brother has shelled out precious money to deliver flowers on a Saturday to a woman he's met once. The same woman I fucked senseless last night and is twenty feet away patiently waiting for a latte and for my tongue to slide into her again.

Not exactly what I'd call the best-case scenario.

"No," he says. "I wanted to tell her the good news in person." He pauses, for dramatic effect, I suppose, aware of the sun illuminating him like the Overlord he thinks he is. "We signed Gia. And JC agreed to the gig."

I blink, suddenly unsteady on my feet. "No, he didn't."

Deep down, I know it's happening. Sawyer, for all his shortcomings —he keeps a spreadsheet on when his condiments expire, for fuck's sake—has made a name for himself. God forbid anything stands in his way of cementing his glory.

Sure enough, with clear-eyed finality, he says, "Yes, he did."

I look up, drawing in a deep, controlled breath. The sky is clear blue with only a few puffy clouds lazily moving across it, and in this moment of tranquility, I feel rage building within me.

Maybe it's Sawyer's shitty, patronizing smile. Or hearing Dad's voice in my head as he griped to Mom about me: *Why can't he get As like Sawyer? Or have a shred of talent like JC? He is nothing but useless trouble.*

Or it could be that I'm overtaken by a clammy sweat.

The sensible thing to do is ask Sawyer to leave.

Which is exactly when I hear Dani's voice behind me: "Rhys? Who are you talking to?"

There's silence for a good five seconds. The thick kind that can be cut with a knife. The pluck in Sawyer's stance melts away, and he whips off his sunglasses to glare into my eyes. It's like having a flashlight shine into my face, but I won't look away.

"I didn't know you had company," he says through a tight mouthful of teeth.

I glance over my shoulder to find Dani frozen in no man's land between the bedroom and us. I'm acutely aware of everything: the terry cloth robe, wrapped and tucked and belted around her; her scent; her panicked eyes. I want to smash my mouth against hers, take her against the wall. Savor her hot and hungry kisses. Live out the morning from five minutes ago.

Instead, Sawyer steps to one side and gives Dani a good hard look. I suppose I should be grateful she doesn't say, *"This isn't what it looks like."*

Because it's exactly what it looks like.

"Hi, Sawyer," she says in a small voice.

My chest tightens, the automatic response of bracing for combat with my older brother. The idea of Sawyer letting this slide is unthinkable.

"Can you give us a minute?" I ask her.

"Yeah. Sure." She eyes the roses in a confused way that twists a knot tighter in my stomach.

I lied to her about Sawyer and his intentions. And the truth is about to bleed out ugly.

Dani slinks into the bedroom and shuts the door. In the suffocating silence she leaves behind, the laser beam of Sawyer's fury burns a hole into me.

"Thanks a lot, asshole," he hisses.

"Listen," I capitulate instead of standing my ground because I might feel a morsel of regret, "it just happened."

His eyes narrow on me. "Let me guess. It happened right after I told you I was interested in her."

"If it's any consolation, she's not your type."

He puffs out a bitter laugh. "Says the guy who lives on another continent."

"Things might be changing." I voice it for the first time, Sawyer uncaring, or rather, too incensed to care.

"Does Evelyn know?" he demands.

"Not officially."

"You're promoting her wine. What do you think the optics are if you're sleeping with the head of marketing?"

His tone. Always that tone. Mr. Superior who knows best.

Not today, says the voice in my head. Not after last night. I am done being the Trenton whipping boy.

"Can something real happen in my life without being shoved through a lens of optics?" I fire back. "And why would it be okay if *you* slept with her? You're now in bed with the winery as much as me."

Sawyer chucks the roses, knocking into the chandelier before thumping to the floor. "I'm not touting Pink Pearl as God's gift to wine, pocketing a million dollars, and shoving my dick into the winery marketing machine. Do you not see the conflict of interest?"

He pulls a face. Anger boils up inside me.

"You're just jealous," I spit out. "You've always been jealous of me."

"Give me a break," he scoffs. "Even as a kid, your calling card was doing the bare minimum. Why do you think Dad wanted to make you his gofer? Because you'd slay the day? You were a listless vagabond. He wanted to drill some common sense into you. And now you just flounce through life, swinging in your hammock, la-di-fucking-da. Zero idea," he snarls, "of what real hard work means."

Sawyer steps forward, his presence filling every inch of space. A flicker of something dark in his eyes tells me he is on the verge of going ballistic.

"You blew the entire family off because I didn't fix your problem. Grow up, Rhys, and deal with it." He jabs a finger into my sternum. "And if this shit blows up, you can kiss your reputation—whatever's left of it—goodbye. Don't expect me to clean up your mess."

My heart is thundering now. Maybe I was stubborn. Maybe I knew my tiny talents would never change the world. But Sawyer glided down the gold-paved road that was his life. No one had to go to bat for him.

And he tucks his fifteen-hundred-dollar shades into the V of his starched shirt with all the smugness of Sawyer. Mr. Righteous.

Maybe that's why I shove him. Hard. He staggers back in his

pretentious Adidas Tiger sneakers, the rubber soles squeaking on the laminate.

"Thanks for the vote of confidence," I blaze back. "I'm good enough to pad out your profit margin as long as I remain a robot going through the motions? Maybe if you weren't a twice-divorced miserable piece of shit who became Dad's puppet without a fight, you might understand. Sometimes you need to follow your heart. Do what you think is right, instead of being a spineless yes-man."

Sawyer doesn't speak, but I can feel the weight of his silence, and his face clouds with something I've never seen.

Hurt.

I just threw down a grenade with the pin pulled out of it. Worse, I smashed his ego. Pain, he can suck up, but he won't stand for that.

Sawyer swings first, air whistling past my face as I dodge him just in time. He spins and flails, trying to recover, but I'm faster. A quick karate-chop to the back of his knee, and he goes down in a graceless swan dive. I slam into him, landing hard on his ribs.

"Fuck you, Rhys," he growls, pushing against me.

He's bigger and stronger, but I continue to punch him, so much anger fueling my fists. He rolls, trying to escape, but I go with him. We crash into a side table, toppling over a glass-bottomed lamp that shatters into a million shrieking pieces.

Seconds later, the bedroom door bangs open, and Dani cries, "Rhys! Don't fight."

But our old wounds have festered to the surface. No Band-Aid can stem the tide of our anger. Not with Sawyer, one arm lynched under my neck, trying to choke the life out of me.

"You have no idea what I've sacrificed for you and JC," he huffs.

I twist and turn, rolling out of his grip, shards of glass biting into my skin. I wince, but the rush of adrenaline dulls the sting.

Bloodshed feels appropriate.

"Don't guilt-trip me," I lash back. "You've made a ton of money off the backs of your brothers."

I kick at the sofa for leverage, trying to scramble away, but Sawyer thrives on an audience. With a gawking Dani frozen on the sidelines, unsure what to do, he crouches, then leaps—two hundred and twenty pounds of solid muscle pile-driving into me, knocking the air from my lungs. And he's panting hard, sitting triumphantly on my chest like an alpha gorilla before he looks me dead in the eye.

"At least I didn't destroy Mom."

I blink back tears of frustration and struggle to breathe, an invisible pressure curling tighter around me. His comment is both cruel and correct. And it cuts deep, stinging more than the unfinished business crackling between us. Dani stands motionless in the kitchen, mortified, hand clamped over her mouth. Deeply immersed in the second-rate drama, none of us clocks the fourth person who has joined our party.

Not until the *clank-clank* of a suitcase rolling over the threshold snaps us back to reality.

Three sets of thunderstruck eyes swivel onto the five-ten ticking time bomb who sashays in on thigh-high, sequined platform boots and not much else, as if she confused noon in Osoyoos for midnight at the hottest club in Ibiza.

Sawyer squints at her like she's a mirage about to swirl away into the desert once he blinks. Dani takes a startled step back, sizing up what she must think is a fangirl who breached security.

Me? The day morphing into something unfixable becomes a brutal reality when Myla lifts her oversized sparkly sunglasses.

Eyes aimed squarely at me and sheened with a scary kind of mania, she squeals, "Hiiii! I'm here!"

Chapter Twenty-Three

DANI

Who is *she*? A lingerie model dragged out of a club at three in the morning? A raver? Because this is no ordinary fangirl. The hard lines of a professional partier pushing mid-thirties are etched deep across her forehead and pulling at the sides of her mouth. Pieces of what looks like confetti sparkle in her purple pixie cut, and barely containing the best boobs money can buy are a collection of see-through crochet panels that comprise her dress.

The tension running through me makes me feel like my heart will explode. I can tell from Rhys's stricken expression that he knows her.

He shoves Sawyer off his chest and staggers to his feet. "What are you doing here?" he asks in a low, spooked voice.

"Oh, babe," she coos, fiddling with an earring laden with so many diamonds, it probably weighs more than her. "We talked about me visiting."

She blows a pink bubble until it pops, then sucks the exhausted wad back into her mouth with a *snap* and makes a kissy face at him.

My soul turns to ash.

Babe?

"No." Rhys stretches out the word like he's speaking to a child who never listens. "I kicked you out of my house, remember?"

"This should be interesting," Sawyer mutters, rising from the floor and wiping dust from his prep-school attire.

The statuesque plaything shoots Sawyer a flirtatious look. "Hi. I'm Myla." She eyes me up and down, doing whatever math she's capable of. "Are you his girlfriend?"

"Dani is with me." Rhys sidles closer to me but stops in his tracks to meet the challenge in my eyes— the one that silently screams, *What is going on?* Somewhere, in a hopeful part of my brain, I wanted Myla to be one of the millions who fawns over Rhys from afar. Who could only dream of touching his golden skin, like I had.

But they've slept together.

A woman always knows.

I clamp my trembling lips together as Myla's blinding psycho smile dips into a frown.

"But babe," she pouts. "I just…"

"Stop calling me that!" Rhys shouts. "You need to leave. Now! This is crazy. *You* are crazy. I told you the other day to stop harassing me."

I feel sickness crawl up my throat. I can see him in my mind's eye— lost in the moment of last night, heavy-lidded eyes, his strokes deliciously deep.

"I can feel your pearls," he whispered. "So, so fine."

And I feel the traces of him everywhere: forgotten muscles tight and screaming, the ache in my core. I trusted Rhys with my body and soul, and now this?

"Why don't you get dressed, and we'll go for breakfast?" Sawyer beckons me to join him, not quite reveling in Rhys's embarrassment, but close. "Let these two love birds sort things out."

"Fuck off!" Rhys snaps. "We are not together. Not in any way. Take Myla for breakfast. Bond over your shared love of money."

Myla plants her skinny ass on the sturdy silver suitcase worth a few beans and crosses both arms. Her upturned tiger's eyes, the prettiest part about her, blaze with defiance. "I'm not leaving."

I hate her irrationally. Because whatever expensive duty-free perfume she douses herself with makes my eyes water from ten feet away. Because she's a bone-thin supermodel type and, judging from her accent and Euro-trash outfit, she's jetted across the Atlantic for this rendezvous. And because she is loaded enough to travel on a whim and track down Rhys, I hate her for that too.

But mostly I hate her because she is exactly who I expected him to like.

Sawyer snatches his sunglasses off the floor and slides them on. "Do you really want to be part of this circus?" he asks me, his tone implying I'd be a fool to say yes. "I'll wait for you in the car."

"She doesn't want to go anywhere with you," Rhys grumbles.

Sawyer's icy stare levels on his brother. "You sound pretty sure about that."

The knots in my stomach have nothing to do with hunger. My mind is blowing up with questions.

So many questions.

And I'm not sure I want the answers.

"Why don't we talk later?" I ask in an unsteady voice.

Rhys spins around to face me. He wears a haunted expression like he's fighting a war I cannot understand. "Ten minutes," he pleads. "Give me ten minutes, okay?"

Perched on her suitcase, Myla investigates her trendy black-and-white-striped manicure. Nails sharp as talons. "We'll need more than ten minutes, babe."

"Shut up!" Rhys bellows, stress radiating off him in waves.

"Jesus," Sawyer mutters, giving Myla a wide berth as he heads toward the door. "Good luck, bro. Sounds like you'll need it."

He finds my eyes across the room and silently says *take your time.* Before I pick the wrong emotion to focus on and regret saying something irreversible, a burly bow-legged man bumps into Sawyer as he's about to leave.

We all lapse into a confused silence, staring at him as his watery eyes scan the stage he's walked onto. They land on the smashed lamp and upended side table. Then they narrow in on me in a robe, porn star Myla, and Rhys half-naked, blood oozing from a cut on his chest. I can tell he's trying to make sense of Sawyer, who, to a stranger's eyes, is the collegiate pimp to our motley crew of degenerates.

Suddenly, the man's puzzled expression becomes as clear as his mission.

Those winery folks, I can hear him tell his wife later as they dig into fried pork cutlets and Caesar salad from a bag. *Bunch of sex-crazed lunatics.*

Because dangling between two of his stumpy fingers is a crinkled Shoppers Drug Mart bag, and he's holding the offending item far away from his JESUS SAVES t-shirt as if it's a skunk about to spray.

"Who ordered the condoms?"

♆

"Is it because he's famous?" Sawyer breaks the silence that's hung like smoke since we peeled out of the winery.

I glance at him, hunched over the steering wheel, eyes on the road. Too chicken shit to look me in the eye while serving up judgment.

"Things happen between people for reasons other than fame." I'm annoyed he reduced me to nothing but a star fucker. I'm also annoyed because it hurts like hell to be blindsided, and I have no one to blame but myself. My emotions are mine to deal with.

"The other day you couldn't stop raving about how much you liked working with Evelyn," he says.

"What does that have to do with anything?"

Sawyer cuts me a sideways glance. "You strike me as intelligent, but have you thought any of this through? Rhys has no plans to live in Canada. You know that much, right?"

"How do *you* know?" I parrot back, his smug tone and underhanded comment that essentially questions my intelligence impressively irritating. "From what I've seen, all you two do is squabble and tear each other down."

"No offense, Dani," he says, "but one week does not make you an authority on Rhys." He shifts in his seat, readying himself to share more Sawyer gospel. "Has he told you anything about our family? Or did you soak up his sunshine and daffodils routine, no questions asked?"

I shut my eyes to steady the roller coaster of conflicting emotions, trying to avoid becoming hopelessly entangled in whatever this mess is. "Is this where you tell me what I should know?"

Sawyer shakes his head as if I'm just not getting it. "What you just witnessed is the real Rhys," he replies. "He's a head case. Always has been. He cannot hold a relationship together to save his life. And he ends up with dumb dingbats because they are who he thinks he's worth."

"Thanks a lot."

Sawyer sighs. "I didn't mean you."

"Are you sure about that?" I ask, heavy on the sarcasm.

"What I do know is that he's not moving back here," he asserts. "Not even for you. Trust me on that one."

Our ambivalent gazes collide over the console.

Not even for you.

His simple emphatic statement sends a shot of ice up my spine. It's as if Sawyer knows how this will end. Like he's witnessed this particular car crash a hundred times.

No, I tell myself. *It does not end like this.*

I stare glumly out the window at another brilliant, scorching day. Sawyer's prior comment stings because maybe—*possibly*—I did get caught up in the fame angle. That's the problem with celebrities: they shine their light on you, and you instantly feel like the best version of yourself. But the light Rhys turns so brightly on me shines on everyone. He doesn't have a shit ton of followers for nothing.

"Where should I go?" Sawyer asks.

We're at the T junction of Highway 3. Weekend traffic crawls in either direction. A wild idea bubbles up out of nowhere—what if I booked it to Vancouver with Sawyer and never returned? Just remember last night and ignore the fact that Myla tarnished what was supposed to be one of the best days of my life.

Oh, the temptation.

"Take a right," I tell him. "There's a Smitty's on Main Street if you don't mind slumming it at a pancake joint."

After a tight silence, Sawyer says, "I'm not the enemy, Dani. If anything, I'm trying to spare you a broken heart."

"That you want to piece back together?"

He shoots me a wounded look. Shit. His fumbling attempt to soften the blow of my sorry fate comes from a good place. I think. But all my nerves are frayed from the fiasco we left behind.

Not to mention, an entire box of condoms has gone to waste.

Sawyer puffs out a breath that says—*whatever.* "If you want me to say sorry for thinking you're hot, it's not happening."

I sink back into the plush leather seat and keep my mouth zippered. The world was like this: you apologize to Sawyer; Sawyer doesn't apologize to you.

Small wonder he's single.

But then, slowly, my compassionate lens kicks in. Everyone struggles. Who knows what Sawyer has had to bear? And what are my fantasies of Rhys based on? Social media, the great truth seeker? The fact is, he and Myla were an item for at least one night. If he's attracted to the likes of her, I had him pegged all wrong.

I flip down the sun visor to shade myself from the relentless brightness. If anything, I'll endure breakfast with Sawyer as a tactical play. Pry as much information out of him as I can. Color in the lines of what Rhys has told me.

And decide what to do from there.

Maybe Rhys creating trouble in my heart flames out like Sawyer predicts.

Maybe we were doomed from the start—thrown together by virtue of forced proximity and not cosmic destiny, which, admittedly, sounds a thousand times more romantic.

Time suddenly feels elastic, like months have passed instead of days. My throat is raw, eyes strangely unseeing. Yes, Rhys Trenton was responsible for the sparkle of diamonds between my legs and a head full of woozy stars. And when the velvet warmth of his tongue dipped into my mouth, I forgot everything.

But maybe what I need to forget is him.

🍸

Every small town has its version of a Smitty's. A basic breakfast joint where a haze of grease hangs thick in the air, and the menus are sticky from jam and syrup fingers. Our waitress, Flo, all hips, jolly laugh and hair dye by L'Oréal, brings two coffees and takes our orders. She hustles back to the kitchen, and Sawyer wets a napkin in his glass of water to wipe his fingers clean.

I bet he jumps in the shower seconds after orgasm.

"So," I start. "What was your fight about?"

Sawyer shrugs—more weary than indifferent. "What is any fight about? Two people who remember things differently."

I say nothing and hold space for him to fill it. I understood the gist of their argument, but I want him to spell it out.

Sawyer rips open and empties a sugar packet into his mug, stirring furiously with his spoon. "Our father had a hard time with Rhys," he finally says. "I toed the company line. Our middle brother, JC, was the musical prodigy. Rhys was wild and unmotivated. They clashed over everything. And one day, he had enough." He pauses to take a sip of coffee and makes a face. I guess coffee snobbery is the one thing the brothers have in common. "Dad gave Rhys an ultimatum—work in the company or live on the streets."

"Wow," I say. "That's harsh."

"Welcome to Peter Trenton."

"What was the problem Rhys wanted you to fix?" I prod. It feels like Sawyer is skimming over the real crux of the matter.

For a long minute, he watches lobster-red tourists shuffle up and down the sidewalk. His eyes remain on the window when he speaks. "JC was off on tour, and I was his only chance to sway Dad's decision. Our father listened to me. Once in a while," he adds cryptically.

"But you didn't say anything."

Sawyer slides his eyes back to mine. It looks like he's aged a decade in five minutes. "Rhys needed to fight his own battles. Forge respect without hiding behind me. How was I to know he'd hop on a flight three days later and never come home?"

I taste my coffee, grimace, and set the mug back down. Even by my standards, it's rough. "That incident started it all, from what I gather."

Sawyer says nothing for a few seconds. Then, "Dad called Rhys an untalented waste of space who needed to get whipped into shape. Do I understand why Rhys left? Yes. And I admire him for having the courage. To not rot away doing a job he hated." Sawyer's hand trembles ever so slightly as he picks up his fork to polish it with the napkin. He looks miserable with his tight, sad smile. "Our mother has never forgiven me, for what it's worth."

So much for biology. You can love something and still ruin a life. Assuming Peter loved Rhys.

"And your father felt no responsibility or remorse?" I ask.

A muscle works around Sawyer's mouth. "Dad was a special breed."

"Was?" My heart does this funny flip-flop. "Isn't he alive?"

"Technically, yes," Sawyer corrects. "He had a stroke a few months ago. The right side of his face became paralyzed, so I took over the company, the day-to-day. That was basically death for him."

If you've followed Rhys as long as I have, you know he touches on many topics. His IQ never goes to waste. But there is one glaring issue he strategically avoids.

"Rhys never talks about your family."

Sawyer takes another pull of coffee. In the dirty light, he looks like a softer version of himself. Less like a warden in San Quentin.

"If you never talk about it, it doesn't exist, right?" he says with a mirthless laugh. "You can gloss over your demons and repackage yourself as Mr. Fucking Perfect Icon."

His tone suggests—not so subtly—that he is jealous of Rhys, that his brother found his way on his own terms despite the odds. Maybe the sacrifices Sawyer has made relate to his own dreams.

"Does Rhys plan to visit your dad while he's here?"

Sawyer's azure eyes bore a hole into mine. "You tell me. I carved out the weekends in his contract so he could get his ass to Vancouver. So far, not a priority. Typical of our prodigal brother." He leans across the table and has the nerve to ask, "Is that the kind of guy you want to hitch your wagon to?"

I can read it in his expression: *A screwed-up slacker like Rhys will drive you to tears sooner rather than later.*

My phone vibrates in my purse, and I hold my breath, scanning the two messages from Rhys.

RT: Where r u?

RT: Can we talk this out? Please.

I feel Sawyer's eyes on me like he knows who's texting, and his innate bossiness will prevent me from replying. I should reply. I know that death spiral feeling when texts go unanswered. A different part of my brain wants to take over, but I refuse to let it.

I'm not ready yet, although Rhys is right. We do need to talk it out. Because where is his safe space without family? How much Blue Mountain coffee can he drink to mask the pain? And if he's kept this hidden for so long, it has to fester like a lesion on his soul.

Chapter Twenty-Four

Have you ever prayed to God asking for a sign that you've done the right thing? I did that once. Buried deep in row forty-three on a British Airways flight barreling to London, my fifteen-year-old heart had no clue what the fuck I'd just done. Flipped the bird to my family, escaping with a knapsack and a prayer that everything would work out.

I landed in drizzle and misery.

Struggled mightily those first few months on the road. Bounced from shitty hostels to shabby couches to filthy floors. Sucked it up and scrounged for grim, under-the-table jobs with meager pay to stay afloat. I patched together a small network of stragglers like me, who hung around until my money ran out.

I tried to make real friends.

A hard task for an introvert.

No surprise that my phone became my best friend.

Instagram was emerging back then, and it felt less lame than Facebook. The only subject I liked in high school was history, so I decided that would be my schtick. I'd share photos of epic battle locations and famous monuments and remind my generation that their precious snowflake lives owe a debt to those who came before them.

That's how it all started.

By the time videos became all the rage, I had a decent following, and my numbers exploded once my face became the primary focus. I never slowed my roll, and I became this thing—an influencer. JC, the wise soul he is, was all over me to capitalize on my pretty boy looks.

Tap the market, little buddy.

Sawyer got me set up. He knew what he was doing, I'll give him that much. We lasted an entire three months with him as my rep before it got ugly, and he swapped out for Bettina.

Suddenly, I had a full-blown career.

More money than I knew what to do with.

A rabid fanbase.

Dream life, right?

Not really.

Behind the shiny curtain lurks the darker reality I've never shared. @Thetrentontroublemaker was born out of necessity, not for some sad reach for fame. I was lonely. And I still am. Crazies populate my world, a sure sign that whatever mystique I've created no longer serves a purpose.

Myla camped out on her suitcase, refusing to leave, highlights everything that is wrong with my life.

"Do you want me to physically throw you out?" I pace back and forth, trying to stay calm. "Because that can happen."

Myla stares me down, absolutely unfazed. "Maybe we need a longer break," she suggests.

I rub my temples and remind myself to breathe, not to hyperventilate. Has she lost it so thoroughly? Does she think we will shack up and craft matching Burning Man outfits? Bake apple pies? Aside from diabolical horniness, why did I crumble for her, of all women?

"Don't you understand how wrong this is?" I plead. "I made a mistake bringing you home. I'm sorry if you got the wrong impression, but I like someone else."

She spends some time trying to work out whether I'm being serious. Then, with a sneer of contempt, she reveals who she really is. "That dark-haired pica?"

One of the benefits of living in Europe is exposure to languages. I can swear in nine different tongues and know enough Czech to understand that she just called Dani a cunt. I'm done playing nice.

"If you're not out of here in ten minutes, I'm calling the police. Seriously. Get the fuck out."

Is it overkill to point at the door? No. This psycho dimwit needs all the bloody encouragement.

Myla blinks. There's a long pause. In the pin-drop silence, her asthmatic breathing sounds disturbingly like Darth Vader. But I feel the first glimmer of hope. That there is a sliver of normalcy buried deep in her gray matter.

Or a healthy fear of authority.

"And where do I go?" she asks.

"Home," I stress. "Hop a flight in the opposite direction. Happy to pay for your return if that helps." If I could charter a jet to depart from the vineyard, I would. It is that dire. "I assume you flew into Kelowna?"

She runs a hand through her hair, and sparkly pieces of silver cascade to the floor. I bet she left a trail across the Atlantic.

"I don't need your money," she says, like I've offended her.

"Then what is it you want?" I ask this openly and honestly, to crack the code of her behavior, because every Crazy was, at one point, normal.

Myla swallows hard, her throat working against the tightness that seems to have calcified her. Her eyes appear glassy, blinking rapidly, but no tears fall. It's like she's trying to hold on to something, anything, to stop herself from unraveling.

I know that feeling all too well.

"Maybe I like you," she says, her voice wavering before she ducks my eyes.

Even if I knew the answer already, it's still surprising to hear those words after the drama and pouts and stick limbs crossed tight. I look into her drawn face, and behind it, the damaged expression scribbled like the mess she is. It makes what I have to say that much harder.

"Fair," I say, buffering what comes next so as not to hurt her feelings. "But if I don't like you in the same way, nothing can ever come of this. Relationships aren't one-way streets."

She slides her shoulder blades together and sits up straighter. I tried not to sound like her teacher explaining a bad grade, reducing her emotions to superficial fluff. My idea to acknowledge them without incorporating any specific language or framing us in any manner of relationship came out of nowhere.

I hope I presented it in the best light possible.

Because plan B is the police.

Her eyes carry sadness as they skirt the villa like she's trying to place the memories of us here—of what could have happened. My lungs start to burn until I realize I'm holding my breath.

And her breathing has changed as well, shallower now, almost hesitant before she asks, "Can I use your bathroom before I go?"

I'm stunned into a brief silence. Myla is out of my hair? It seems too good to be true.

"For what?" I ask because, well, with her, you never know. Maybe she'll nest in the shower.

She rolls her eyes. "What do you think?"

Unless she plans to steal my toothbrush, what do I have to lose? And with momentum on my side, no time like the present to usher her out as fast as humanly possible.

"Go ahead. I'll call you a taxi."

She stands up slowly, wobbling on her ridiculous boots. I feel her expectation that I should say more, but what else is there to say?

The faintest quiver in her lips gives away the battle raging beneath her calmness before she says, "Such a gentleman," with all the disgust she can muster.

She stalks off to the bedroom, and I rest a hand over my eyes in full-blown exhaustion.

Holy smokes.

I'm not made for this emotional turmoil.

I bolt to the kitchen island to check my messages on my phone. I'd snagged it out of the bedroom after Sawyer and Dani took off, charged it, and fired off two texts to Dani.

No reply.

I sag with the weight of my sinking heart. What did I expect? When a guy claims not to have a girlfriend, and his one sexual misstep materializes dressed like a Vegas showgirl…

It takes everything in me not to fire off a third text. Dani lives here. Eventually, she'll return. But what garbage and family dirt is Sawyer feeding her at breakfast? Nothing that will put me in a good light, that's for sure. I put in a call for another taxi, wondering if they might start blocking my number.

Pizzas. Condoms. European starlets.

What other items will I have them transport?

Thankfully, word hasn't gotten out yet about the drama, and Dispatch cheerily informs me my ride will arrive shortly.

Thank Christ.

I hear the toilet flush, and Myla reappears with one of my towels bunched in her hand. "You mind if I borrow this?" she asks and quickly clarifies her request. "I might need to kill some time at the lake before my flight."

"In Kelowna," I repeat, to be clear.

"Yes, Rhys," she says condescendingly. "In Kelowna."

If I need to cover the cost of a hundred fluffy towels, fine. Take as many as you want.

"Sure. Okay." I glance at my phone again. Nothing. "The taxi will pick you up at the tasting room," I add distractedly.

Myla unzips her suitcase and angles herself, backside facing me, as she tries to jam the towel inside. But she has to force it in, her bag likely jammed full with a hundred bikinis and vape sticks in every flavor imaginable.

Task complete, she touches up her hair. Her eyes are brittle when they find mine.

"Dmitri offered me money to sleep with you. He was under the impression you like men. I only proved him wrong, so don't think you're all that."

I bite my tongue. Do not take the bait. I've heard those rumors more than once. Maybe Dmitri has his doubts, but no need for him to fly Myla here to substantiate the rumors a second time.

If she needs to save face, so be it.

"Tell him I say hi."

Myla purses her lips. Or tries to shape those injected skin flaps into something other than a bittersweet smile. There's a sameness to the prowling Euro elite that makes me think they all went to the same school and drank the same Kool-Aid. Myla has cheekbones like sharp knives. Hard eyes. Implants that could survive nuclear war. Running so hot and cold, how did I ever miss it?

"Have fun with your new girlfriend. And fuck you," she adds for good measure. "You're so overhyped."

She trundles out, and the settling of my rapid-fire heartbeat feels like an acre of space suddenly opened up. I fight the urge to slam the door and engage every lock, standing guard on the porch until the taxi arrives and Myla slips inside.

Chapter Twenty-Five

DANI

chest is dull and formless, a giant sprawling ache. Rhys texted to say he kicked Myla out and wanted to talk, and I should feel relieved. It shouldn't hurt so much. But the lusty magic of our morning has evaporated with the realization that seven days does not a forever guy make.

Still, part of my mind went there.

It's only been a week, but it feels bigger.

When I look at Sawyer, I register that he's been studying me. The gray hairs on his temple shimmer silver from the sun spilling through the sunroof, and I see the miles on his face, forty not so far away.

"I'll be in touch about Gia and JC," I say. "Thanks for breakfast."

I gather my purse and open the door, but Sawyer halts me with his hand before I slide out. He revealed a different, softer side this morning. He fiercely loves his brother despite their dynamic. We even managed a few laughs sharing office politics stories over bitter drip coffee that would've made Rhys cry.

"It kills me to say this," he starts. "But you might be the breakthrough Rhys needs. Go easy on him, okay? He's more fragile than he lets on."

"I will," I say, my heart heavy. "I promise."

Sawyer draws his hand away, the corner of his mouth twitching with an almost smile. "And maybe don't tell him how surprised I am that he made it this far."

As he drives off, I'm grateful for the clarity he brought to the Trenton family mess. He explained a lot. Explained everything except Myla—a choice Rhys cannot pin on troubled family history.

But then again, I remind myself he had a whole life before this. One that I hold no claims to. And who am I to judge? The woman who kneeled under Brett's desk while he gripped my hair and set the tempo?

Not exactly Snow White.

And there's the bigger issue about his father. Rhys has never once mentioned a trip to Vancouver. And I plan to ask him about that once he gets here.

Inside my villa, it's fever-hot. I open every window, but the limp breeze only pushes the hot air around. Rhys suggested we meet at my place to talk, and I hated the first thought that flashed through my mind: *because it's more neutral or less tainted?*

I apply a fresh coat of lip gloss in the bathroom, my hand lightly shaking. I felt calm-ish on the drive here, but my world is now buzzing and popping. Rhys will explain, I listen, and a decision lies at the end. One that Sawyer insisted had Rhys on a plane back to Corfu.

I'm prepared for that. I think.

What I'm not prepared for is to find Rhys, right in my living room, simmering quietly in a wrinkled black t-shirt. Fists shoved into the pockets of his shorts.

Taller, somehow.

The beautiful chaos of last night rushes over me. How we both lost ourselves, melting into each other and coming undone.

My insides start to quake.

"Hey," he says. "I let myself in."

"I can see that."

He shakes out his hair like it's a nervous tic. "Sawyer left, huh? He sent me a text."

"We had an interesting breakfast."

Rhys pulls a face. "How much did he shit on me?"

"Hardly at all. Most of the conversation involved you and your family."

His eyebrows shoot up in disbelief. "That so?"

Without knowing all the details, a portrait of his life has emerged. One that he needs to color in. "I didn't know your father was ill."

A little tremor works around his mouth. "That's one of the reasons why I took this gig. To check in on him."

"When were you planning to do that?" I ask as gently as I can.

He pins me with those heart-stopping eyes. Instead of humor dancing in their depths, a brewing storm rages. "I'm not here to talk about my father."

I sit on the sofa and pat the space beside me. "I know."

He perches on the edge of the sofa, his body tightly coiled. I breathe in his spicy vanilla scent, the fragrance that swirled around us this morning in bed, while his touch, the gentle stroking of my hair, radiated through me like a burning fire.

Rhys stares at the floor, his expression blank. "Myla was a one-night stand. A mistake I truly regret. Should I have said something? Yes. Eventually. But no one confesses their dirty secrets when you're about to make love to someone for the first time." His eyes meet mine with such a sorrowful gaze that my breath catches. "I swear there is no one else. There hasn't been for a long time."

That reveal doesn't compute with the delicious shock of Rhys battering me senseless. I guess I found a winner in the stamina department.

"You showed no signs of rust."

I crack a smile, but Rhys keeps a lock on his serious expression. "The likes of Myla is not how I roll. It's the furthest thing from the truth."

I lay a hand on his knee and squeeze it. "I know."

His bewildered expression clears into a look of *ah-ha*. "So, you and Sawyer talked about many things."

"He loves you," I say, side-stepping the details. "Even though you drive him crazy."

"Yeah, well, that goes both ways." Rhys makes an indeterminate sound and fixes his attention somewhere behind me. He looks years younger, and vulnerable. "I wish we had a closer relationship. Like you and your sister."

After Rhys held me tight during last night's aftershocks, he smoothed my ruined hair from my face, and we rambled about life in that free-association, deep dive way when you're awash in pheromones, inhibitions loosened after intense first-time intimacy. I shared my frustration with my permanent second-place standing, forever in Amelia's shadow. But he congratulated me for never allowing that to supplant our bond.

Maybe that's inspired him to do the same.

After a heavy silence, I address the elephant in the room. "Where did she end up?"

He faces me dead on. "I stuffed her in a taxi. A one-way trip to Kelowna. She can find her way back home from there."

"She seemed a little off-kilter."

"Ya think?" He laughs, but there's no humor in it. "I call women like her the Crazies. The scary thing is, there's an endless supply of them. If it's not her, it'll be someone else next time."

"There was another gang of women holding a vigil this morning at the entrance," I reveal. "They swarmed the SUV before security stepped in."

With a depleted-sounding sigh, Rhys slumps back and tilts his face skyward. A long minute passes. "It's not fucking worth it anymore, Dani," he finally says. "No amount of money validates this insanity."

I curl my legs underneath me and hold space quietly, sensing we are shifting into a more profound territory. "Are you thinking of giving up the influencer stuff?"

He tips his head left to look at me. "I've been thinking about it for a while."

"What would you do instead?"

"I don't know," he says with a shrug. "Last night, you got me thinking. About your agency. Maybe I can help you set it up."

"From here?" I clarify, not believing for a heartbeat Rhys would slum it in Osoyoos. "But you live in Greece."

"What if I didn't?"

My pulse races as fast as my mind reels. I'm half in shock, half wishing Sawyer was here to eat his words.

"Oh," is all I say.

He sits up and repositions himself on the sofa to face me, eyes bright and no longer dull. "You have the brains; I have a ton of money, more zeros than I know what to do with. Might be an option to explore." He scratches the back of his neck like he's itching away his fears. "I'd rather do something purposeful with my life. Not just be a face that sells random shit. I mean, not Pink Pearl, obviously," he's quick to point out. "That stuff is the bomb."

He searches my face with frank confidence that unnerves me. What he's inferring is huge. And the logistics of starting a new venture together when I'm still finding my feet at Nero Vino are beyond my grasp. Never mind the personal implications of merging lives. Suddenly this conversation is moving in a direction I'm not prepared for.

"I'm flattered by your offer," I say. "But maybe we should, you know, let things unfold at something other than a breakneck pace?"

The shine in his eyes dims the tiniest bit. "Yeah. Sure," he says, disappointment creeping into his voice. "I mean, no rush."

Oh, god. Did he expect an immediate yes? Even though it feels like time has folded in on itself, it has only been seven days. Still, I sense he feels what I feel.

That there is potential in us.

I gather his hand in mine and kiss it. Tuck it to my breast. "Please don't interpret that the wrong way. I like you. I like you a lot." My accelerating heart rate cracks open the tightness I'm holding on to inside, and a nervy giggle erupts from the depths. "Honestly, I've had a stupid crush on you for years."

A silence falls. So sudden and absolute and weighty, it becomes the third entity in the room. Rhys stares at me, head tilted like he's trying to parse if he heard me correctly.

"Years?" He sits with a sudden stillness that feels dangerous. "I thought you recently followed me."

A bad crampy feeling takes over my entire body. I can almost taste his unease. "Uhm, actually, my sister discovered you first. She hosted a podcast called *Easy A Gets the Scoop*. She interviewed you three years ago. That was when I officially started following you."

Very slowly, he extracts his hand from mine. "Your sister was Easy A?"

"Yes," I say when, intuitively, I know the only answer to remove the heaviness that settled around us is "no."

Rhys stands abruptly. Tall, trembling. I can see it on his face—pieces falling into place. But what pieces?

"Is that what went down at Yvette's?" he asks, a wariness in his voice. "Some kind of sisterly payback?"

Huh? Sisterly payback? I'm utterly confused. A patch of voice escapes my mouth. "What does that mean?"

"I didn't understand the look of triumph in your eyes," he says, his voice gathering steam. "But now it makes sense. Was that the plan all along? For Amelia to show up here and orchestrate a tag team?"

His words land like poison darts. My whole body seems to wilt because he's accusing me of something untrue.

"Honestly, I have no clue what you're talking about," I say. "Can you—"

"Right," he scoffs, cutting me off. "No clue. Just like you started following me two months ago."

I feel a prick of panic at how fast everything has tilted not in my favor. But he has to understand. In what universe does it make sense to lead with *Hi, I'm Dani, your boss. And by the way, every night I cyberstalk you and think nasty thoughts. Welcome to Nero Vino!*

I wring both hands, guilt brimming inside me. "I didn't say anything about knowing who you were so you wouldn't feel weird."

Jesus. It sounds pathetic, even to me, and his eyes drill into mine like I've lost the plot.

"Yeah, well, so much for that." He crosses both arms, his gaze liquid fire. "Last night you said you and Amelia have no secrets between each other."

Suddenly, I feel queasy. Amelia was adamant I keep mum about the podcast—to keep my interactions with Rhys untainted is how she couched it. But his anger. That can only mean... Oh, shit. I rise to my feet, hoping that movement will shed the devastation building in my bones.

"Please," I plead. "Tell me what happened with Amelia." Because there is a story, although every nerve fiber in my body revolts against hearing it.

We stay locked in a silent standoff. An entire wordless exchange happens with his eyes locked on mine, and behind the anger is a flicker of despair.

"Today is already my worst nightmare, Dani," he says, his voice stripped raw. "And I have zero interest in rehashing the past. Ask Easy A what happened and keep her far away from me. The last thing I need is more Crazies in my life."

And Rhys marches out, slamming the door behind him.

Chapter Twenty-Six

RHYS

"IS EVERYTHING OKAY?" NICOLE LEANS FORWARD ON HER STOOL, TRYING to catch my eyes. "You've been quiet today."

"I think it's something I ate," I reply, the hitch in my voice betraying me. "Not feeling one hundred percent."

Nicole isn't buying my fake smile. Why would she? I feel numb. The darkness of Saturday was so complete, Sunday a complete drunken write-off, not even the surgical-grade lighting in Nicole's mad scientist office could brighten my Monday mood. I'm trapped in a room full of beakers with sticky notes pasted on every inch of available wall space. Energy sapped from tossing and turning all night.

Focus is nearly impossible.

Nicole powers down her computer and swivels to face me. Francis and Rita left to get lunch, but the emptiness in my stomach couldn't be filled with food.

"Do you want to talk about it?" she asks.

For the past hour, she's schooled me in her secret sauce system on how she grades grapes for readiness. She tracks acid, sweetness, and tannins daily, grading them on a one-to-five scale in her Moleskin notebook. When I asked how she knew the wine was ready, she offered a coy smile. "That's why Evelyn pays me the big bucks."

But we both know the topic has veered away from rosé production.

I meet her eyes and try to sound pulled together. "The weekend was a bit rough."

Nicole nods, tapping one finger thoughtfully on her lower lip. Dani has dropped in every day during filming. Every time she did, we joked and played off each other, thinking we were being so discreet. But it's like me sneaking home at midnight when I was thirteen, raiding the fridge for munchies when Mom wandered in. She sniffed the air and asked questions while I denied everything, a haze of pot smoke clinging to me.

With no sight of Dani today, Nicole puts two and two together. "I was walking the lower vineyards after lunch on Saturday," she says. "A lot of commotion drifted down from your place."

One dark eyebrow rises in my direction. How lawyer-like of her, giving me just enough rope to hang myself. My chest tightens uncomfortably. I've almost forgotten what it feels like to have someone give a shit. For a tense moment, I debate if this is a line I want to cross, revealing my disappointment and frustrations.

But if not now, when?

One quivering breath later, I ask, "Have you ever felt that no matter how much you try to outrun yourself, you smack back into whatever it is you're trying to escape?"

Nicole hums a sound of agreement, sun-bronzed biceps flexing as she crosses her arms. "Welcome to the frustration of life, kid. I worked a hundred hours a week, a slave to the system and the money I thought would make me happy. Killed vacations to take on new cases. Killed my marriage," she says, a matter of fact, remorse in the rearview mirror. "Not that it wasn't slowly dying anyway. Turns out all the big dick energy, dicks in general, had to go. Best decision I ever made. I'm poorer on paper, but ecstatic on every other metric." She taps a finger on my knee. "Where are you at?"

My smile flickers, then fades. "The slowly dying part?"

Nicole digests that, smart enough not to jump to conclusions without working over the available information. "What would make you come alive?"

To stem the pain of having to rethink every life choice I've made until this moment? is what flashes in my mind.

What I say is, "Not being alone. Patching up the relationship with my older brother. And having the courage to face my father. Not to blame him for how things turned out."

Nicole rolls her stool closer, eyes bright and blue and steady. "Can you tell him that?" she asks gently.

And there it is—The Question.

The silence stretches for several seconds, an abyss as deep and long as all the lost time I need to make up.

I've tried to imagine the scenario. Me, the black sheep, emboldened enough to crumble the Peter Trenton dynasty of arrogance and bullying? Would he allow the toxic loop to close? Let me finish a sentence for once? Or will it be business as usual? King of the shit birds picking at me, finding something to complain about.

Even my birth pissed him off.

Mom assumed her thirdborn would arrive early—stats show that is often the case. But I arrived late into the world by four days (typical slacker, Dad huffed for years) on a cold December night that coincided with the Trenton Talent Management Christmas party. With Dad stuck in the hospital waiting for my ass to show up, he missed out on signing Sarah McLaughlin. Ever since, he's bitched to anyone who'll listen that I'm the reason he missed his own party, allowing "dirtbag opportunist" Terry McBride to snatch up Sarah over drinks.

I was a curse from day one. Can he ever see me in a different light?

"I can," I say haltingly.

"When?"

Nicole slides my untouched glass of water in front of me. I take measured sips, feeling a deep urge to hug her. I bet she and Dad would've been besties back in the day—ruthless, focused, miserable even in victory.

"Soon?"

She taps my knee once more. "Commit. That's the only way it happens. For your father, your brother. And Dani."

With her tender smile, my breath steadies. Life is never about easy answers or a single magical fix. Nothing happens without trying.

But what should I do about Dani?

The door suddenly flies open, and Evelyn swans in, abuzz with energy. But she skids to a stop, shy of the doorway. The heaviness of our conversation lingers like sludge in the air.

"Oh, dear," she says. "Am I interrupting anything?" Her gaze flicks to Nicole, who silently conveys with a nod that it's cool.

"How's it going?" I ask.

Evelyn insisted on hugs from day one, and I like the old bird, so we embrace. Decked out in an all-black Adidas tennis outfit with nails painted gold, she's rocking the 'tude.

"You'll never guess who I saw at the Home Hardware," she rolls a third stool over to start the gossip train, "with what looked like a stripper hanging on his arm! Honest to God, women these days try to get away with wearing nothing. So déclassé."

Nicole chuckles. "Our old friend Tomas at it again?" To me, she says, "He latches onto every piece of fresh tourist meat in town. The younger the better."

"Thank goodness he didn't see me," Evelyn huffs. "Too enamored with the boobs spilling off Miss Russia."

A thought flickers at the back of my mind, the briefest thing. But I shelve it for now.

"Is he the one giving you grief?" I ask. "Dani said he was stirring up shit at the meeting the other night."

Evelyn grumbles, "That's him. The pride of Osoyoos. And then," she continues, "I dropped in to visit that battle ax, Gail. She gives two hoots about Tomas and his attempts at character assassination. Droned on and on about how the community is pushing her to clamp down on Nero Vino and Divine Debauchery." She glances at me. "Mind you, she and Dani didn't see eye to eye the other day. About your following descending like locusts."

"How is Dani?" I ask, trying for casual. "I haven't seen her today."

"Horrible!" she exclaims. "Poor thing has food poisoning but powering through the day."

With a knowing glance in my direction, Nicole says, "Must be something in the water."

"What?" Evelyn's head is on a swivel, eyes darting back and forth between us. "Are you not feeling well?"

"I think it's just a twenty-four-hour bug," I lie.

Nicole and Evelyn share a loaded look. These ladies aren't stupid. My mystery illness is a condition called "heartsick."

What guts me is that Dani lied about something so basic. Half of my followers are women. I mean, fair, no need to gush on and on about me, but her lie points to one thing. She knew about Amelia. That's what cratered my heart so completely. It left me in knots after I bailed from her place. I knew I recognized Amelia's voice over the phone, but what were the odds of those two being related?

And if they are as close as Dani said they were, how could she not know?

Also, that look at Yvette's called her bluff.

I suddenly feel so tired. Of pretending I have everything under control, that the baseline for normalcy is everyone dazzled by a guy who plays it cool on camera but is a flailing hot mess, terrified he's lost the very heart of his essence with zero ideas on how to recapture it.

If there was ever the time for an existential dice roll.

I clear my throat, weirdly nervous. "Is it cool if I take off for the city next Friday?" I ask Evelyn. "I'll be back Sunday night."

"Of course!" she says without hesitation. "The weekends are yours. And with your fans creating chaos in town, it might be wise to escape. Can you create a fake post about a trip to Calgary? Something to dislodge them from their makeshift camp?"

"I can get an old colleague on their case," Nicole chimes in. "Scare them off with some threats and legalese."

"Alas," Evelyn shakes her head, "this new generation comes pre-baked with righteousness. And determination that would put you to shame. As long as you're here," she says to me, "they're here."

The dark hum in my body accelerates. One morning I'll find a new girl on the doorstep, acting all chill before the inevitable high-stakes drama.

I need out.

Nicole and Evelyn graciously allow me to excuse myself. I wander back to my villa, swamped with an empty kind of helplessness. The hot sun reminds me of Corfu, but my palazzo, my life, everything about Greece—it all feels disarmingly unreal. Do I want to go back? This intense bonding with Dani has opened up something in me. It's unsustainable and unhealthy to keep going at it alone. One day soon, I'll crack, just like JC did.

This sense of uncertainty amplifies once I'm inside the villa. The maid has spit-shined every surface to perfection, and something about the dustless, lifeless ocean of greige depresses me. I escape to my safe space and swing in the hammock, mind in overdrive.

Nicole was right. Nothing will change on the outside if I don't change on the inside. I need to commit. With everything, starting with my family. Dad needs to hear me out—every regret, every moment of yearning for a connection that never came.

No more running, no more avoiding.

My resolve slowly gathers. Later tonight, I'll write a heartfelt speech. Practice it every day before I leave. Deliver it with an ice-cold calm.

If Dad still refuses me, so be it.

At least I tried.

Y

The answer always comes to you at night.

And it hits me at the lake like a cold, swift punch to the gut.

I'm out on the raft, the water black and calm, the sky cloudless and starlit. I sigh and wonder how much longer I can tolerate being haunted by thoughts of me and Dani. Our textervations have dwindled to nothing. Last night I drank myself into oblivion to stop the hurt. I tried to fall asleep early tonight but stared wide-eyed at the ceiling, the walls starting to close in.

That's when I came down here.

To think.

About life, Dani, the speech I have yet to write.

I silently rearrange the words in my mind and curse myself for not having the foresight to grab my journal.

And that's when the world around me dimmed, or maybe it was just my vision tunneling—everything outside that single, awful realization blurred and faded into the background.

My journal.

I bolt upright, breath stripped from my lungs, throat thick with dread. In the darkness, everything is still except for my brain. It stumbles over itself, reaching for recall.

When did I see it last?

The morning after with Dani. I remember thinking I should shove it in a drawer. (Not that she would snoop, but on the off chance, what would she say to all the lustful positions and details? My feeble attempt at erotic prose?) But then the Sawyer and Myla show came to town and blew the morning wide open. Have I seen the journal since? What I do recall, with sudden bone-chilling accuracy, is Myla walking out of the bedroom with a towel bunched in her hand.

My temples pound as the buried visual floats back to the surface.

She stuffed the towel into her suitcase, her back facing me. She had to put muscle on it like her bag was too full.

Or something other than terry cloth was bundled within it.

My mouth goes dry as dust.

I stagger to my feet and try to convince myself this is all a terrible dream I will soon wake up from.

How could I not suspect something fishy with her?

Because I was preoccupied with Dani and why she wasn't replying to my texts. Who cared about a towel if it meant Myla out of my life? I would have handed off the goddamned bed had she asked.

Fuck!

I slice into the water, swimming hard and fast toward shore. I charge up the stairs, taking two at a time, my chest on fire when I blow past Dani's place and the parking lot. My villa is shrouded in shadows, nothing but blackness upon darkness. I rush inside to the bedroom and snap the light on.

Nothing.

My palms go humid, the knob to the bedside table door slippery under my fingers.

Maybe…please.

I yank it open. Empty.

A wave of nausea makes me flush with sweat. My head suddenly feels too heavy for my body, and I sink onto the bed, face cradled in both hands. Listen, I'm no serial killer creepily cataloging my victims, but I have an active imagination. And my drawing skills are decent. Not that Van Gogh will be rolling over in his grave or anything, but the pages and pages of excruciating details reflect my Dani-obsessed brain.

To calm the fuck down, I tell myself Myla won't do anything stupid. Maybe she gets red with fury and rips it all to shreds. Or chucks it into the Mediterranean with a feral scream. Lights it on fire in a parking lot, muttering an incantation. I project all of those scenarios into the universe without a shred of hope. Wishful thinking only takes one so far.

Because I saw it in her eyes.

That unhinged sheen of someone with nothing to lose.

All the air in the bedroom contracts around me like a vise. How does that saying go? "Hell hath no fury like a woman scorned?"

I blocked Myla on Instagram so she can't post on my account, but if she rage-blasts on her socials, the pick-up will spread faster than a code red virus.

I'm spiraling into full-blown panic when my phone chimes from the kitchen. A terrible, sinking feeling hits—like Myla somehow knows I know— and I brace myself to face the damage. But when I check the screen, it's *See Saw* lighting up, with stacks of unread messages from both JC and Sawyer beneath it.

Urgent. Call me. 911.

I feel untethered, light as air, as a different kind of horror takes over.

The phone keeps shrieking in the dark.

Every cell in my body screams, *Don't answer.*

Chapter Twenty-Seven

DANI

"Excuse me?" Amelia shoots back, but we both know she heard me just fine.

"What happened between you and Rhys?" I ask again, an eerie calm to my voice despite the churning in my stomach that started on Saturday and hasn't stopped.

It's ten p.m. I'm sprawled on my bed, exhausted from a day that refused to let my mind focus on anything but this call. Amelia and Dean took off for a couples' weekend retreat in Whistler—their first since the twins arrived—and I had the decency not to sabotage their little getaway by unloading on her.

But now it's time for her to come clean. Sisterly payback.

After a long silence, Amelia asks, "What did he tell you?"

"I don't have the energy to talk in circles all night, Ames. You owe me a straight answer."

In the background, I can hear the TV in her bedroom and Dean whispering, asking if she needs space.

Amelia's voice returns, tighter now, "Give me a minute, Dani. I need to make a tea and walk you through this."

I hear the rustle of movement, the soft padding of feet as she heads downstairs into their dream of a kitchen that my entire apartment could fit inside of. At a future date, will we sit at the marble counter, eat home-baked cookies, and gossip? Or is this an unfixable rift?

The silence stretches, punctuated only by the muffled sounds of Amelia preparing her tea. Every second without closure is an unbearable burden.

"Did you sleep with Rhys?" I blurt out. "Yes or no."

My heart seizes. Three agonizing seconds pass before she says, "No."

But it's not a definitive no. It comes out cagey, loaded down with gravitas.

"Don't lie to me, Ames. Don't you dare!"

"Nothing happened," she insists. "Not like that."

My throat stays tight. "Then what?"

The kettle starts to shriek, then silence. I imagine her pouring hot water over a teabag, watching the color seep out. She always did this when she was buying time, gathering her thoughts.

"Hold on," she says, and I bet she's heading into the great room to curl up in Gramma's rocking chair. The one where we sat in her lap while she read us bedtime stories. It's her favorite place in the house. Her safe zone.

I feel robbed of breath, an icy grasp locked around my throat. Trying to make sense of why my sister has fibbed to me for years.

She clears her throat before taking a noisy slurp of tea. "When Dean and I went to Europe that summer, we had a stupid fight. Over nothing, really. And because I was drunk, and I'm petty, I ditched him. I hopped on a plane to Greece while he partied in Munich."

"Greece," I say tonelessly. "As in Corfu?"

"Yes," her voice is strangely quiet, "I tried to connect with Rhys. I thought, why not? We had fun on the podcast."

"Seriously? You were on your honeymoon."

She sighs, and it's the heaviest sound she's made in months. Maybe years. Even through childbirth, she barely whimpered.

"You have no idea, Dani," she says in a barren voice I barely recognize. "I've fucked the same guy since high school. Every night it's the same damn thing. You've had the luxury of sleeping around. That was my moment. A chance to experience something different. Now, I'm trapped."

"Trapped?" I repeat. Amelia wanted nothing more than to marry Dean. "I thought you were like two peas in a pod."

"Because that's what I make sure everyone sees," she says with a trace of bitterness. "The anointed child who can do wrong."

My mind rushes to process everything. Do I even know my sister? She's pure as the driven snow. The one with the pristine life. And yet— she was ready to throw it all away by cheating with Rhys?

"So, then…"

I can almost feel her grimace over the phone. "I texted him and said I was on the island. Could we meet up for a drink? He said no, politely. It wasn't his thing to hang out with the media. And I was pissed," she admits. "I'd come all that way for nothing. I got hammered, and you know what the Rialto sisters are like after too much booze."

"Go on," I say through gritted teeth. I remember damn well Amelia line dancing on the bar in Mazatlán while I, the eternal wing woman, buffeted her from breaking a leg.

"Some locals at the bar told me where his house was."

My heart gives a sharp little pulse. "You stalked him?"

"Listen," she says, as if there is some legitimate excuse for her behavior, "I was a train wreck. Angry at Dean and Rhys. Men in general. Eventually, the police showed up, and I spent the night in jail. Or whatever they call it in Greece. A holding tank for drunks."

I feel a mix of shock, disappointment, and pure incredulity. This is insane. Valedictorian Amelia in jail? "Jesus, Ames. I have no words."

"You cannot tell Mom and Dad," she stresses. "I managed to get out of there without Rhys pressing charges."

"Did you apologize?"

"Yeah," she says. "But Rhys warned me if I ever pulled a stunt like that again, he would call me out, no hesitation. Rake me over the coals of the public jury."

I absorb that as best I can. The reality of this is weirder than I ever imagined. But now it all makes sense. "Is that why you shut the podcast down?"

"How was I supposed to carry on? My credibility went up in flames. Not to mention I was humiliated and embarrassed."

If Rhys scoured my Instagram feed, he wouldn't have recognized Amelia in our photos. Hair so blond, it was almost white with an adoring Dean gazing reverentially at his wife who made marital vows she had no intention of keeping.

"And Dean?" I ask. "Does he know?"

"Dani," she drifts back into her authoritative voice, "when you get married, you'll understand you pick your battles. Nothing happened in the end, so why open that can of worms?"

Holy shit. After living in Amelia's shadow for years, always the screw-up compared to her flawless life, will I ever see her the same way now that the illusion has shattered?

"What did Rhys say?" Amelia asks, a sliver of uncertainty embedded in the question, like maybe there's more to the story she never shared.

"Same," I lie.

"How did this topic even come up?" she asks, her tone more fraught. "You promised me you wouldn't say anything."

Before I remind her that this is her cross-examination and not mine, I hear a light *tap* against the window followed by an urgent whisper. "Dani? Are you awake?"

I jolt upright, breathing in sharply, practically a gasp. Rhys. I yank the top sheet around me, my heart pounding as I slide off the bed. I creep to the window, open the blinds, and peer outside. Right away, I know it's not good. The moonlight washes over Rhys, turning him a Sawyer-like ghostly pale. He hums with dark energy, an unnatural presence that sends a shiver down my spine.

"I have to go," I tell Amelia, abruptly ending the call. Tossing the phone onto the bed, I slide the window open and face Rhys, standing as still as a statue.

"What's going on? Are you okay?"

His face is a storm of emotion, and he swallows in a broken, defeated way. "My dad had another stroke," he says. "I need to get to Vancouver tonight. Can I borrow your truck?"

It feels like the world tilts beneath me. I want to rage at Amelia for lying, for stalking Rhys, and for adding herself to his Crazy list. Because of her, I had the shittiest weekend, unsure if Rhys would even hear me out if I tried to convince him again that I knew nothing. But when all is said and done, I know my feelings will level out. I will love my sister for the mess she is.

I will love and forgive her as I should because, in the end, family is everything.

And that's why my response to Rhys comes without a second thought.

"Give me fifteen minutes. I'm coming with you."

🍷

"You don't have to do this," Rhys says a somewhat pointless fourth time as I roar up the highway heading west. "And I can drive."

We crest the hill, the shimmering lights of Osoyoos disappear, and absolute darkness engulfs us. There are no streetlights on this remote section of road.

"It's not safe at this time of night," I tell him. "You have too much on your mind to navigate all the winding passes."

The prognosis for his father remains shaky. Sawyer's most recent text said he might not walk again. If my heart feels like it's gone through the wringer, Rhys's must be near the point of collapse. On cue, he jams both hands into the kangaroo pocket of his hoodie and blows out a sigh that sounds raw and jagged at the edges.

I get it. I was stressed to the max all weekend. Thankfully, Amelia killed my greatest fear and the panicky ache eating me alive has subsided. But I'm dying to hear his version of the event.

I approach it in a roundabout way.

"I spoke to my sister tonight."

After a charged silence, he asks, "How did that go?"

I replay the conversation, leaving out the bit about Amelia and Dean already married to spare her some dignity.

"I swear on a stack of Bibles she never told me," I finish, hating the wobble in my voice. "There was no plan for her to come up and have us ambush you."

Rhys nods, but not the way you nod where you're agreeing with someone. His silence stings. The refusal to comfort me with a morsel of confirmation or denial.

"And I'm sorry I lied about knowing you," I blabber on. "But…" I exhale slowly, my voice barely rising over the low hum of the engine. "I'm not sorry about the other night. Not in the slightest."

Rhys looks over. Dark eyes, his pupils dilated, black smothering brown. Does he want to hear all this right now? Likely not. But this feels like a game-changer night. One that requires brutal honesty.

"I'm not sorry either," he says. "And I should have believed you. Forgive me for storming out the way I did. Bad form."

A funny feeling takes over in the blanket of silence. This weird sense of déjà vu. Hurtling on the dark highway to the unknown waiting for us in Vancouver reminds me of the drive up in the dead of night two months ago. Nursing a broken heart but full of hope. If I had known then that Rhys was part of the equation—rather than Evelyn offhandedly informing me the day after I arrived that my internet crush was my five-week summer project—would I have jumped so high at the opportunity?

Yes.

I would have jumped fifteen feet. Cleared the moon, if need be. I liked Rhys then, and I like him even more now. Or should I say, I actually do know him, a little. He's more complex and intriguing than I ever imagined. And he made my guarded heart bloom again.

If there is a chance for us, he deserves to know it all.

"About that shit I pulled at Yvette's…" My knuckles tense on the wheel before I continue. "It had nothing to do with Amelia."

"And," he says, the slight rise in his voice a question to know more.

His gaze flickers toward me, a softer look now, the tension in his shoulders easing slightly. I take a deep breath, slowing the car a smidge as I process what to say. It's now or never. If I can't be upfront on this raw, hurting night, I have no business being with Rhys.

I tell him everything. How I let Brett abuse his power, minus all the gory details. My insecurities and self-doubt, starting with the Dani of eighth grade, taller than every boy and hiding her boobs with baggy sweatshirts to stop the stares and teasing. Dani with a mouthful of braces mortally ruined at grad dance when Steve Ashe walked past without a second glance and into the arms of blonde, petite, and perfect Emily Reynolds with her venomous smirk that said, *you have no chance, ever.*

All the promotions I got looked over for.

"Why did you like him?" Rhys asks, zeroing in on Brett.

Why indeed? I've asked myself that question many times on too many wine-soaked evenings. Tonight is when I'm finally honest with myself. "He promised me the moon, and stupid me fell for it."

"You're not stupid, Dani," he says. "You are smart and talented. I can draw, but what you create is real art."

"What do you draw?" I ask, genuinely curious.

It's the tiniest ripple, but in the tight confines of the truck, the energy shift feels seismic. Rhys rearranges himself in his seat and it strikes me that he wants to say something unpleasant.

"Things that catch my attention," he says vaguely.

"You never mention drawing in any of your posts," I say, unable to stop myself. But whatever. The cat's out of the bag. Brand me a super fan and call it a day.

"Believe it or not," he says, "I'm an introvert. Sharing my sad excuse for art is too personal, and the world already knows enough about me. I need to hold some things close to my chest."

"I'd like to see some of your work."

He glances at me with a look I can't figure out. Pensive? Nervous? Worry? A little of all three. Maybe what he draws is actual garbage, and he knows it. I don't push the matter.

Instead, I circle back to his question that I left unanswered.

"You asked me if what happened at the vineyard turned me on. The answer is yes, if that wasn't glaringly obvious."

A ghost of a smile flickers on his face. "I'll never forget that."

I swallow hard and say nothing. Embedded in his reply is a hint of nostalgia, as if Osoyoos and I are already a distant memory. Was I reaching to believe we were back on track, even if the direction was still unclear?

Damn you, Sawyer. For nailing it.

Because in what rational world does Rhys leave Greece to shack up in an old tractor shed and demean himself with double-doubles from Tim Horton's?

I stare out the windshield at the headlights slicing through the dark, illuminating the sparse landscape with cold slivers of light, making everything feel distant, suspended in time. Maybe this is the Rhys-less world I need to prepare for, but all I can think about is the moonlit memory of us, naked on the raft under the stars, when I thought I could live inside that moment forever.

Chapter Twenty-Eight

RHYS

I would rather be anywhere than here. Weighted down with heaviness, my legs are like two pillars of concrete, doing everything in their power to slow down the inevitable.

To walk headlong into the past I ran away from.

"I think this is it." Dani points at a hallway that looks like all the others we passed. "The waiting room is at the end."

Her grip is steady on my hand as we shuffle down, passing rooms I'm too freaked out to look into. Money may buy you the privilege of a private room—of course, Dad has one—but the end game in a hospital is the same whatever number lives in your bank account.

Thank Christ for Dani.

We stopped in Manning Park three hours ago for a bathroom break and a quick nap. She asked how I was holding up. By then, exhaustion had kicked in, my foundational walls crumbling, and I was a mess, admitting I was nervous as hell. She kissed my trembling chin and whispered, "Whatever you need. I'm here."

I'm trying to act like I'm not a basket of nerves and center myself before we hang a right and step into the waiting room. Fluorescent lights buzz at that annoying level of high-end fatigue, adding a layer of tension to the blank white coolness of the room. Sawyer watches the morning news on a tiny TV mounted to the wall. Almost approachable in sweats and high-tops.

But he faces the other direction and doesn't see us walk in.

JC does.

And his face lights up as soon as he sees me.

"Little buddy," he pushes himself out of the sad, worn chair with that famous winning smile, "you made it."

He's gotten lankier, his face bristled with a beard, and he sports gold hoops in both ears, but some things never change. Our bond is ironclad. As timeless as his uniform of jeans, Converse, and leather jacket.

We lock in a tight hug, and I bury my face into his neck. He smells like dryer sheets and some fancy cologne.

"Fuck, man," I mutter. "It's good to see you."

We disengage, and JC playfully ruffles my hair while Sawyer flicks a cool gaze in my direction. "Morning."

"How goes it?" I ask, both of us remarkably civil, considering we smacked each other with Mike Tyson shots two days ago.

"As good as it can be."

His gaze drifts to Dani with a look of reproach—like she should be at his side and not mine. She offers a brief smile and hello while JC tips his head in her direction, implying *introductions, please.*

"Shit," I say with a sheepish grin. "Right. Dani, this is JC."

Dani smiles, a little starstruck. "Hi. I've heard so much about you."

Do they shake hands or embrace? Dani looks unsure, but JC solves that problem. He's our resident hugger.

"Nice to meet the woman my brother can't stop yapping about." He shoots me a wink over her shoulder, unbothered by my hot glare. Forever the shit disturber.

"Where's Mom?" I ask because her signature perfume, Cool Water, lingers brightly in the stale medicinal air.

"Rhys," a familiar lilting voice says from behind me.

I spin around as Dani untangles herself from JC to observe how I cope with this reunion. Mom's eyes widen before they soften into something painfully tender. Silver hair swept back, and very put together for nine a.m., she is the classic Shaughnessy matron in pinstriped slacks and cream blouse, clutching a Styrofoam cup with what has to be the world's worst coffee.

Despite our Zoom calls, seeing her in person throws me off. A round-shouldered heaviness has replaced the steel of her posture. Worry and grief have permanently etched her features.

But she's still fucking beautiful.

Even with tears streaming down her cheeks.

"Hi, Mom."

"You're so tall," she whispers. "And you look so much like your father."

JC gives me a shove in her direction. "Hug already, will ya? Sheesh. It's only been what? Sixteen years?"

I step forward, my arms hesitating mid-air as if seeking permission before fully committing. Mom closes the gap between us, allowing me to embrace her. She's stiff at first, as if her reciprocity might mean I disintegrate before her eyes. Then her fingers grip the fabric of my hoodie, holding on like she's afraid to let go. In her arms, time spins backward. Her warm, steady touch was always the quiet assurance I needed. Mom cries softly, her frame so fragile as I rub away the shudders, careful with the fine silk of her blouse.

Sawyer watches us, the tension in his shoulders as rigid as the silence. JC was the apple of Dad's eye—the musician he always wanted to be. Mom doted on me. That left stoic, dependable Sawyer with the leftover scraps of their affection. Perhaps that turned him into the steely authority figure that has always made him the glue keeping our family together.

Very slowly, with Mom resisting, I ease out of our hug to introduce Dani.

Mom acknowledges her with a watery smile. "Pardon me," she wipes away mascara streaks with the back of her hand, "I'm a little overwhelmed."

Dani nods, handling the situation like a pro. "Pleasure to meet you, Marilyn. Although I wish it could be under different circumstances."

Mom reaches for Dani's shoulder, her voice thick when she says, "Thank you for bringing him home."

"Well." JC claps his hands together, bringing us out of the emotional cloud. "You two must be beat, driving all night."

He throws the question at Dani, who looks anything but. Ridiculously hot in her glasses, hair in a messy ponytail, and stunning without makeup. He flashes that smile, and I feel a surge of irrational jealousy. My brother will go to the ends of the earth for me, but he can also have his tongue down any female throat in half an hour without even trying.

I inch closer to her, signaling, *this one is mine.*

Dani stifles the cutest yawn. "I am a little bleary," she admits.

"Why don't you scoot home and get some sleep?" I suggest. As much as she's a trooper, who wants to hang out in a hospital and watch someone you don't know drool all over themselves?

"Okay," she says. "Text me whenever. I'll pick you up."

"Are you two staying at the house?" Mom asks, quick to intervene, looking at me for the answer she wants.

Dani and I never discussed where I'd crash. The Trenton mansion has enough rooms to house a hockey team. And JC has a sweet bachelor pad on the water, overlooking Stanley Park. But if I can lie beside Dani tonight in her condo, I'll take that, thank you very much.

But I can't crush Mom's hopes right now.

I peck Dani on the cheek. "I'll keep you posted. Leave your phone on."

I wish I could say it all went like clockwork after that. The Trenton family unified. Me and Dani snuggling after sex in her bed, bellies full of sushi. Hope for a better future shining bright.

Not the ring of my phone shattering the silence, and Sawyer grumbling, "Typical."

Or me skimming the screen to see Evelyn's name with a sense of foreboding. Dani had texted earlier to inform her of our midnight emergency run. She's probably calling for an update.

Or so I hope.

"Mornin', Evelyn," I say for the benefit of Dani, her head tilted. Curious.

"Rhys," Evelyn says, her infamous cigarettes-after-sex voice sounding grittier than usual. "Are you two in Vancouver?"

"Yeah. We just got to the hospital. Sorry, but I can't talk long."

The silence that follows carries a weight. And it isn't a peaceful silence. It buzzes through the phone like static before a storm.

"Oh dear," she says. "I'm sorry to interrupt you, but we have a situation."

🍷

"Jesus, Rhys!" Sawyer fumes, throwing his arms wide. "Can you, for once, not be the full-fledged fuck-up?"

"What?" I shout back. "You think I planned this?"

"That would mean you have the foresight to plan. Not live day to day with your head in the goddamned clouds." His chest heaves with a disgusted sigh. "Why would you trust that woman to be alone with your stuff?"

JC motions at Sawyer to settle down. "Bro, chill. Both of you. Keep it down. We don't need a scene."

"I can't be calm," I say, halfway to hysterics. "How do I fix this?"

Other than I can't.

"Maybe you should have thought of that sooner," Sawyer yells. "Before our mother ends up in the bathroom on the edge of a nervous breakdown."

I had no choice but to share the disastrous news with everyone. They all stared at me, the scandalized gasps yet to come. Not only did Myla swipe my journal, but she ditched Kelowna and detoured back to Osoyoos where she and Tomas hooked up at a coffee shop.

When Evelyn shared that news, I felt my blood coagulate. She had mentioned Tomas parading around with a woman during her visit with Nicole and me. Her description of a half-dressed European ditz should have set off every alarm in my head.

Because what do you get when two scheming weirdos hell-bent on revenge collude?

The end of the world.

In the form of photocopies of my illicit drawings plastered on every business door in Osoyoos. My innermost, dirtiest thoughts stapled to telephone poles. And scrawled over the top in flaming red ink were Tomas's twisted call to arms:

Nero Vino is a disgrace.

Boycott Evelyn.

Is this how Nero Vino promotes their wine???

And so on.

Mom swooned and started to hyperventilate, prompting Dani to escort her to the bathroom. And I stood there with the universe crashing down around me, shame-faced for being such a fool. We skirted the topic of my drawings on the drive down. That was my entry point. I should have prepped Dani for the worst.

I should have done a lot of things differently.

Like, not sleep with a Crazy.

To have this hit Dani in the face like a plateful of scissors is the lowlight of my life so far, and I've had plenty. I feel sick to my stomach and turn away from Sawyer's wrath and endless disappointment. Nero Vino and Evelyn so disgustingly discredited when she has been nothing but a champion for me swallows me alive in guilt. And my Instagram account is a damn firework show, the hits coming and coming. Myla tagged me and Dani in her revenge postings, and the algorithms have shut down the most depraved pictures, but the damage is done.

Why does this have to happen when I'm an emotional wreck, about to face my father, or what's left of him, for the first time in years?

Dani suddenly reappears, pale as milk, shoulders concave with defeat.

"Where's our mother?" Sawyer immediately asks.

"Taking a moment," Dani says. "It's a lot to process." She wheels around to face me. "I just spoke with Evelyn. She asked Francis and Rita to rip down what they can."

Christ. Why didn't I think of that? Maybe I am that useless. And Rita agreeing to help me? If that doesn't throw the morning on its head.

"What else did she say?" I press.

Dani retreats a step, and the subconscious movement rings deep in my hollow bones. "She thinks it's a good idea for you to stay down here. And definitely no posting. About anything."

JC takes a seat and blows out a long, decompressing breath. "And I thought touring was stressful."

Sawyer's acidic expression changes into something calculating, like he's just been reminded of something. "I need to smooth things over with Evelyn. Let her know that one part of the Trenton clan can deliver without a monumental shit show."

"That's your concern?" I snort, anger coating my skin.

"It's one of them," he glowers back. "Aside from keeping the company afloat, I also ensure my two brothers have a pipeline of money flowing to them. But thanks for lightening my load. Good luck getting a gig after this."

He shoulders past me, knocking me hard enough that I stumble back. JC watches him storm out and then rises to his feet with a weary sigh.

"I'll deal with him," he mutters. "You and Dani sort out Mom."

JC goes off in search of Sawyer, leaving Dani and I squared and facing each other. Every line of her body speaks of uncertainty.

Sparks of despair flicker around my brain. "How is she?"

"Devastated," Dani says, her voice colorless.

My body feels leaden. All I can manage is a small, helpless shrug. "I'm so sorry. This is horrible."

The breath she draws in sounds painful. "She really is a Crazy, huh?"

"Whatever you do, don't look at the photos, okay? Don't feed the insanity."

"You need to talk to your mom." Dani fidgets with her hands in a detached, distant way, and I feel this numbness consuming me. "I'm going to go home now."

My tattered heart wilts. Will Mom be anything other than repulsed? Her youngest son reappears, delivered to her by a dark-haired angel she had already envisioned, I could tell, in a wedding dress. And I upend her moment of motherly glory with this?

She won't understand. Mom never understood my struggles with women. She figured a man with looks had the world at his feet, the pick of the crop, like how the great Peter Trenton rolled. Not a wallflower who became more and more isolated with his increasing fame.

"Can I see you later?" I ask. Hopeful, borderline desperate.

Dani bites her lip. Even a reluctant maybe would prevent my future mental health from imploding. A hard no, and I may never recover from the damage I've created from one careless moment.

I cross both sets of fingers, feeling light-headed, unaware my lungs have stopped working.

Finally, she says, "Let's play it by ear, okay?"

Chapter Twenty-Nine

DANI

At midnight, I sit on my balcony, drinking jasmine tea and trying to stay awake. Darkness swirls around me, my blood half anxiety. I've tried to read but can't concentrate. I keep checking the time. Even The Ramones are a pulsating sound that rearranges my atoms and squashes all thoughts.

God, if Joey fails me, I'm in serious shit.

My mind tries to pick apart the reasons why Rhys hasn't shown up. Visitor hours ended at eight, and his last text landed at four when he asked if he could swing by. I said yes. I need to see him. I need him to cradle me in his arms and protect me from this exploding shitty day.

To tell me it will be alright, even if it isn't.

Because I've been a woman in meaningless motion. I tried to eat but picked listlessly at a poke bowl Uber left on my doormat. I vacuumed, Windex-ed, and laundered. Nothing could occupy my restless mind, or make me forget my clit was now, in Osoyoos, arguably as famous as Rhys.

The only comfort I will feel is when we are here, no more than two feet apart.

At twelve-fifteen, the waiting game finally ends. Rhys buzzes from the intercom, my nerve endings tingling the entire time it takes him to ride up the elevator. As soon as he steps out into the hallway, the energy shifts. An ominous kind of stillness floats around him.

"Hey," he says. "Sorry I'm so late."

I step aside, holding the door open. "It's fine. Come in."

He kicks off his flip-flops, eyes sweeping the living room in a way that bubbles up the same self-consciousness as when Brett first came over and detailed what I needed to upgrade.

"I'd invite you in," I joke through my insecurity, "but you're in. It's no palazzo."

He quirks a brow. "This is cute. It suits you."

I shut the door, and a silence falls, me trying to figure out where to start. Rhys is tired-eyed, far from immaculate, and still takes my breath away.

He's also impossible to read.

"Can I get a glass of water?" he asks.

"Sure. Are you hungry? I've got—"

"I'm good with water. Thanks."

I gesture at my sofa that, admittedly, has seen better days. "Have a seat."

Through the opening that divides the kitchen from the living area, I watch him sink onto the cushions, attention fixed on the blackness outside. I was low-key hoping his mood might have picked up because he was right. The algorithms shut down the worst of the images. Being a sucker for torture, I tracked the comments on his feed. Lots of support, surprisingly, with Myla universally trashed for being a vindictive bitch. A small drop of mercy in an ocean of bad luck.

"Here you go." I hand off the water to him, and he downs it in three thirsty gulps.

"Thanks," he says. "I didn't realize how parched I was."

He sets the glass on the coffee table, and we stare silently at it. There is so much hanging in the air, unsaid.

"Did Evelyn reach out with any updates?" he finally asks, eyes half-closed in a giant cringe.

I curl up on the opposite side of the sofa. "Gail is having a field day," I admit. "And Tomas is talking to anyone who will listen, but Evelyn is all over the damage control."

"My ass isn't fired?" He shakes his head, incredulous. "That lady is a mensch, considering I fucked up her brand for the near future."

"I mean, it's not great," I hedge, because it's not. No point in having our heads in the sand. "The crazy thing is, I had a ton of media requests. Long-term, this could play out in our favor," I add, spinning a hopeful angle.

Rhys nods, less than visibly cheered. "The long-term residue is what worries me."

He meets my eyes, and a spark of worry erupts inside me. It's like peering into a deep well and seeing nothing but darkness.

"Are you sure you don't want anything—"

He stands abruptly. Solid but trembling. Hands coiled into fists. "I just … I need some air."

"The balcony," I say, my outstretched hand indicating where it is.

Rhys takes two tentative, stumbling steps and stops, weaving slightly like a marionette doll pulled by invisible strings. The air is strange, heavier somehow. Thick as velvet. His eyes squeeze shut, and a low, strangled noise hums in his throat.

Then it's as if his bones, his very core, dissolve.

He collapses, landing on his knees with a thud that my bitchy neighbor below will surely complain about tomorrow. Rolling onto his back, he becomes one with the floor, limbs spreadeagled, every muscle and tendon visible wound to the breaking point. His chin starts to quiver, and he shoves the heels of his hands into both eyes.

"Fuck," he says, his voice rising in pitch.

Something twists in my chest. I move slowly, kneeling beside his shattered state. "Rhys," I say as gently as I can. "Talk to me."

I watch his throat move up and down, the corners of his mouth tightening. Rhys's shoulders rise and fall with his labored breathing before the words tumble out with a shuddering sigh. "I sat with Dad all day. The nurse told me even patients in a coma can hear. Their subconscious retains words. So, I blabbed about how sorry I was. That I disappointed him. That we never bonded."

He inhales a stuttered breath, eyes glittering as he swipes away fallen tears. "And when the nurse came around and said it was time to leave, I was about to get up, and Dad reached for my hand. His grip freaked the hell out of me. He wouldn't let go." In the shadowed light of my living room, I can see the vein in his neck pulse dangerously. "And I'm like, now? When it's too fucking late?"

His mouth screws tight, holding it all in. I blink fast, trying to absorb one crisis after another.

"Maybe—" I start.

"And Sawyer," he interrupts, anger leaking in, "he's picking me up so we can have dinner with Mom and JC, and he starts reading me the riot act the moment I'm in the car. Bettina already texted me that a bunch of bookings got canceled, so I told him to fuck off. But he wouldn't stop." His shoulders sag as if lying motionless on my Pottery Barn rug is too much effort. "I had a full meltdown. We were hurling horrible, toxic shit at each other. He said I didn't deserve you, and…" After a few seconds of flat-lipped silence, he adds hoarsely, "And he's right. You're the first real connection I've had in forever, and I messed that up."

Emotions crash inside me, hot and fast. But I can't lose it here. I have to be the strong one.

"There's so much going on right now," I remind him. "You need to focus. Make your family the priority." I swallow past the squeeze of my throat. "And I don't blame you. This wasn't your fault."

His red-rimmed eyes burn into mine. "Everything's my fault."

I try to tune out the sound of his voice cracking, but then all I can hear are his aching waves of grief. My own tears rise up in sympathy and shock. Broken doesn't begin to classify it. This is a complete breakdown.

"I feel like I'm drowning, Dani," he says, his voice knifed with desperation.

Tears stream down my cheeks, dripping off my chin in a slow, wet tempo onto his arm. He looks at me, gutted, and reaches for my hand, our fingers trembling before they settle. The room feels like it has its own center of gravity, pulling us into its depths.

"Don't cry," he whispers. "Tell me we can figure this out."

I breathe into the dark. Thoughts of him alone and unhappy break off another piece of my heart. I touch his lips and trace the path of the hard lines etched on either side. His kind smile, the blazing warmth of it. Will this crumpled soul find the will to smile again?

With my touch, his fingers tighten around mine. "Every time I close my eyes, I see you. No way I can recover now that I've fallen for you."

He searches my face, his still shaken. Healing from the drag along rock bottom will take Rhys days, perhaps weeks or months, but all the uncertainty within me crystalizes into a singular truth: my whole body knows he's the one for me.

I tuck a loose strand of silken hair behind his ear, and a forlorn *mmm* spills out of Rhys. "I fell for you a long time ago, Mr. Trenton."

I let the words hang, not as a dare, but as a recognition. That I lied, and if we plan to get beyond this, he needs to forgive me.

"C'mere," he says, sweetly tugging on my shirt.

He draws me into a deep, lusty, and desperate kiss. I can taste the salt of his tears and feel the heat of his skin. In me, emotions too powerful to name churn, a dangerous uptick of urgency in my blood. Our soul-stirring kiss turns urgent and torrid, saying everything words can't. It puts both our engines in gear. He pulls me onto the hot sauna of his body, and I feel him swell against the parts of me in need of release.

"Make love to me," he murmurs. "I need to feel us together."

I catch my breath, mumbling, "Here?"

He cups my ass, drawing me closer until our breaths mingle. "Yes. I don't want you to go far."

"Because there are so many places to hide in eight hundred square feet."

His laugh. Unbridled in a way that felt impossible minutes ago. It's the release of tension we both need. I push up and sit back on the hard platform of his thighs. I unbutton my shirt, caressing my curves as I uncover them bit by bit. He eyes my best bra—black, satin, barely affordable—and the goods spilling out when I unclasp and shrug it off.

"I love your body." He rises up to kiss my delicate flesh, my C-cups warm and heavy. He fingers my nipples into taut buds, playing, teasing, making me moan as a delicious shiver shoots up my spine.

The idea of coming apart in my house. With Rhys. And his zero-to-sixty-to-holy-shit brand of pleasure.

Yes, and yes.

"Stand up for just a second?" he asks.

I wish I could say I made some effort to help things along, but in a single fluid move, he peels his t-shirt off, tossing it into the ether. Then he wriggles free of his shorts and sends them flying across the room with a flick of one perfect foot.

He's rock hard, and upon release, the swollen flesh smacks lightly onto his torso. Leaning back onto the rug, he cradles his dick in his hand and gives me a wide-open look.

This is me, is what it says. *Not Instagram Rhys. The Rhys who just lost it, broken and crying on your living room floor. Nothing more, nothing less. Are we cool?*

Yes, yes, and yes.

He is my kryptonite.

I ease out of my jeans, taking the silky fabric of my thong with them. He sucks in the view like a starving man. Before yesterday, I had no clue how my pearls affected him. No idea how talented of an artist he was.

He did draw me perfectly; I'll give him that.

Me and my scandalous pearls straddle him, my fingers curling around his hard, satin skin. *Fuck the foreplay* is what my scrambled brain shouts. I'll never survive slow and caring. We need to tear into each other and ride wave after wave of pleasure.

I angle him to my warmth and push onto his tip. A fluttery sigh escapes his lips, and Rhys pulls back slightly, the question of safety in his eyes.

"I'm in the clear," I say. "You?"

He nods, and I ease myself down, eyes closed to savor every inch of sensation.

"Yes," Rhys moans. "Yes, to everything you do."

As we're locked together, his fingertips draw slow tickling circles on my ass cheeks. He pauses there, watching me.

"Lean forward a little," he whispers. "But keep me inside you."

Hands planted on either side of his chest to bear my weight, and careful to keep him snugged tight, I lower to brush my lips hungrily against his. "What do you have in mind?"

He trails one finger over the curve of my butt, moving lower and lower until I feel the smallest hairs tingling. Destination: rosebud. His finger pad, rough and warm, circles in a maddeningly slow tempo. I quiver and clench, and we both go still for a breathless pause.

"Is that okay?" he asks in a hushed voice.

Aware of nothing except the force field we make touching, and unable to form a coherent reply, I nod consent.

He wets his finger, teases me for a moment, then slowly pushes his finger inside. No buildup. A sudden rush of warmth and pleasure rolls into my head.

"I've never done this," I say, my voice trembling on the edge of discovery.

He licks his lips. "Me either."

He pumps a little deeper, his moves slow, calculated, tender. A small tight spot in my throat begins to dissolve, melting down into my breasts and stomach. Untamed noises spill out of me, my flesh so profoundly alive from his touch. How deep my hunger dwells is the lesson here, taught for the first time. It's exhilarating and terrifying and so intimate all at the same time.

I rock tight against his dick while my ass clenches around his finger, pulling it in deeper. He makes a feverish noise from the back of his throat, bitten-off sounds of need. His gaze brims with the same amazement I feel vibrating in my blood.

Eye to eye, the message is clear: we both need to get this day out of our systems.

"Dani," he murmurs. "You look so beautiful."

I thrust my hips forward, grinding my pearls hard on his erection for maximum damage. He swells inside me, and oh, what a wicked feeling. My heart unlocks, my soul opening wide, beckoning him to join me wherever this darkly inquisitive journey takes us. I ride the delicious shock of his finger, my body burning with the forbidden pleasure of two blinding sensations.

He drives into me with steady, deep strokes, harder the louder I moan. Is this what it feels like to give yourself in full trust? He's making me feel sexy and wild in a way I never have before. No choice but to give in to that feeling, letting it carry me over the edge into bliss.

Within minutes, that familiar warm tingling curls up inside me, reverberating through my body from the inside out. I'm rocking forward and back, reaching for the high.

Rhys never lets up, building in tempo, pushing into me again and again, the sounds of our choppy frantic breathing becoming dim as I fall into a deep oblivion.

"Fuck, Dani," he rasps and gives up control. With a clipped groan, he thrusts his hips in one final, marauding command, his warmth spilling into the tightened space of my spasming flesh. Shudders slam through me, leaving nothing but a dazzling trail of stars in my brain.

Chapter Thirty

RHYS

When I wake up, my eyes feel sore and crusted with sand. I peel them open and blink into the half light of an unfamiliar room. Dark purple walls. Frilly curtains and a flower-patterned duvet that smells of lavender. There's a fretful moment of uncertainty and a grasp for recollection—to figure out exactly where I am.

And then it hits me.

It all hits at once.

The sweet scent of her. All my achy limbs. Dani's side of the bed is cool to the touch, but her pillow still has a Dani-sized dent in it. I snuggle into the downy softness, a relieved breath shuddering out of me. I was an absolute train wreck last night—everything inside of me angry and tense, heart breaking all over her floor. It was insane (and maybe stupid) to go where I did. Never felt the urge before. But you hold tight on to every available lifeline when you're falling apart. And I needed her entire being to stop me from skidding into the depths.

I roll onto my back, fingering the chain around my neck and the familiar ridges and curves of the Seneca pendant. The elderly Italian woman who clasped it around my neck in Rome on my sixteenth birthday freaked me out at first. She had the air of a fortune teller—head scarf, a lazy eye, and giving off cryptic vibes. And she refused to take any money, claiming it was a gift—*for someone who looked like he could use a wise friend.*

Engraved on the back is a Seneca quote that became one of my favorites: "Time discovers truth."

How apropos that, last night, I had the years peeled back to reveal a different me—the quiet, shy teenager gone up in smoke, replaced by a man ready to live his best life, rising from the ashes with his beautiful phoenix. All this time, I've been waiting, wanting, and searching for a woman too impossible to believe in anymore. And then the universe delivers me to Dani. On the hallowed grounds of Nero Vino, no less.

It was all so dreamlike.

So fucking meant to be.

"Rhys?"

The door creaks open, and Dani's there, dressed in nearly nothing. Her nipples shine through the black lace slip trimmed with red bows. Sexy as hell, hair falling in loose cascades around her shoulders. Once again, I'm a guided missile locked onto my target.

I can't take my eyes off her.

"Hey there," I say, my voice thick with sleep.

"I just wanted to check in on you," her voice low and sensual behind that killer smile. "It's almost eleven."

"Almost time to wake up," I joke. "Come join me?"

I lift a corner of the duvet, and she climbs in, my arms banding around her. The smell of her leaves me reeling, and I bury my head into her neck, dizzy with the sudden wave of desire. Last night, we talked and talked and talked. At the crack of 3 three a.m., we finally dragged our exhausted asses (hers still tingling) into bed and conked out cold. Sleep came easy because we staked our ground rules to ride out this mess. No engaging with media, especially social media. If friends, family, or foes tried to dig for dirt, we shut them down. Dani said a fire without fuel fizzles fast, and we need this reduced to ash as of yesterday.

"Did you sleep okay?" she asks.

"Like a rock."

"Me too," she says. "I liked having a bath with you. It felt good getting clean together."

Right. The bubble bath. My skin smells like coconuts for a reason. But I can be excused for a momentary memory lapse. Dani left me with a functionless brain and a quivering mass of shot nerves.

She curls into me, her fingers weaving through my hair, massaging my scalp, turning me into mush.

"Your mom called and invited us for lunch," she says.

"At the house?"

"One o'clock."

Uncertainty ripples through me, paranoid thoughts crowding in. To step back in there after all this time—what would it feel like?

My body tenses against hers, and Dani asks, "Is that okay?"

"Yeah. But you don't have to come if you don't want to."

Dani reaches out and fingers my pendant. She asked me last night if I ever take it off. All I said was no. One day, I'll tell her how Seneca's words carried me through the rough patches. He's the father I never had.

"Correct me if I'm wrong," she says, "but I think you need me right now."

Call that the understatement of the year. Last night, we were both caught between a helpless surge of arousal and raw, new sensations. And when her moans turned into sharp cries, and I looked at where my body entered hers, both places, I knew life would never be the same.

She's my new world, and I can only pray that I'm hers.

"My mom really likes you," I say. "JC, too. And Sawyer," I add, somewhat reluctantly.

She snuggles into me, the sun reflecting off her pale skin, making her glow like some kind of apparition. "There's this other Trenton. You might know him. His name is Rhys. What's the verdict with him?"

"Last I heard, he wants to light you up. All day, every day."

Dani's hand slips under the duvet to stroke my finger, the one that went rogue. "Tell him he makes me want to do things I've never thought of before."

I smirk, loving this. "As the evidence shows, I've thought of many things."

Last night, her body rewarded mine with a sweet release of passion, while I technically did nothing. Hardly fair to let the woman of my dreams do all the work, as capable as she is. When I roll her onto her back, I take me with her. Her lips mold onto mine, our bodies crashing together. I want to yell out in happiness.

This is it. Pure ecstasy.

I inch lower and spread her thighs wide, settling between them. Her eyes look down into mine as if nothing in the world existed outside the two of us. I ignore the pain in my chest that isn't from facing more ghosts but the thought of future days without her in them.

I brush my lips against her wet folds, and Dani throws back her head with a low, sexy groan.

"I love how you respond to me," I murmur.

"It's cause and effect," she says, her voice mellow. "And you are one hell of a cause." She weaves her fingers into my hair again and draws me closer to her womanhood. "I want you inside me."

"Trust me, I'll get there."

No one deserves the burden of making me feel whole, but Dani makes me so much more than the sum of my broken parts. If this giddy, uncertain feeling that won't leave me alone is what I think it is, bring it on. Even if it's a big scary space of doubt filled with no guarantees. To feel love, however brief it might be, is better than never knowing the feeling at all.

But first, I need to dip my tongue into her center and slowly lick my way to the deviant pearls that got us into this mess in the first place.

♈︎

"You have that glow," JC says, "of a man getting serious action."

"It's called a tan." I help myself to the grapes Mom's housekeeper laid out for us, doing my best not to let my embarrassment show. JC can blab about sex like it's no big deal, but what happens between Dani and me under the sheets is our business.

JC munches on the banana he just peeled, his mouth twitching into that smile that is a free pass for almost everything—bottomless drinks, dates, forgiveness. It's funny how he felt larger than life to me growing up. Now, under the soaring ceilings of my parents' enormous kitchen, he looks normal-sized.

Or maybe the perception of myself has changed.

"If your drawing skills are any indication, she's a definite keeper."

I stare at him, inordinately proud of his mistimed humor. "Did you have to go there?"

He laughs, half-choking on the mouthful of banana. "Consider this a marketing coup. I don't even like rosé, but I'm willing to try it now."

I pelt a grape at him. Hard. "You're an idiot."

"Takes one to know one," he teases and lunges for the remaining tower of fat green grapes at the same time I do.

We rip off clusters of ammunition and prepare for battle on either side of the kitchen island. Our favorite childhood pastime involved launching grapes at each other. The best kind of war, if such a thing exists. A well-thrown grape can sting like hell but leaves no real damage.

Other than a sticky floor that needed constant mopping.

JC launches his tried-and-true attack—a rapid-fire succession that kept me cowering for cover as a kid. But I'm stronger now. And he's unprepared for the hurl of fruit pinging off his body.

"Dude!" he yelps. "Since when did you get all aggro?"

"Consider this making up for lost time," I say, ducking his green bullets.

"Oh, yeah?" He winds up his arm to launch a handful in my direction.

I duck, the buckshot spray of grapes whizzing over my head to connect with the impenetrable wall of muscle that enters the kitchen at the exact wrong time. Seeing JC's look of surprise, I turn, and there stands Sawyer, wearing a suit and his eternal frown.

Arms crossed. Eyebrows slashed into knives.

Like clockwork, time spinning backward, JC and I snap into our poses of obedience, waiting for the reprimand.

Sawyer flicks a piece of grape from his lapel and arches one dark brow. Despite his stiff exterior, his eyes are soft. Not quite welcoming, but that might have more to do with me.

"Not much has changed here, huh?"

No, but also, yes.

When Dani and I walked through the front door earlier and all the ghosts I'd been dreading didn't swarm me, it dawned on me that everything can change.

For the better.

Mom and I talked it out before Sawyer arrived, and she's (sort of) come to terms with the reality of what happened—made palatable by my promise never to let Dani out of my sight. And now I have to set aside my bruised ego, follow Dani's advice, and make things right with Sawyer.

I clear my throat. "Listen," I start, my voice sounding as awkward as I feel. "I didn't mean half the shit I said yesterday."

A flicker of profound uncertainty passes over his face. "And the other half?"

I fall quiet for a moment, recalling the endless messes JC and I created that Sawyer was tasked with cleaning up. Always looking out for us.

Like that long-ago night at the Commodore Ballroom, Vancouver's famous concert hall. JC was giving 'er on stage with his band, and me, smuggled in as an underage roadie, prowling in the dark corners so the bouncers wouldn't nab me.

When I came out of the john, I saw Sawyer hunched against the back wall by the bar, doing everything he could to stick out like a sore thumb in his blazer and dress shoes. He stood in the shadows, arms crossed, acting like it was a crime to smile. Eyes on the dude selling merch, because cash was king in those days, and it tended to disappear.

He was managing JC and his band even back then.

Representing the family biz because Dad gave him no choice.

At one point in my life, having to be related to Sawyer was its own special kind of misery. Maybe having a big brother pushing me to be better isn't the worst thing after all.

"You never went to bat for me when I needed it the most. That stung," I admit. "But I understand now why you didn't."

"There were only so many times I could save you." And with what sounds like grudging respect, Sawyer adds, "So you saved yourself."

"Is this where you two kiss and make up?" JC chirps in, his dumbass smile more blinding than the wall of stainless-steel appliances behind him.

Before either of us smacks him one, Mom and Dani enter the kitchen. Arms linked. Ear-to-ear smiles. Bestie patrol.

"Oh, Sawyer," Mom says. "I didn't hear you come in. Dani and I were in the study, looking at old photos."

Dani lays a flirty wink in my direction. "You were pretty cute with your long hair. All those ringlets. Pudgy legs."

A grape bounces hard off my forehead, and JC chortles a laugh. "Always a looker, that Rhys. Remember all the girls who used to call here, giggle and hang up? Mr. Heartbreaker."

I can feel my face go red from the collective gazes of everyone in the room landing squarely and humorously on me. "It's not like that ever amounted to anything."

Not like the scorched earth of smitten groupies JC left behind in high school. Or the emotional devastation of every girlfriend when he moved on to the next target.

Mom lays a protective hand on my shoulder, her sensitive third-born. "I spent the morning with your father. He's perked up immensely since yesterday. The nurse couldn't believe the transformation."

All the emotions of last night flood through my veins like a narcotic, making me feel woozy.

"Really?" I clear my throat to get the shake out of it. "That's great news."

And the little smile Dani gives me is one I tuck into the safety of my heart for all of eternity.

"Can we eat?" Sawyer asks. "I have to get back to the office."

"Isabel has set up everything in the dining room," Mom says, referring to her devoted housekeeper, now gray-haired and long in the tooth. "Tomato soup and grilled cheese sandwiches."

She beams at me, and my stomach flip-flopping has nothing to do with hunger. Lunch happens to be my favorite childhood meal.

"Let's go." She links her other arm through mine. "We have so much to catch up on."

Her loving gaze travels across all three of her children before landing on who is very obviously her newly adopted daughter-in-law. JC gives me an exaggerated eye roll. I'm done for, and he knows it. But who would have guessed that emotionally awkward Rhys scores big in the relationship department? Or that, in the house where I never felt remotely important as my brothers, where I lived in fear of punishment for being me, I can enjoy a meal untroubled, no longer pathetically in search of my father's approval.

I never thought I would say this, but it feels good to be home.

Chapter Thirty-One

DANI

I FIDGET WITH MY HAIR, KEEPING AN EYE ON THE HOMELESS GUY PUSHING his mangled shopping cart of bicycle parts along Hastings Street. Rhys finishes paying for our coffees and sets the tiny cortados on our table.

"Are you ready for this?" He eyes the tower of stacked sugar packets. My restless hands have been busy.

"Yes." I blow out the breath I've been holding. "And thank you for coming with."

He leans in to steal a quick kiss. "Are you kidding? Would not miss this for my life."

Four weeks in Vancouver have blown by in a haze of hospital visits, family time, and working out our frustrations on my standard-issue mattress. A certain someone keeps coming after me, and Rhys has had enough.

Today it ends.

We actually have two meetings on the agenda today, and I chose this coffee shop on purpose for our first tussle.

Brett will seethe when the low-profile tires on his precious Maserati touch rubber on the grimy streets of the downtown east side. Plus, Rhys can fly under the radar. In this neighborhood, the residents are on the lookout for their next fix, not an Internet personality.

I down the coffee in two gulps, just as Brett rolls in at noon on the dot. Suit impeccable. Two-hundred-dollar haircut and million-dollar ego. He struts over like he owns the place, heels of his hand-tooled tasseled loafers clicking on the tile floor. It gives me immense pleasure when his smug smile curdles, recognizing Rhys.

I accidentally forgot to mention that he would be at my side today.

"Is this your legal counsel?" He throws a disdainful look at the mesh tank top I asked Rhys to wear on purpose.

"Yes and no," Rhys takes the lead like he wanted to. "No, in that I don't hold a law degree. Yes, in that I have enough cash to drown you in lawyers if you don't back off."

Brett whips off his sunglasses and scowls, the emerald green of his eyes I once found alluring flashing with indignation. "Is that a threat?"

Rhys stares him down, zero submission. Giving no shits. "Absolutely."

"Why are you doing this?" I demand. "Slow news day? Time to kill?" I cut to the chase just to annoy him. Brett has an infinite capacity for combat. He loves to bicker as much as he loves to play power games.

In response, Brett shrugs, like *duh, do I have to ask*? "Any businessman protects his assets."

"You know those designs are mine. Created on my time, not yours."

"No, actually," he flips back, "I don't know. And if your hobo friend here wants to waste his money in court, bring it on."

"Are you that thirsty for attention?" Rhys shakes his head, beyond appalled. "Why else would you throw shade on Dani other than propping up your crushed ego?"

In the sticky silence, they size each other up. Brett is smaller than Rhys in every way. Uglier and meaner. A malignant little tumor. Hair blacker than his soul.

"Last I heard," Brett says with a snigger, "your artwork embarrassed Dani and an entire town."

Like a snake uncoiled, Rhys strikes. "Are you going to claim ownership of my drawings too?"

Brett laughs like it's the funniest thing he's ever heard, his bone-white teeth on full display. "I'm not interested in amateur hour from a fucking influencer who's eating my sloppy seconds. Is this the best you can do, Dani?" he asks. "Your version of 'Reach for the stars'?"

I feel the air between me and Rhys shift, his entire body tensing. Brett's abominable behavior deserves a punch in the face, but we promised each other to keep things cool. Yet it still feels like I've been slimed. At one point, I swallowed my pride for this fool. Now I fight back bile.

And try to keep my voice steady.

"You used me, for my work. For your own pleasure. And then you replaced me when you got bored. We both know I could have come after you, and still could, for the bullshit lay-off."

"But you didn't," he flips back. "And you won't."

"Because I've realized my worth."

Finally, his air of doing us a favor evaporates. "And you think this airhead stud muffin is going to bow down to your precious altar for the rest of your life? Better and younger is always around the corner. Right, dude?"

I'm not the kind of person who gets violent. But Rhys proved the other day that, when push comes to shove, his fists could do the talking. What he and I have brewing together is too big for a tiny annoyance like Brett, but it all happens so suddenly, it's beyond my ability to stop it.

Rhys stands, his chair screeching across the hardwood floor. His fingers twitch into a fist. I watch his arm swing and brace myself for the crunch of knuckle against bone.

But there's nothing but silence.

Between the curtain of my fingers, I peer out to assess the damage.

Rhys's fist hangs just shy of smashing Brett's pompous nose. Thank god for restraint. And I'll take to my grave the endless enjoyment of witnessing Brett cower.

"Why don't you spread your dirty dogma somewhere else, asshole?" Rhys bites out. "Dani is my person. I plan to make her morning coffee for the rest of her life. We're going to get old together. And you're just going to get old *and* ugly because that's who you are on the inside."

Brett adjusts his blazer, red-faced. Uncomfortable that he didn't live up to his personal standards of cutthroat idiot. This is a fitting place for him to go down: in a sketchy coffee shop, emasculated by an Adonis in board shorts who doesn't take shit from anyone.

Me? I'm so fiercely proud of Rhys, my heart wants to explode. My lover, all business.

"To summarize," Rhys says, "if you don't retreat your sorry suited ass to whatever hole you crawled out of, prepare for war." He crosses his arms, totally flexing in both manners of the saying.

I glare at Brett in utter disgust. The gaze he returns is dull at best, although I get the sense he is searching to find a biting reply.

"Screw both of you," is the best he can come up with. Then, in a truly shining example of douchebaggery, Brett shoots his final lame bullet at Rhys. "You'll be in her rearview mirror in no time, useless fuckboy."

Brett kicks aside his chair like a tantrum-throwing child and storms out. The lone barista, who watched the drama unfold from behind the pastry display, fiddles with her nose ring. There seems to be nothing more to add.

But then she says, wise beyond her twenty-odd years, "Adulting much?"

For some reason, Rhys and I find this outrageously and immensely humorous. I laugh until my stomach aches and Rhys pulls me into his arms. His eyes, rimmed with thick lashes criminally wasted on a guy, shine with victory.

Seeing me for not only who I am, but who I can be.

"Who are you and what have you done to Rhys?" I ask.

Smiling like a fool, he says, "Not bad, huh?"

"You might have a career in law after all, my little pit bull."

If anything calls for a celebratory kiss, this is it. Rhys weaves his hand up into my hair, tips my head back, and kisses me hot and open-mouthed. His demanding tongue punishes mine into the dark corners as the room, the sunny day, everything fades away, and I feel this ache of desire to take him right here, on any flat, available surface.

God only knows what else would have happened if the barista hadn't cleared her throat, sending us stumbling into the table and our cortado thimbles flying to the floor.

"Sorry," we sing-song simultaneously, giggling like pranksters.

Not sorry one iota.

🍷

Meeting number two—the Amelia Summit—commences at sundown. The sky has shifted from a brilliant bright blue to the indigo of approaching dusk, the moon hidden behind thinning summer clouds. My sister squirms awkwardly in her chair, caught between the past and the present.

The karmic journey of the three of us converges here, in my apartment, sitting at the Restoration Hardware dining room table I scored on Facebook Marketplace.

"I'm sorry," Amelia mutters, eyes downcast to her untouched bagel and cream cheese. "For everything. I'm not proud of what I did."

Rhys doesn't respond right away. He wants the power dynamic made clear from the start. She can sweat it out until he's ready to forgive and forget.

"I'd hope not," he finally says, arms banded tight across his chest.

After wading through the sludge of Trenton family drama and Rhys at my side earlier to banish Brett, the baton now passes to the Rialto sisters to clean up their side of the yard.

"The past is the past, Ames," I add. "And today is all about the future. Our future." I reach for Rhys's forearm, moving my thumb back and forth on his tanned skin like windshield wipers to soothe him. Now I can add "feisty" to the adjectives we use to describe him. "We need your word that what happens between us remains between us."

"Because if I can't trust you," Rhys interjects, laying it on heavy, "that will only hurt Dani in the end."

239

"I get it," Amelia grits out, a touch hangdog after the fifteen-minute browbeating Rhys laid down shortly after she arrived. "And I'm not the same person I was back then. I'm a mother. I have different priorities. Better priorities," she stresses.

Rhys leans back, his gaze landing on mine with the question, *what do you think?* We had intense discussions about this get-together all week. The ground rules he wants in place with Amelia. No hidden agendas or scheming intentions. No acting like a Crazy. If we're moving forward together, the slate starts fresh.

Amelia reaches across the table and waits for my hand to twine with hers. She's on fire, skin burning hot, no doubt from the heat of Rhys's interrogation. God, he's surprised me today. This entire *week*. How he's navigated it all with tenacious resolve.

"I'm sorry I never said anything. Hopefully, you understand why."

"Of course I understand." I tilt my head gently at Rhys, the gesture implying we've put her through enough. "And we will never say anything about why your podcast ended. Or utter a word of this to Dean."

Something flickers in the depths of Amelia's baby blues. Surprise? Definitely shock. An understanding that we mean business. (With some low-key flexing if required.)

"Thank you," she says, the words sounding snagged in her throat. Then she tucks two freshly ash-blond locks behind the pink shells of her ears and offers a peace pipe in the form of dinner with Dean and the twins.

Rhys takes a few seconds before replying, "If Dani's cool, I'm cool."

From the simmering intensity in his eyes, I know tonight when he touches me, it will be fierce and unforgiving.

I'm cool with that.

Chapter Thirty-Two

RHYS

It still feels like summer in Osoyoos if heat is the benchmark. But the leaves on the trees have shifted into bright fall yellows and reds, and the orchards heave with apples. With the zoo of cars and families packed up and gone home, Main Street feels like a ghost town. As we drive down the strip, I quietly tally all the businesses—the ones Dani and I will hit tomorrow during our apology tour. I owe Osoyoos and Evelyn that much.

Idling at a red light, Dani looks over. "What are you thinking of?"

I pop a few jellybeans from the bag in my lap, chewing thoughtfully. "How different it all feels."

Dani's hand drifts off the gearshift to scrub my bare knee. "Because you feel different."

Isn't that the truth? Nothing plays out guaranteed is the lesson I've learned from this trip. From misplaced bitterness (Sawyer) to delusional ex-bosses (Brett) to woefully off-the-mark sisterly obsessions

(Amelia), situations—and yes, Sawyer, the optics—can change if I allow them to.

And change me in the process.

"Oh, hey, I forgot to mention, Bettina called when we stopped at the fruit stand," I say. "She's happy to help out once we get up and running."

"Really?" Dani is downright shocked by this news. "She recovered from the trauma?"

Chic and stark in a black Helmut Lang dress, dark bangs cut viciously straight, Bettina sat stony-faced in her office when Dani and I dropped by last week to share our plans. For years, I thought nothing could dent Bettina's Teflon coat. But her blazing blue eyes misted over, and her Bavarian accent shrilled with despair.

"Rhys!" she wailed. "You've worked so hard to get here. You can't quit now. Please reconsider."

I suspect the anticipated drop in her income fueled her unusual display of emotion because I've actually worked very little. The fundamental thing I want to change.

Together with Dani.

"We have to tell Evelyn at dinner tonight," Dani says, mirroring my thoughts. "I can't pull off Divine Debauchery with this hanging over my head."

The party to end all parties continues, despite Gail's protests and the community upheaval. Calvin lands in three days. Gia and JC, tomorrow afternoon. Evelyn insisted I attend as part curiosity, part adhering to one point of my mostly unfulfilled contract. But also to prove she stands behind me and Dani one hundred percent.

Gotta love that lady.

"You know she'll be cool, right?"

Dani mulls that over with a sound of uncertainty. "I hope so."

"What else is going on in your mind?" I can tell from how she bites her bottom lip that she hasn't told me everything. I'm catching on to the ways of my girl.

The light turns green, and she guns it. "The day you arrived, we chatted in my office, and she said all the good employees leave her eventually, and that I would too." She sighs, a little wistful. "Not that I expected to work here forever."

"Judging from that," I say, "she won't be too shocked."

She sneaks a quick look at me. "I feel like I owe her indefinitely. She's afforded us so much grace."

If there is such a thing as a one-woman battle, Evelyn stormed the goddamn Bastille. She took all the haters to task, claiming that every woman and man has fantasies, and why string me up for mine? Especially in the form of personal, vindictive slander. How would they feel if their private thoughts were aired to the world?

Apparently, most of the Osoyoos citizens sympathized.

The truth will unfold tomorrow when we go door to door.

All I can do is show my utmost regret and pray they accept it. The bright spot is that the fangirls jumped ship weeks ago, disillusioned after I cut out and my feed went dark.

What a relief to drive into the winery without a security check or the need to look over our shoulders. But as Dani drives up the hill to drop me off, a hint of sadness creeps in. This is the place where our story started.

It will always hold a special place in my heart.

Parked, with the engine idling, Dani kisses my cheek. "I'll swing by just before six."

"You'll be sleeping in my bed tonight, right?" I clarify.

She affects a pose of surprise. "I thought that was a given after weeks of suffering on my shoddy mattress?"

Suffering? Does she mean tangled up and sheened in sweat, breathing deep and calm? The idea of that makes me laugh. "Like I said, I'll sleep on rocks as long as I have the most important things surrounding me."

She beams back a smile as bright as mine. "Have I moved up the ranking list? Bumped your precious coffee from the top slot?"

I wind my fingers in her hair and gently tug her over the console. She provokes the same reaction, day after day. "You are my new number one, Dani. Now and forever."

Our lingering sinful kiss would steam windows in winter but gets cut short with a sharp *whack*, followed by, "Well, well, well. Look at you two lovebirds."

We both jump back, startled to see Nicole, who must have wandered up from the vineyards when she saw Dani's truck.

"Hey there," I roll down the window, "are you joining us at dinner?"

She leans on the sheet metal with a lazy smile, dressed in her best farmyard duds and face smudged with dirt. "I would, except this grubby little number has a date."

Dani squeals excitedly, leaning over my lap to say, "Congrats! A local?"

"She manages one of the hotels in Kelowna." Nicole cuts me a genial smile. "Not as hot as you, mister, but who is?"

"Good luck. And you'll be at the party?" Dani asks.

Nicole belts out a laugh. "Are you kidding? The biggest ticket in town? I am so primed. And if you don't mind helping this old grape get Roman-ready, I could use your guidance. Seems I need some help in the fashion department."

Dani side-eyes me. My grin is just as impish as hers.

Love is in the air, and it's catching.

"Well, dears, here's to a great and final Divine Debauchery." Evelyn raises her wine glass and waits for us to cheer back, but Dani and I falter, caught off guard.

"Final?" Dani isn't ready to believe it.

Evelyn sips her wine and sets the glass beside a plate piled with BBQ chicken, herbed salad, and roasted yams. Golden hour drenches the patio in warm, magical light and the emerald-hued lake shimmers in the heat waves.

"I took a time out while you two were gone," she says. "Some good old-fashioned soul-searching. With all the commotion, it felt like the apocalypse was no longer avoidable."

"But this event is legendary!" Dani's voice flies to a heavenly register. "It's *you!*"

Evelyn smiles fondly at her. "All legends eventually retire. Or get put out to pasture."

I voice my surprise, just as astonished as Dani. "You're not giving up Nero Vino, are you?"

"Not yet," Evelyn assures us. "I have a few more good years in me."

"But?" Dani asks. Because it's there, waiting for us.

"Not a *but*," Evelyn hedges. "More like an acknowledgment. That living and dying inside my comfort zone lacks verve. A change of the guard can do wonders. And Tomas, irritating shit that he is, does know the land and the business inside and out. And before you lose your cool," she says to Dani, who is on the verge of doing just that. "He and I had a sit-down after the dust settled. A tête à tête, as they say in France. He *is* family, after all. The only family I have left. If my poor Hugo hadn't been run over by that tractor, we might have patched things up sooner."

Dani pauses, a forkful of salad hovering on her lips. "Is that how Hugo died?"

"I know, tragic. But, yes. Anyway, Tomas and I have decided not only to be civil but work out an arrangement where he can eventually take over."

Dani looks crestfallen. I have yet to meet this character, but if Evelyn is willing to give him a shot, he can't be a total idiot. I finish chewing my mouthful of chicken. "What will you do when you give it up?"

"Work on my slice serve," she muses. "Stop and smell the roses. All that gobbledygook they keep saying is good for the soul."

I'm speechless. In this short time, Evelyn intertwined with her vineyard felt as constant as the sun rising in the east—perpetual and enduring.

Evelyn nibbles on a piece of charred yam. "In the interim, with an eye to handing off this operation in its most stellar form, I need solid hands and brains to help me out. What do you think? Are you two up for it?" She lowers her sunglasses to peer at us.

"Us?" It squeaks out of Dani like she's sucked on helium.

"Who else?" Evelyn asks with a shrug.

"Well, uhm..." Dani looks nervously at me.

"Actually." I clear my throat. Our secret sits on the tip of my tongue, waiting for release. "We have some news to share."

Evelyn's face gives away nothing. No surprise, or alarm. And she listens to every stumbling, fumbling word that spills from our mouths. Our vision for the agency is still forming. Half-ideas and concepts. But we are undeterred. And our optimism shines through.

"Well," Evelyn says, and I can tell she's impressed. "This delights me to no end. Dani, I'm so proud of you. I know this was your dream. And what better way to start than with a loving partner?" She reaches across the table to squeeze my hand. "I had a feeling about you two from the start. Dani was so nervous about your arrival. I figured it had more to do with a jumpy heart than jumpy nerves."

Dani blushes. I have no clue why her crush remains an ongoing source of embarrassment. Based on the very vocal proceedings of the past few weeks, every neighbor in her building knows how she feels about me.

"And what role will you play other than financial backer?" Evelyn asks me.

I take a swallow of wine. "Dani's assistant? Office boy?" I smile at the irony. I'd escaped a similar fate sixteen years ago only to come full circle to the same entry-level job.

Evelyn tips her wineglass in my direction with a crafty smile. "I believe you might have a career in illustration."

Dani laughs so hard, she starts choking. Me? I'm clapping her on the back, stricken for a millisecond. "That could be in the cards."

Dani's choking fit settles, and Evelyn pivots the conversation back to the immediate future. "Knowing all this, how long do I have you for?"

"We can discuss. I don't want to leave you high and dry," Dani insists.

"No, of course not." Evelyn waves off a pesky fly that's been buzzing around then gives us the full measure of her attention. "I'll have to hire a replacement to handle the day-to-day, on-the-ground stuff, but what if Nero Vino was your first client?"

Dani and I share a look. Excitement creeps into my soul. Who says no to a golden opportunity like that?

"We'd be honored," Dani says, a little breathless.

"We can create all your marketing materials," I jump in, every stitch of me full of belief. "Manage your website. All the ad campaigns."

Evelyn beams at me. "Look at you go. She'll make an executive out of you yet."

"Hold all the discussion," Dani says. "I need to use the bathroom."

Evelyn waves vaguely in the direction of her three-thousand-square-foot ground floor. "Take a right after the pool table. The powder room is the first door on your left." As soon as Dani is out of earshot, Evelyn's face brightens. "I love this," she gushes. "For both of you."

I lean back in the chair, profoundly, quietly happy. I'm grinning now and buzzing too. "We're psyched. And to help you out would be dope." The crust of my joy cracks a little as I continue, "And I wanted to say, it's not fair for me to keep the fee. I did a week of work. And you shelled out for Francis and Rita."

Evelyn waves off my offer like another bothersome fly. "I have enough money. You tuck that into your pocket. With the caveat that you splurge on something grand and sparkly for Dani when the time comes. She deserves the best."

Damn right, she does.

Not only is she deserving, but I will support, encourage, and fulfill all her dreams because she makes me feel like the best version of myself.

What more can a guy ask for?

Chapter Thirty-Three

DANI

The final edition of Divine Debauchery is underway, and what a spectacle. Evelyn transformed Osoyoos into ancient Rome, and no picture can do it justice. Ten-foot-tall Doric columns ring the outdoor theater, and actors clad in gladiator regalia prowl the property carrying thick shields and glittery sharp swords. The crowd is buzzing, high on life and assorted things, nibbling on the platters of Italian delicacies offered by servers in linen tunics and sandals.

The only thing missing is Nero himself.

But I have my own Roman god—debauched in his own, special way and looking mighty fine tonight.

After a solid hour of socializing, Rhys and I are soaking it all in from the stage where Calvin Harris will momentarily light it up. The lake behind us is dark and still under a dome of stars. The late summer air holds just the right amount of heat.

"You look amazing in that toga." I adjust the crown of olive leaves tucked in his flowing locks. "And you are rocking the eyeliner. I told you it would look fierce."

He fixes me with his pleased eyes, blazing bright with desire and sexy as hell rimmed in black kohl. Evelyn insisted we wear the same outfits from our infamous photoshoot—we'd kept them, for obvious reasons—and I felt very self-conscious strolling past a poster-sized ad capturing our most scandalous moment in the vineyard.

But I blushed harder during ice wine aperitifs last night when a tipsy Evelyn admitted they all knew what had happened.

"The polite thing was to pretend," she'd said. "You were so out of sorts."

Rhys had slid his eyes to mine and gave a hopeless shrug. Unbelievable. He knew they knew. I'd been the lone one out, hyperventilating in Yvette's bathroom and praying for the earth to swallow me whole.

Not fair.

I could blame them for stretching out my agony.

But in a full circle moment, I, Dani Rose Rialto, have made peace with blame. And with the internet. Because, without it, my wine label designs would not have flown through cyberspace to spark Evelyn's interest. She never hires me, and I don't end up here, on a star-soaked night in Osoyoos, wrapped in the easy, masculine strength of Rhys Trenton's arms.

"I better keep you on a short leash," he murmurs, nuzzling my neck with soft kisses. "All these Hollywood players have been casting looks."

The double bill of Calvin and Gia in dusty Osoyoos proved too iconic to miss, hence the star power on display. Half of young Hollywood wanders the grounds, their desperate agents promising me obscene amounts of money, along with their firstborns, in exchange for tickets.

I felt like a powerful wizard holding the cure to cancer.

"Dani! Rhys!" Unrecognizable in a hot-pink tinsel wig, Evelyn waves at us to join her at the champagne bar, where she holds court with a stately redhead dressed in sensible pumps and a knee-length skirt. "Let me introduce you to the princess!"

"A real princess?" I whisper to Rhys as we make our way over.

He scopes out the modestly dressed woman, far less impressed than my awestruck booty. "I think she's from the Netherlands."

While we gab with modern-day royalty, I spot Gia and JC huddled under a pop-up tent near the stage. Their conversation looks intense. Are they discussing the setlist? Or how to outdo Calvin? My money is on the latter.

Not that they have to try hard.

Rhys and I dropped in on one of their rehearsals in Vancouver and, holy shit. The noise was astounding. The cinder-block studio could barely contain the explosive energy. JC's blistering solos acted like a fire starter to Gia's flame, coaxing her throaty howl into earth-shattering octaves.

Passion seared into every note.

Hotter than lava.

Panty-soaking sexy.

What will happen when they throw down their incendiary heat onto this hedonistic crowd? I can hardly wait!

The stage lights suddenly illuminate, and a murmur of excitement ripples through the crowd. Kinetic humans swarm to the front, flowing, charging up. Ready to rock.

We say our goodbyes to the princess, and Evelyn shouts after us, "Enjoy! And thank you for the music."

Hand tight over mine, Rhys shoulders his way to the front of the stage. Spotlights beamed up into the sky create dizzying circles as roadies blast dry ice, shrouding the stage in smoky mystery. The energy feels tightly coiled. My skin tingles. Anticipation times infinity.

Silhouetted in smoke, Calvin wanders onto the stage with a casual wave, and the heavily wasted crowd roars their approval. Rhys introduced me to him earlier, and he was the sweetest guy. Unassuming. Tired from the long overnight flight. One of the hottest DJs on the planet, and he was just like you and me, drinking hot tea and shooting the shit with Rhys.

It was funny to see him in fanboy mode. Obvs obsessed.

Settled behind his wall of tech, Calvin throws on headphones, and the first notes crackle through the loudspeakers.

Wine glasses toast the sky with a chorus of *Fuck yeahs!*

"Good evening, Osoyoos," Calvin says from somewhere in the smoke cloud. "Thank you for having me."

Rihanna's opening lyrics of "This is What You Came For" ring out, and a surge of party bros and damsels crush around Rhys and me. He protects me from the mob, arms cradled around my shoulders like a human cage.

"Stay right here," he whispers in my ear. "I got you."

"You're not going to dance?"

As if. The music has kicked in, and his body sways to the beats.

"Hell yeah," he says with the biggest smile. "Get ready to shake that fine booty."

I'll never be like him—inhabiting the music, becoming it—but whatever.

This buttoned-up woman can shake it just fine.

Calvin's massive hits keep rolling, pounding the crowd with bone-rattling bass and rave-worthy speed. By the time the final notes of "We Found Love" drift into the summer night, the sweat-soaked audience is utterly exhausted. They scatter, seeking bathrooms or complimentary rosé refills.

Rhys excuses himself to hook up with JC before their set, and I encourage him to take his time. When Rhys stumbled into his brother's arms at the hospital, it felt like Jesus moving into the light. Their deep connection struck me all the way to my toes.

Thick as blood.

A bond he needs to nurture.

Along with his other brother.

I rehydrate and do a lap of the property, checking my phone for an update from Sawyer. Nothing since his last message when he said he'd be here by eight. It's almost nine-thirty. Per town guidelines, Gia and JC have to wrap by eleven, and there is no way Sawyer will miss their act.

I send a quick *Where are you?* text and fire off a few celebrity photos to Amelia, who is living vicariously through me tonight. She promptly responds, shouting via text:

AR: Olivia Rodrigo? FAWK!!! If Taylor Swift shows up, I will hate you forever for not inviting me.

DR: Gotta run. Looks like I have to say hi to Lily-Rose Depp.

AR: Did I mention I hate you???

I tuck my phone back into my bra, smiling. Proud. And yeah, a little triumphant.

Sorry, sis. It is finally my time.

Rhys and I stay camped out front and center for the main event. Mild-mannered Calvin let his beats do the talking, staying silent through his one-hour set. But when Gia struts onto the stage with a booming, "Yo, bitches!"—welcome to the new world order.

The crowd goes bonkers.

Gia's all hair flips and snapping fingers. A saucy little minx in fish-nets, a leopard-print onesie, and ballet flats, she leans on the mic stand to take a sip of Fireball whiskey she brandishes from a gold fanny pack draped around her tiny waist.

"Are y'all ready to burn this place down?" She holds a hand to one ear and leans toward the crowd, inciting drunken bellows of approval. "Because Nero, that crazy motherfucker, burnt Rome to the ground. And if I follow in anyone's footsteps, it will be a notorious legend. Capiche?"

More hoots and hollers.

Someone screams, "Fuck ya!"

"Sorry," Gia says, motioning for more noise, already a superstar with an innate ability to work a crowd. "I can't hear you. Are we burning this place to the ground?"

Just when I thought Calvin had sapped all the energy from the crowd, a thundering howl erupts that would wake the dead.

Or all the senior citizens of Osoyoos who watched TV and went to bed early.

I glance up at Rhys. He's shaking his head, primed and ready. "This is going to get crazy."

How can it not when you have a mad scientist as a musical ringleader?

"That's the spirit, MOFO'S," Gia continues, grinning wide. "Yeah, yeah, yeah. Now, I want y'all to dig deep and give it up for our very special guest star. The man, the myth, the legend. The guy who can make the guitar orgasm…Mr. JC Trenton!!!"

For a split second, there is absolute silence. Sawyer kept the lid tight on JC's appearance, and not a soul here expected to hear his name. But he is a legend, a living one with a legion of fans who never saw him play live. And now, he's going to burn down the house with Gia?

Not even fingers jammed into both ears deaden the surge of sound, louder than a jet plane taking off. I'd be scared shitless accosted by such torrid reverence, but JC wanders onto the stage, no sign of nerves beneath his beaming smile.

Beside us, two young actresses are having meltdowns, fumbling for their phones.

What the actual fuck? Oh. My. God. This can't be real.

Gia introduces the rest of the band, and they settle in for last-minute tuning before blasting us in the face with Pop My Cherry's biggest hit, the fiery sing-along, "Blackest Nights."

And we're off.

For most of the set, Rhys's erection throbs against my butt. He's had a few drinks. Handsy and kissing me sloppily, just missing my lips. Giving off wild, untamed energy. When Gia announces their final song, he makes his move.

We're squished like sardines in the packed, blissed-out crowd, but no one notices his hand disappear between the folds of my toga. He slides a finger past my thong, teasing my barbell with sharp little flicks.

"Mmm," he mumbles. "You drive me crazy."

The encore kicks off with a familiar refrain. Gia launches into the lyrics about leaving a good job in the city, working for the man. Big wheels keep on turning.

"Proud Mary"? No way!

I scream my approval, and Rhys's finger starts moving in devastating, precise circles until my clit hardens into a tight bud, blood rushing to my pussy. I melt into him, grinding twerky ass movements onto the solid wall of his desire until I feel his short, clipped breath raging hot in my ear.

"Are you ready to get lit?"

Gia stalks the stage, belting out lyrics like she's Tina Turner reincarnated. She blasts into the first chorus, and Rhys plunges his finger deep inside me.

"Oh, fuck!" I gasp, my body faint with sensation. Stars in my head.

"That's the intention," he mutters, finger-fucking me slow and steady, talking dirty into my ear.

No space between us. Just raw, burning desire.

What happens next is a full-blown musical/erotic climax that will live in my memory forever.

The band is swinging, tightly flawless even as they sound warm and loose. JC hoists his guitar skyward, a roar from the drunken masses to blister them with one last solo.

Someone yells, "Burn the house down!"

Gia catches that, flashes a thumbs-up, and grins. As the band surges toward the peak, she takes a long swig from her water bottle, tosses it over her shoulder, and plants her feet wide in a commanding A-stance. At the same time, Rhys starts working my clit over until I'm gasping for breath, tension building in waves.

And then…

JC charges across the stage and drops to his knees, sliding clean between Gia's spread legs. His back arches as he tears into the solo, the noise bruising the air, slamming into me like a physical force. Gia leans back, and a strong and mighty stream of water arcs from her mouth. Backlit by the dry ice smoke, the water sparkles and tumbles into JC's open mouth. Perfectly timed. Impossible.

I watch it happen, but I swear my eyes are playing tricks. Because how???

"Rhys," I pant. "What the hell?"

And he answers with grunts and dark animal sounds, driving his hot hardness into my ass. Not that I blame him. If I had a dick, it would be pointing due north and then some because JC and Gia are real-time possessed. Sonic soulmates synched on some higher level, conjuring up sexy black magic impossible to rehearse.

The band speeds up the tempo, the deep, punishing bassline thundering faster and faster, drums going manic. Rhys responds by frantically tag-teaming between scrubbing my clit and fingering my seam. Shockwaves of pleasure spiral through me, tension building and building like the music. Nothing has ever felt like this: ruinous and dirty and so right.

I ache for him. Burn for him to slide inside me.

I'm barely aware of JC, playing like he's not hearing the crowd flip out, utterly lost in a torrent of furious notes, like I'm lost in the waves pushing me higher and higher. And Gia sways in the hot wind, a genie conjured by her musical magic lamp writhing on the stage between her legs.

Her voice pitches louder and louder.

Rolling. Rolling. Rolling.

I feel the muscles of Rhys's chest tighten against my back. If he thrusts any harder into my backside, I'm going to blow apart. "You can only want me," he growls into my ear.

Exquisite pain funnels lower between my legs until I'm all feeling and floaty, with no sense of time, space, or reality. The musical crescendo hits at the same time the obliterating spike of release rips through me. Black dots smother my vision, me bucking hard against his hand in the desperate desire to be one with him, the climax so intense, a shattered groan leaves my lungs in one delirious exhalation.

Rhys slips his thumb into the dark wetness of my mouth, muzzling my cries. His other arm clutches my waist as he drives into my backside with deep, rhythmic spasms, biting my neck, the feral sound of his release lost in the ear-splitting roar of the crowd and the spray of fireworks lighting up the sky.

Everyone wants a piece of future history. The crowd is ten deep backstage, jammed shoulder to shoulder under the pop-up tents. There were so many fireworks for the finale, it still smells like a bomb went off.

Gia spots me and drags me in a fierce, sweaty hug. "Whadda ya think, sistah?"

"Oh my god, Gia. That was like…" I trail off, and she fills in the blank for me.

"Like we were having sex?"

I stifle a laugh. Both them and us. "Kinda."

She runs a hand over her mop of raven hair. Eyeliner melting down her face, lips stained scarlet, she's the hottest thing in a crowd of a thousand hotties.

"Sweet. I wanted that effect. No time for basic in this world. And you." She stands back to admire my ensemble. "On fleek, snatched, and lit, baby!"

She grooves to some silent beat in her head, wiry, jungle cat energy humming off her as she scans the crowd. I follow suit, triangulating on unfamiliar faces when my gaze collides with Sawyer's. He's on the sidelines, slightly removed from the craziness. Dress shirt buttoned to the neck. He holds up his highball glass in greeting.

Gia waves back and shouts into my ear, "What do you think of Mr. FBI?"

"I think you're in good hands," I yell back.

Gia nods, not quite agreeing. Skeptical, like any creative wildcard would be with a suit. It looks like she has more to say, but a fan storms between us, fawning and gushing praise. I take that as my cue and cut across the crowd to join Sawyer.

"You made it." I elbow his arm, and he loosens up by one percent. "What a performance, huh?"

"Classic JC," he says. "Bringing down the house."

"Your instinct to pair them was spot on. You can't buy that level of chemistry."

His eyes slide off mine as he drains his drink. "Rhys might have convinced you otherwise, but I know what I'm doing."

A flash of low-level shame passes through me. Rhys didn't exactly sell Sawyer when I asked if he had designs on me. And I judged Sawyer—lumped him in with the likes of Brett. If that's not deserving of penance...

Clunkily, I try to change the subject. "You should join us on Corfu for New Year's if you have the time."

He considers this and offers a slight shrug. "That might work."

A silence falls. Ninety-nine percent of me wants to find Rhys, but I hang back, observing Sawyer as he catalogs the famous crowd. Sizing up future clients? Probably. But this time I don't lay down judgment. After the shock of Amelia's secrets wore off, I sat with the idea of how even the people closest to us harbor thoughts and feelings we can never understand.

In Sawyer's case, what is the personal cost of being on the money all the time? Of always being the strong one?

Maybe he doesn't know any better.

And, maybe, work is all he has.

Last night, when Rhys cooked a big fat Greek feast for me, JC, and Gia in the villa, he mentioned a woman named Jasmine King, the feisty daughter of a Hong Kong billionaire and Sawyer's long-term girl-friend. They were destined for the altar, and something blew up. Exactly what, nobody knows. Jasmine disappeared. Sawyer refused to discuss it. JC said he's never been the same.

I think of that now. Deep down, a vague ribbon of hope runs through me. I touch his arm and smile. "Rhys would love it if you came. JC and Gia will be there too."

Sawyer glances at my outfit and then lifts his eyes to mine. Written all over my face is the message: we're in this together. Let's make the best of it.

His brow cocks. "Party like it's 1999?"

"Toga optional."

Finally, a laugh. "Bedsheets were never my thing. Not a good look on a paper-pusher."

I gauge his expression and find it as light as his tone.

"Dani!"

At the far end of the tents, Rhys wildly motions for me to join him. His golden, bright beauty blazes in a brilliant smile. So different from thirty minutes ago, us trembling under the night sky, my body twitching from aftershocks. Rhys was very hot, his skin on fire against mine. What we witnessed was once in a lifetime. A fusion that knocked the breath out of me. Never mind that Rhys came all over my toga for a second time.

"That was incredible!" I'd gushed, meaning in every way possible.

And Rhys, still breathing hard, had said, "I told you he was the Trenton with real talent."

"Number one, I beg to differ. But," I paused to catch my breath and center my still-melting core, "those two. Together."

His eyes swept over me, a quick, loaded glance. "That's what I'm worried about."

On a quiet and still August night in Vancouver, Rhys and I watched the sunset at Kitsilano Beach while he shared what went down with JC years before. Online news stories tell the tale of JC's musical career and subsequent breakdown, but my heart crumbled with Rhys's first-hand account of how burnout took his brother down. It feels like something still lingers with JC, but Rhys wouldn't say more.

"It will be okay," I assured him. "We'll both watch out for him."

Rhys hugged me tight, squeezing all the remaining air out of my lungs. "Thank you," he had whispered. "For being my person."

Sawyer elbows me, and I snap out of the memory haze.

He chin-nods at the still-waving Rhys. "Go make my little brother happy." And then, with softness in his eyes, "He deserves it."

I drop a quick kiss on his stubbled cheek that smells like musk and expensive leather. "Thank you for everything. Don't leave without saying goodbye."

And I wind my way through the spirited crowd to that smile of pure joy, shining on me, the luckiest woman in the world.

Chapter Thirty-Four

RHYS

December 29th
Corfu, Greece

LIKE FORREST GUMP INFAMOUSLY SAID ABOUT A BOX OF CHOCOLATES, YOU never know what you're going to get with a Corfu sunrise. The morning sky is as delicate as a sigh. An unfiltered, jaw-dropping canvas painted bright pink with streaks of golden yellow. With the colors reflected on the glassy, still surface of the Ionian Sea, it's impossible to tell where the sky ends and the water starts.

Hands down, this will be my favorite sunrise.

The first one with Dani in my heart, and in my house.

She landed late last night. As soon as she fell into my arms, not even the fragrance of eighteen hours of travel wafting off her could dampen the thrill. We threw ourselves into each other, making up for three days of lost time. Full-blown, unfiltered, soulmate-perfect mayhem.

Sheets stained with desire.

I swing in my hammock, strung between two gnarled olive trees, and a quiet buzz of happiness thrums through me. I listen to the bird-songs and the tide slapping at the rocks far below on the sugar sand beach. Breathing in the scents of sea and earth, the thyme and rosemary growing wild, I can't help but smile and think of her. Dani lives in my brain, in my soul, somewhere beyond sense and reason, and I'm trying to reconcile the depth of my longing for her with the reality that she also needs to sleep.

I kept her awake until the first light of dawn, poor thing.

I'll give her at least another hour.

That gives me ample time to process my new glittering, hopeful world. Since ditching the insanity of influencer life, I've filled up my days with one mission in mind. Well, two. The launch of our agency and pulling off the biggest job of my life: Dani's partner.

So far, so good.

We left Osoyoos at the end of September and moved (with the damn bed) into the house I bought in Vancouver. Thanksgiving and Christmas had us shuttling between her parents' place and mine. Gordon and Deb Rialto welcomed me as their own son, and not once did they bring up what Dani had quietly informed them of when they returned from South America.

The two nicest people I'll ever meet. I appreciate how chill they are.

Unlike Mom.

She has fixated on us like one of her renovation projects and manages the upgrade of Rhys to serious coupledom with a vigor that borders on extreme. Emails clutter my inbox with decor suggestions for the house in Vancouver or cooking classes for couples. Honeymoon-approved vacay destinations.

Just in case you need some help, darling!

And I'm like, Mom, settle down.

I have survived for sixteen years on my own.

If I can call the endless meandering of my hazy hot mess years surviving.

Now I have an actual purpose, and I become lost deeper in the fantasy of us by the second. Living our dream life in Corfu and

Vancouver, cuddled in each other's arms, drunk on love and possibilities.

I can hardly fucking wait for it all.

"Hey you," Dani says.

I startle, an unbalanced mess of arms and legs trying to sit up too fast in the hammock. And there she is. Bundled into one of my hoodies, barefoot with bedhead, and hands down the sexiest woman alive.

"Morning. I didn't expect you to surface for hours."

She pads over with a delighted laugh. "I couldn't sleep. I'm too excited."

Palming my cheek, she brushes her mouth over mine with a soft, sleepy kiss. I can smell the tangy musk of us on her breath when she says, "And I missed your warmth."

"We can fix that."

I spread my legs to accommodate her. And she does an okay job for a hammock rookie, laughing as she clambers in, utterly graceless. She burrows against my chest, snuggling into the fleece blanket to ward off the chill as a giant sigh escapes her mouth. The sun is a golden ball of fire, slowly rising out of the clear blue water, and I can taste salt at the back of my throat, cut with the faint scent of chlorine from the infinity pool.

"It's so pretty," Dani murmurs. "The palm trees and all the flowers. Your garden and pool. Exactly what it looked like in your videos."

When the chatty real estate agent toured me through the palazzo a decade ago, I snapped it up, no questions asked. All the security measures I craved came pre-baked into the design: at the end of the road, high on a cliff, and fortified like a bunker. And now it finally feels less like a jail and more like a home with Dani here. I band my arms around her, nuzzling into that secret pocket of her neck where she goes wild when I nibble the delicate skin. I never want to stop touching her.

"Speaking of videos..." I fix on a spot on the horizon, readying myself. "I wanted to bounce an idea off you."

"Go for it," she says.

A quick recap of what's happened since August. I haven't posted at all. Bowed out of pre-existing commitments and turned down new ones. With radio silence on my feed, the comments on my last reel have tipped the ten thousand mark. Variations of the following:

OMG. Is this the end of Rhys?

Dude, I'd be a no-show if I were you.

WTF people???? Leave the poor man alone.

I wasn't sure how to end it all, but on the marathon Boxing Day flights back here, the vision became crystal clear.

Dani listens carefully, weighing each word. "I think that's brilliant," she says. "But is it wise to kill your account?"

"The Trenton Troublemaker era feels done. I'm over it. This is the Rose Dylan Agency era."

She twists her head to face me. "You like that name?"

"It's grown on me," I admit. "It sounds classy. Not too feminine or masculine. Just right."

I balked at first. Did I want Bob Dylan haunting me? Dad was obsessed with Dylan and drilled into me as a kid that I should be honored to carry his name. And me, Rhys Dylan Trenton, giant shit-head and lover of beats, argued that a creaky whine was a horrible choice to be the voice of a generation.

That did not pave the way for a better relationship between my father and me. But now that he's on the mend, the dark periods behind us, we're bonding. One small step at a time.

"I like it because it links us together, without being obvious," Dani says. "Only our closest peeps know our middle names."

"And the R and D also represent our first names," I point out. "Did you realize that?"

She glances up at me with a look of *come on*.

"Careful," I mock-warn. "I might be your lowly assistant on paper, but I wield considerable power."

She pokes my ribs and laughs. "Are you talking staying power?"

"The first time didn't count," I remind her, poking her back.

We're both chuckling as she sets the hammock in motion, rocking us back and forth. "Every time counts," she says. "The Rose Dylan agency is a team effort."

I reach for my phone, buried between our legs. Galvanized. "Then let's do this. One take. No time to overthink it."

"Now?" she asks like I'm losing my mind, when, in fact, my head is in the clearest space it's been in years. "I haven't showered."

"Me either. Level playing field."

She blows out a deep breath. Attempts to wrangle her hair. Pulls the blanket over us because she is naked from the waist down. "Okay. Ready."

I open the camera app like I've done a million times. Find the best angle. Against the rising sun, we're backlit, a little blown out. Time is of the essence.

My finger hovers on the record button, pausing a moment to let the rush of memories spool through my mind. Will I miss this? Maybe here and there. But like Evelyn said, living and dying within your comfort zone cripples your ability to do more. And my man Seneca said it best:

He who is brave is free.

I press record.

"Hey, everyone," is how I start it. "Long time, no post. As you can see, I have my hands full." I kiss Dani's cheek, and she bursts into a nervous giggling fit. Adorable as ever. "I just wanted to say thanks for all your support and love over the years. It's been a wild ride. I hope I inspired wanderlust and the importance of history. Now it's time for me to carve a new path, and me and my girlfriend have big plans for the world. Right, babe?" I zoom in on Dani, who curls into my chest, mortified with by the close-up. "Oops," I say. "She's a little gun-shy on camera. One of the reasons why I'm shutting down this account."

As soon as those words leave my lips, the weight and significance of the moment hit me unexpectedly. I'm verklempt. A deer in the headlights forced to carry on with a live recording. "Yeah, so…" I clear away the lump thickening my throat. "I'm moving on. We're moving on. New adventures. New ventures. This is our official goodbye to my old handle, but keep your eyes peeled for the Rose Dylan Agency launching in the new year. You can follow us there."

I whisper into Dani's ear, and on the count of three, we both flash my famous two-fingered sign, smiling like idiots as we say, "Peace out! And Happy New Year!"

Thirty seconds later, our goodbye video is out in the universe. Then

I shut the phone off. On New Year's Eve, I'll delete the account. Start the year fresh on every level.

(And that was my other inspiration for jetting back early from Vancouver—to scrub clean any lingering remnants of Myla before Dani arrived. Dmitri, weasel that he is, informed me that Myla slunk back to Prague to hide under a rock. Her Rhys smear campaign backfired big time, and the privileged gates of Glitterati-land slammed shut in her face. And for good reason. All the posers I used to pal around with have perverted skeletons lurking in their closets that make my drawings look tame.)

But I digress.

Dani and I sway in silence for a long minute. I wait for the bleak nothingness to blanket me—sixteen years of The Trenton Troublemaker, my entire identity, soon to vanish with the press of a button. Tellingly, a weird peace settles over me instead.

"How do you feel?" Dani asks.

"Good," I admit. "Relieved, kind of."

She glances up, searching my face for unspoken truths. "It might hit you later, like an aftershock."

"Bring it on," I say, snugging her closer. "I have my safe zone right here."

(Little did I know that this post would become my most-watched ever, with over ten thousand comments. It spreads like wildfire across mainstream media. Fucking CNN picks it up. Our new agency explodes from that level of free exposure.)

"We'll have to brainstorm a great tagline for our agency," Dani says, moving right along. My efficient, can-do woman. "Something memorable. Catchy."

"What about *An intoxicating pairing*?"

"That's Evelyn's line, you brat!" she says, giving my ribs another hard jab. "Sounds like you and she are angling for my job."

"No," I chuckle, bumping her to one side, "but I do need you at a different angle."

She inhales with gleeful, childlike wonder. "Does this finally mean…?"

Of all the drawings that went public, her favorite remains the one of me going down on her on this very hammock, on this very patch of grass.

"Are you ready to break again?" I tease, her slick sensitive parts the obvious answer. My rascal hand, always up to no good, has zeroed in on the mother lode.

"I'm always ready for you."

With a smile I recognize as dangerous, she pops off my hoodie, rearranging herself in the hammock widthwise, legs spread and dangling off the side. Using the hoodie to protect my knees, I kneel in front of my muse, my everything. I spread her legs wider, as wide as the hammock allows. Dani gazes into my eyes with such naked acceptance, so happy and relaxed that I feel strangely out of sorts. Me, responsible for that look of utter serenity? I try to catch my runaway breath, but it's galloping too fast, like my heart.

I ache everywhere. For her. For us. Our life together.

"I love you, Dani Rose."

"I love you, Rhys Dylan," she whispers back.

The sun rises behind her, casting us both in warm, golden rays. A cloudless sky of blue waits for us to welcome the morning.

And welcome it, we do.

Thank you and free bonus!

I hope you enjoyed *My Grape Crush!*

Reviews are the lifeblood of an indie author's success. I'd be honored if you took a moment to post a review on any of the sites below. If you're not comfortable putting your thoughts into words, a star rating works just fine.

Amazon

Good Reads

Book Bub

Listen to the *My Grape Crush* playlist! Scan the QR code for the Spotify link.

Thank you and free bonus!

What's next? Book two in the Trenton Troublemakers series! My Cherry Duet stars spitfire singer Gia Barlow and flirty guitar god JC Trenton. What's the mystery behind JC and his past? Read this delicious age gap rock and roll romance to find out. It's going to wreck you in the best way.

Save 25% on future eBooks by buying direct through my Rowan Rossler Shop. All eBooks delivered immediately through Book Funnel. Signed books also available, mailed with love & bonus swag!

Scan to shop!

Also by Rowan Rossler

The Hustlers Series

The Cruiser (book 1)

The Challenger (book 2)

The Closer (book 3)

This jet-set romance series stars three BFFs navigating dreams, desires, and all the beautiful complications of falling in love. Glamour, spice, and sexy drama. Pack your bags and follow your heart!

The Trenton Troublemakers Series

My Grape Crush (book 1)

My Cherry Duet (book 2)

Book Three (coming soon)

Three brothers and the fiery women who tangle with them star in a trio of interconnected but standalone romances brimming with sibling drama and shameless fun. Trouble always comes in threes…

Acknowledgments

Where to start? So many emotions churned through me writing this story! Not only is *My Grape Crush* dedicated to my first love (who sadly left this earth far too young), it is my love letter to the sun-kissed town of Osoyoos.

My family vacationed in Osoyoos every July, and god, the memories! No computers or cell phones. Hot sunny days. The beautiful lake where we floated for hours on air mattresses. I was too young to enjoy the wine this region is famous for, but I have more than made up for lost time!

Canada is not the first country people think of when it comes to wine, but the combined provincial wine industries of BC and Ontario are significant. The regions produce award-winning wines that compete on a global level and are exported around the world.

A quick snapshot of the Okanagan Valley's wine history. Grapes were grown by settlers in the mid-1800s and early 1900s, and in 1932, Calona Vineyards was established and remains the oldest continuously operating winery. But it wasn't until the 1980s that the BC wine region started to flourish. As of 2024, there are 326 licensed grape wineries.

And here is another cocktail party tidbit for you. Did you know that Osoyoos is Canada's only desert? Yes, we have a desert! And the temperatures in August can be extreme. The threat of wildfires exists every year, and the region has lost many acres of crops in the past decade. I'm grateful for the sacrifices made and the love these wine farmers bring to their craft. Cheers to all of you!

During my June 2024 research trip to the Valley, I spoke to the following winemakers who graciously shared their insights.

Richard da Silva - Da Silva Winery. What a wonderful two hours we shared. Your family's long tenure in the area was especially fascinating, and I drew on that to shape Evelyn's back story. And you gave me some amazing quotes which I had to use.

Mohan Gill - Bordertown Winery. Your story was so inspiring! The Gill family came over from India and built their reputation as fruit growers before starting their winery. I witnessed your storage facility filled with a million dollars of wine inventory, and I was impressed, to say the least.

Rebecca and Matthew Mikulic - Thee Sisters Winery. What a joy to interview a dynamic husband and wife duo. And you introduced me to the delicious and deadly frosé—a Slurpee concoction of rosé, ice, and strawberries. Watch out, folks! Two of these are dangerous.

Severine Pinte - Le Vieux Pin. This gorgeous winery evokes the best of France, and Severine kindly shared her rosé methodologies with me. Nicole Tanner's carefully noted balance guide is a nod to her system, tracked daily in a notebook.

Daniel Bontorin - Bottega Wines. Daniel is a true rosé specialist, creating his own wines and consulting with other wineries on their rosé production. Thank you for all the insider information and the delicious glass of Cabernet Franc straight out of the barrel. Yum!

Paul Jordan - My long-time friend and liquor rep, thank you for arranging meetings and doing everything with a smile. Your energy and passion are always appreciated.

Kelly Josephson - Wine Growers of BC. Rock star alert! I appreciate your support of the book. It's folks like you that make the writing journey so much fun.

Aaron - what fun we had that afternoon running into each other at various wineries. Thank you for your humor, recommendations, and the term 'diet oak.' It never found a home in this story, but it will crop up somewhere, someday.

On a creative note, thank you to my editor Krista Venero. It was a pleasure working with you. Your sharp eyes steered this book into the story it could be. Hugs also to the beta readers who provided excellent feedback. I knew this story had legs based on all the positive notes.

A special thank you to the fabulous Mikayla Greenwood. This ultra-talented DIY and beauty influencer became a dear friend through the film and TV world. She graciously answered many questions about the influencer life with her usual flair. Thanks babe! Follow her on Instagram! @missmikayalag.

And now for the emotional part…

I absolutely subscribe to the notion that authors write stories for reasons buried deep in their souls. And when I let all the emotions bubble through me, I knew what, or should I say who was calling me to tell this tale.

My first boyfriend, the lovely and troubled Jason Robertson, is forever linked to summer in my mind and heart. Not only did we spend a glorious week together in Osoyoos, but his family owned a wonderful oceanfront estate in Qualicum Beach, a cute town on the east side of Vancouver Island. And yes, there was a killer hammock strung up between two cedar trees overlooking the Pacific Ocean. Jason and I spent hours in that hammock, rocking together as the sun turned gold over the Pacific. Endless love in our souls, unaware our bliss would be tragically cut short.

No surprise, whenever I think of summer and hot star-soaked nights, I think of Jason. I miss you always you crazy, beautiful man.

Last, but never least, a huge shout out to all the booksellers and my dear readers! Without your support, none of this would be possible. Grateful for every one of you!

Love,

RR

xo

About the Author

Rowan Rossler is an Amazon Top 100 bestselling author and travel junkie living in Vancouver, BC. She loves bringing bold and flawed characters to life in her contemporary romance tales. If you're a lover of sultry moments, sexy drama, and heartfelt emotion, Rowan is your one-click author.

A lifelong book lover and former financial planner, her pivot into TV production inspired her to put pen to page. If she's not writing, you'll find Rowan stage left at a concert, cooking, whipping her abs into shape, or enjoying la dolce vita on one of her many travel adventures.

CONNECT WITH ROWAN: